D0903449

FELICITY

CORAL LANSBURY
FELICITY

E. P. DUTTON  NEW YORK

Copyright © 1987 by Soldina Company Ltd.

All rights reserved. Printed in the U.S.A.

Publisher's Note: This novel is a work of fiction. Names, characters, places, and incidents either are the product of the author's imagination or are used fictitiously, and any resemblance to actual persons, living or dead, events, or locales is entirely coincidental.

No part of this publication may be reproduced or transmitted in any form or by any means, electronic or mechanical, including photocopy, recording, or any information storage and retrieval system now known or to be invented, without permission in writing from the publisher, except by a reviewer who wishes to quote brief passages in connection with a review written for inclusion in a magazine, newspaper, or broadcast.

Published in the United States by E. P. Dutton,
a division of NAL Penguin Inc.,
2 Park Avenue, New York, N.Y. 10016.

Originally published in Great Britain.

Library of Congress Catalog Card Number: 87-71363

ISBN: 0-525-24561-8

OBE

10 9 8 7 6 5 4 3 2 1

First American Edition

For
Rita Korn

CHAPTER ONE

'If I am not mistaken,' and when President Garland used that particular phrase to the Board of Governors of Pequod College everyone knew the truth stood tall on battlements of commonsense and right reason, 'If I am not mistaken, these alleged rapes were pure fantasy in one case and an attempted mugging in the other.'

There was a murmured protest from two women governors but they were silenced by the chairman, Lester Marcus, who made up for his diminutive stature by an ability to mobilize his face into expressions that resembled Chinese theatrical masks. They subsided and President Garland immediately forgave them with a generous display of superlative dental work.

'In the case of Jane Brociewicz,' he stumbled slightly over the name but settled for 'brush' instead, 'Miss Brush admits that when the alleged attack took place she lay with her eyes closed saying that she was weak, worthless, and would submit to anything, and when she opened her eyes, lo and behold! The assailant was gone!'

The rising note of wonder in his voice satisfactorily implied that adolescent female hysteria had been responsible for this delusion. Angela Tidworth shifted uncomfortably and said, 'That's the worst possible scenario. The man could become violent if provoked.'

Lester Marcus glared, 'We're not even sure there was a man present. It could have been—' He was going to add that it might well have been one of the local feminists run amok, but the President had smoothly intervened.

'In the case of Miss Benita Collini, we cannot deny that the girl—'

'Young woman', Mrs Tidworth retorted sharply.

'I stand corrected, Mrs Tidworth,' and this time the President added a deferential bow to the toothy glitter. 'Forgive the usage of an earlier day.'

Three of the men present nodded approvingly as they recalled that happier time when any woman between the ages of seven and seventy-five was happy to be called a girl. Pequod College had not retained its position as one of the top ten small liberal arts colleges in the United

States by abandoning its traditions. When the revolution of the 1960s swept across the land obliterating all course requirements, President Garland's successor had calmly made Old English a prerequisite for every major in the college and then waited while the storm raged past and beyond him. 'We have our own way with revolutions here at Pequod,' he said at the time. 'Instantly restore the past and you have saved the future.' Other colleges burned and fell apart over Vietnam; Pequod was convulsed by compulsory Beowulf.

President Garland's accent shifted from his native Michigan to the pleasant two years he had spent at Cambridge where he learned to pronounce schedule without a 'k' and developed a taste for weak tea. It was that flavour of Caius, three published papers on Hugh Bigod's eyre and the recommendation of the local Republican senator that made him so appealing to the Pequod Board of Governors.

'This young woman, Miss Collini, was brutally mauled barely a hundred yards from her own dormitory.'

'No one would seek to deny that, Mrs Tidworth, but was the assailant, or perhaps we should more accurately use the plural form – Chief Flyte assures me that there may have been more than one miscreant involved – were, and we must be precise about this, were the assailants predators from Hempstead, or perhaps New York, since we must accept our neighbouring metropolis as the potential source of violent crime in this area, appreciating as we do that the inhabitants of this area are not prone to crimes of this nature, but more often bent on larceny than sexual harassment?'

Most of those present slid comfortably down the Ciceronian terraces of President Garland's subordinate clauses and arrived at the expected conclusion. Only Angela Tidworth was still dissatisfied.

'You seem to be forgetting that her clothes were ripped off, she was cut and bruised and—'

'And her wallet was gone by the time that campus police arrived,' Lester Marcus said sharply.

'If some students hadn't heard her screaming, she could be dead by now.'

'Mrs Tidworth, I know you speak for several women's groups here on campus, but there should be no uneasiness on the part of the ladies,' President Garland said, flourishing his teeth again.

Morton Jacobson coughed and pointed significantly to his watch.

'Dr Jacobson, Mort, forgive me,' President Garland's voice was tremulous with concern. 'Forgive us all for intruding on your Passover.'

Lester Marcus was about to pound the table with his little fist and announce the meeting adjourned when the President sketched a graceful coda in the air with outstretched hands, 'Every security precaution has been taken to ensure that there will be no further violence of this sort on the campus of Pequod College.'

Mrs Tidworth's ally then tried to speak but her words were lost as chairs were pushed back and Dr Jacobson hurried past them for the door.

'Chief Flyte has doubled security and all the main walkways are being patrolled after dusk,' President Garland said, and invited Lester Marcus to have one for the road.

Less than twenty minutes later, Dr Betty Levin of the library staff also realized that she was late for Passover and decided to take a short cut behind the gym and through Sufferin and Mollock, the two main blocks of faculty housing. She had left her car in the students' parking lot and when she turned the corner of Sufferin she almost fell over the mounded April snow piled high at the side of the path. The car keys slipped from her red woollen forefinger and as she bent down to pick them up something took hold of her and pushed her face into the snow. She struggled and screamed but the snow was filling her mouth, and fingers like stones were pressed against her windpipe. Now, unquestionably, everyone in Sufferin would have heard her cry out had Felicity Norman not shrieked at precisely that moment. When Felicity's voice came echoing down from the top floor, the whole building stopped to listen.

Methodically and without haste the man cut Betty Levin's throat and sliced into her breasts and thighs. Only then did he stop and take her with a few urgent thrusts that left him gasping. For a moment he looked down at his handiwork with satisfaction and slowly turned the long razor where he had just spent himself. Felicity was still screaming above him, and he looked up and laughed, then dragged the hacked remains under the azaleas and crouched there, unseen by one of Chief Flyte's men who chugged past on a campus moped, his cap pulled down to cover the earphones, his head wagging in time with Tina Turner. The blood seeping out from under the bushes melded to a darker shadow in the fading light and the man vanished.

'I am not going to let you deconstruct me any longer!' After she had screamed, Felicity took a deep breath and tried to argue with Bernie. She felt as she always did when they quarrelled; as though she were standing under a grinding avalanche of words about to fall and obliterate her. His last remarks had reduced her to hysteria, and all she could summon up now was a choking gasp, 'If I stay with you any longer I'm going to end up as a litter of footnotes.'

'Litter! This—this is the litter!' Bernie stepped back and gestured around the room, almost tripping over a small mountain of grubby clothes, muddy sneakers, old newspapers and a desiccated plant which was once, he recalled, going to be repotted and had then mysteriously disappeared. He looked into the bedroom to a vista of chaos: sheets dragged across the rug and the mattress hanging half-way to the floor as though a gang of grubby-fingered thieves had just ransacked the place looking for a clean corner. There was a heavy aroma of burnt cheese and rotten oranges laced with turpentine and glue. Felicity had been painting last night and, as he turned, he stepped on a tube of citrine bisque that oozed across his bare foot like dog shit.

'My God!' he screamed, wiping off the muck which had now picked up some pencil shavings and a limp potato chip, 'If I stay with you any longer I'm going to be buried alive in a garbage tip.'

Silence descended over Sufferin. One floor above, Des Freskin began to clear his dissection table in the kitchen and decided to invite Felicity for dinner tomorrow night. Downstairs, Cissie Curlewis was in the middle of some energetic foreplay with Michael Dempster when she suddenly slapped her hand across his mouth.

'Keep it down!'

'Huh? What – I thought you liked your nipples squeezed first.'

'Shut up, Michael! I want to listen. Bernie and Felicity are splitting up.'

Cissie hoped she could get the phone into the bathroom and call Bernie from the shower recess when Michael was doing his post-coital back exercises. She decided to make it a fast and very athletic session.

Felicity was distractedly gathering up handfuls of clothes. 'Don't bother to pack, Bernie. I'm leaving. I can't exist like this either. Nobody remotely normal could. You don't treat me like a human being. I'm just one of those texts that you pick up and pick at until there's nothing left but your verbal droppings.'

Bernie restrained himself from saying that no woman had ever suggested in the past that he should vacate his own faculty apartment. Instead, he reached down, grabbed a load of books tangled in a frayed Indian shawl and almost threw them at her. Possibly for the first time in his life he felt that words were inadequate to describe the chaos around him. He fell back against the wall and croaked, 'A sewer rat would die in this environment.'

'Bernie, when we first started living together, it was obvious we were both messy.'

That was a lie, Bernie thought; all he had done was accommodate himself to the quirks of his current housemate because he was by nature tolerant, considerate and sensitive.

'Now suddenly, just when you've got tenure and everything you ever wanted – poetry published, a book accepted – you decide you want a nanny-cum-housekeeper. If I thought security and tenure would turn you into a dreary, picky little—' She was going to add a number of

10

adjectives, having become quite a connoisseur of Bernie's failings over the last six weeks, but he interrupted. She knew what they were really arguing about; everything else was just a subterfuge and a screen to conceal her desire to have a child.

The feeling had grown upon her like a hidden warmth, a stirring that made her stop and watch the children in the college day-care centre, and with that feeling the sudden awareness that she was thirty and a biological clock was counting the years of her fertility. Yet the morning when she leant over Bernie in bed and said they should think about getting married and having a family, he had almost fainted with fright, then laughed and said they'd never find a baby in the accumulated garbage. They never spoke of it again, but the sense of time passing and her body's need remained with her. It really didn't matter what he said now.

'Oh no, that is definitely not it, Felicity. Don't expect me to respond to any more of these infantilizing regressive traumas. It's you – this is a perfect example of displacement and surrogate identification.'

'For pity's sake, Bernie, that's what's wrong with you. One minute we're talking about something real, something ordinary, and the next it's become gobbledegook. I don't know what you're saying,' she cried, and wanted to add that she didn't think he did either. Then she found herself crying because she remembered how much she loved Bernie despite the fact that he could be such a selfish little twit at times. 'I'll come back later,' she said, 'and collect my belongings. Stef will take me in.'

'How? How do you propose to pack? Are you going to send in a forklift truck and a brigade of sanitary workers? You – you have forced me to live in conditions that would have appalled a peon peapicker. You're a slob – you – if we had coal you'd keep it in the bath. You—' As a counterpoint to the theme of English scruffiness he was about to introduce his mother who used to wash bananas after she peeled them, and who regularly cleaned the bathroom tiles on her knees with a toothbrush soaked in ammonia on the maid's day off, but decided not to mention her after all. Alison Graham, the psychologist he had lived with before Felicity, had told him on too many occasions that he was anally fixated on his mother.

'I'll come back and get my things when you're teaching, Bernie. And don't,' she pointed to the four posters of Whistler's nocturnes on the wall, one partially obscured by Bernie's plaid cardigan, 'don't touch the Whistlers, I'll take those down myself.'

'I never wanted that second-rate impressionist on my walls in the first place. It will be a pleasure when James McNeill Whistler moves out of here. Before you came I had a room full of Miros. Nineteenth-century

British impressionism, if you can call it that, makes me feel the inadequacy of all English art when compared with the natural force and genius of French—'

Bernie felt he was about to make a particularly neat point but Felicity had stepped over a pair of skis, two squash rackets, trodden on his clean shirt and was gone. He could hear her knocking on Stefan de Mornay's door across the hall: a few moments of blurred speech with Stefan's voice climbing to a falsetto of protest and disbelief, and then silence with only murmuring as the other inhabitants of Sufferin resumed their activities. Bernie sighed with enormous relief and satisfaction and decided to call Martin Harris for a fresh shirt. Before that he would clean the apartment until he had scoured and vacuumed Felicity out of every crevice and bulging closet. He was half-way down the corridor when Cissy Curlewis called from her bathroom with the phone under two towels. Gone already, she thought bitterly as Michael Dempster grunted on the television rug, and she knew of at least half a dozen women who were waiting to climb under the covers with Bernie.

Pushing past old crates and climbing over ancient steamer trunks that had been left to moulder by a long-dead faculty, Bernie finally managed to find six suitcases and pack them into each other like Chinese boxes. Panting, he dragged them up the back stairs ignoring the cheery greeting of Des Freskin who passed him on the landing carrying a plastic bag of dismembered and still twitching frogs down to the incinerator. Methodically, Bernie ranged the open suitcases against one wall of the living room and began to drop all of Felicity's belongings into them. A stabbing ache twisted across his chest and Bernie told himself sentimentally that memories were being plucked from his heart, then realized the pain was from so much unaccustomed bending.

He had known Felicity for eleven months and lived with her for eight— eight months during which he had converted his dissertation on narrative closure into a book, published the acclaimed poems, *Absence and Omission*, and been rewarded with a letter from President J. Trustcott Garland giving him tenure in the English Department of Pequod College.

Established in the late nineteenth century as a Methodist school, Pequod owed its name and reputation to one man, a robber baron who had embezzled more railroad stock and financed more bogus mining companies than any of his contemporaries. However, it was not his great wealth which made Horatio Marcus remarkable, nor the story that at Halloween you could hear the wailing of dead shareholders in his bogus companies from every stone on campus, but his lack of height. Horatio Marcus needed all his money and more to rise above his contemporaries, since, measured in his embroidered silk socks, he was barely five feet. He had passed his wealth and a certain recessive gene to his descendants who were all diminutive despite their passion for statuesque women. Horatio's son, Baldwin, had continued his support for Pequod and discovered gymnastics, leaving a scholarship fund to the college for the pursuit and development of excellence in all aspects of the sport. It was Baldwin and his son who had seen gymnastics made an Olympic sport, and a Marcus carried off a bronze medal at the Berlin Games. If Pequod College claimed to enrol some of the brightest students in America, it also had some of the smallest. Tiny figures, extravagantly muscled, would burst out of the gymnasium and hurry off to their classes, and whenever he passed them on his way to a board meeting, Lester Marcus would always stop to smile and wave. He too had been one of their special company, and three miles from Pequod at his colonial mansion with its long avenue of osage orange trees, two little boys tumbled and bounced on a miniature trampoline.

Felicity had appeared unexpectedly one morning in the faculty lounge with a long cashmere shawl stuck in the door, and a lump of fringe anchored to her waist by a convoluted Victorian onyx brooch. There was a sudden sound of rending silk and a frantic flapping until Bernie managed to disentangle Felicity from the door and an aged sociologist who had tried to get in under her arm and was now swallowing silk fringe and straw flowers in large quantities – a far cry from the sugared doughnuts and coffee for which he had been salivating for the last hour. To Bernie it seemed as though Botticelli's *Primavera* had jumped out of a hamper of theatrical costumes, shaking sunlight from a dazzling halo of brilliant yellow hair. She smelled of saffron and jasmine, and her face entranced him with its ascetic moulding and enormous lavender eyes; a face that seemed to be gently rebuking the promise of a body of baroque proportions with spreading hips and richly full breasts. It took him less than ten minutes to discover that Felicity was a visiting research fellow in art history and to decide that she was definitely going to be his next live-in mistress.

He threw a muddle of scarves and a leghorn hat crowned with knots of ribbon and wildflowers into a suitcase and stamped on it all to make room for a down coat with ermine tails on the sleeves. What he crushed was the sudden memory of Felicity's hair which stood out from her head in a flaming yellow aureole, like a sunflower or some radiant cactus. Her hair— He picked up the phone and asked Martin Harris to bring down a clean shirt before the pain in his chest got worse. That was how it began this afternoon, Bernie thought, just as he had laboriously assembled what he would be wearing to his parents' Passover that evening. He had found the dark-blue suit and a pair of matching socks, and one, he was sure, had not been worn more than once. Delicately and with care he'd

13

unfolded a shirt from the laundry and spread it on the bed, hovering over the virginal whiteness of the polyester-cotton as though he were Juliet's nurse smoothing out the wedding sheets. He hadn't worn a pressed shirt for so long that he'd felt a slight responsive stiffening at the thought of its crisp folds yielding to the warmth of his body. Felicity was tinting her hair and the smell of saffron gusted from the bathroom where several handfuls of marigold petals were soaking in a saucepan with nine pinches of pure saffron.

The Frauenfelders were calling to announce that their car had broken down again and that meant five of them would have to cram into Bernie's Fiat, five that included their eleven-year-old son who combined genius with homicidal intentions towards all adults. The precise sequence of events was still clear in his mind: he'd asked Felicity to remind them that the Fiat was a two-seater sports model and they should ask a gentile neighbour to lend them a car for the evening. Within a week of knowing Felicity he realized that when she spoke in a melodious English accent the whole campus reacted as if it were in direct communication with Camelot. He next went into the bathroom to shower and when he came out Felicity was laughing at him from the bed and telling him that young Frauenfelder had just returned the car's spark plugs which he'd borrowed for an experiment that had successfully electrified the iron bannister and several tenants of the faculty apartment complex.

Felicity had brushed past him smelling like a paella and when he looked down on the bed he'd wondered if Jackson Pollock had used his shirt as a canvas. A damply pink depression surrounded with an aureole of brilliant yellow petals was reaching for his socks and his folded red tie; a giant anemone with creeping yellow tendrils. He forgot most of what he'd said then but he could still feel a medley of demented drums in his ears and marvelled that he had survived for eight months without succumbing to nervous collapse or a heart attack. Without thinking, he took his pulse and the counting calmed him. Felicity Norman was gone and at last he could put his apartment and his life in order. Almost absent-mindedly he answered the phone and accepted Cissie Curlewis's invitation to dinner the following night, puzzled that Betty Levin had not called first. Immediately he realized that she would now be well on her way to Passover with her parents in New Rochelle. He wondered if she would phone when she got back to campus, or wait until the next morning, and, knowing the depth of Betty's passion for him, decided to expect a call around midnight. Over the years he had grown pleasantly accustomed to women lusting for him, but with Felicity he had almost forgotten what it meant to be an object of desire for women.

Sex with Felicity had always been more than satisfying and this time he felt the ache in his groin; yet even when they were making love,

Felicity had been eccentric. And it wasn't as though she were a militant feminist. On the contrary. She had been invited to give a lecture on women in art in the women's studies programme and refused, saying there was no sex in art, which had produced a howl of rage from the junior female faculty who insisted they spent half their working lives being chased around drawing boards by libidinous, tenured male professors. He had been forced to extricate her from that little debacle by explaining to some irate maenads that Felicity was using a different terminology and what she really meant was that she had been so traumatized by masculine oppression that she simply couldn't express her outrage in a patriarchal language system. Then there was the time when Brenda Minkoff asked her if she wanted to be a sex object, and Felicity had said that on certain occasions she was delighted to be a sex object which was far better than being a sexual reject. His relations with the feminists were far more relaxed that Felicity's, and when Mrs Tidworth of the Board of Governors suggested that a group picket the administrative building after the second rape, he had volunteered at once to carry a placard, but Felicity said she preferred to paint. If it came down to basic principles of gender, he was far more of a feminist than she was, the first member of the male faculty invited to give a course in the women's studies programme, and twice admitted to the local lesbian caucus to address the lack of gay role models on campus. He was truly a liberated male who did not feel his masculinity was threatened when he used a vacuum or tossed together some zucchini bread for a party. Women admired and liked him and once it got around that he had split up with Felicity there would be a long line of eager flatmates outside his door ready to move in with their woks and organic sprouts.

There was now a clear space in the middle of the room and an open track to the bedroom. Without Felicity there would be order and serenity in his life and someone like Cissie or Betty Levin who would know how to appreciate a professor who could fill the first five rows of any classroom with palpitating sophomores. Bernie flung open the wardrobe and a reflection glowered back at him from the mirror. He stared, and the image so mollified him that his expression became almost benign.

There was no question about it – he was more than ordinarily handsome. Very different from his brother; but Seth was dead, and Bernie felt the slightest twinge of satisfaction that he no longer had to measure himself against his brother's Nordic good looks. No, he was certainly not the typical blond beach boy or football hunk, but something more darkly attractive with the primordial appeal of Nijinsky. Unconsciously he fell into the pose of the Fawn and turned sideways staring at himself with half-closed eyes through the hollow of his raised arm. Small, catlike feet and taut straight legs and, thank God, his buttocks were still hard and jutting. Nothing flabby there to indicate that he was thirty-four and spent most of his time sitting down. The first sign of age in men, he knew, was the buttocks. He always felt vaguely uneasy in the washroom when he saw some old academic trying to hitch his pants over a lank, creased haunch that had succumbed to long sitting, abandoning hope and muscle to a scattering of grey hairs and sagging skin.

Bernie shifted slightly and frowned. The shoulders were a little rounded but a few sets of tennis would straighten them, and he would definitely use the weights in the gym next week to keep his upper arms in shape. A scroll of white hair above his ears could have been painted on to his glossy black hair and only made him look more like a fabled creature of the woodland or an Aubrey Beardsley satyr. Dark hair sifted from his neck in waves to his chest and out across his back, spreading down his legs and arms, all of it reaching a glistening turbulence in his groin. Bernie stood now, legs apart, hands on his hips and marvelled at the glory of his manhood. From the back, old men were flat from the neck to the thighs, and when they walked their testicles dangled on frayed ropes, but his balls were like round, glowing nuts in a dark forest, and above them rested an organ of such beauty and strength that women had pretended to collapse under the weight of it. He was, Bernie thought, remarkably well furred and magnificently hung. Felicity used to stroke him with the backs of her nails in a way that made his skin seem a separate part of himself, but the moment he thought of Felicity the forest shuddered and fell back as the mighty serpent rose, then wavered and collapsed as irritation supplanted a momentary excitation.

She had been astride him and he was looking up into the swinging softness of her breasts when he felt the sudden instant of stillness before the tide took hold of him and threw him to the stars. The bow pulled back to its uttermost limit, his whole body ready for the ecstatic surge . . .

'Say something dirty to me – quickly!'

Felicity leaned over him, his face was framed by her breasts, and her voice was muffled and throbbing.

'Scroom me, darling. Oh, scroom me now – please!'

He couldn't actually say that she spoiled it for him, but for a split second he was put off his stride and his attention flickered. The orgasm was perfectly satisfactory, but it could have been better, he knew that.

'Scroom?' he said to her afterwards. 'Is it Anglo Saxon?'

'No, Bernie, it's mine.'

'What do you mean, "It's mine"?'

'I scroom.'

'You mean "screw", don't you?'

'You may screw; I scroom.'

'Are you actually trying to tell me that in the middle of a terrific fuck you invented a word?'

'Of course I didn't make it up then, Bernie. I've always known that men screw and women scroom. It's something a woman just knows.'

Bernie was still puzzled the next day but he did not tell Felicity that he had spent over an hour poring through the Oxford Unabridged to find the term. And she had other words that she used when they were making love that he couldn't find in any dictionary either. Yet all the feminists he knew made a point of swearing like locker-room quarterbacks, and a lot of women who made no pretensions to being liberated had been able to curse very satisfactorily in bed. Felicity had never sworn and said that was the main reason she found the campus feminists so unutterably dreary. When men used four letter words, she said, it was offensive, but when women used them it was unnatural. Instead, she preferred to scroom.

Thank God, Bernie thought, he was now rid of a woman who was permanently out to lunch. He was half dressed when Martin arrived carrying a pristine lawn shirt on a padded hanger.

'I brought you some links in case yours were lost.'

Martin sank into a chair, gasping like a marathon runner who had run his race in the tropics.

'She didn't leave until four this morning. Bernie, I can't go on like this. She's demonic – nothing satisfies her.'

Bernie had always marvelled at Martin whose sexual prowess was only eclipsed by his impenetrably arcane scholarship. Martin was a mathematician who was on the point of breaking Hendrik Lenstra's algorithm for factoring. First he had challenged Pollard's r.h.o. method and shown quadratic functions to be clumsy and aberrant, then, last year, at a national congress, he proposed that instead of elliptic curves, the factoring could be accomplished by a series of rhomboid spheres. He had only published six brief papers but each one had been seen as the revolutionary demolition of an existing theory. Bernie, who had a fine nose for success, admired Martin enormously even though he never had the faintest idea what a r.h.o. was or did. At Pequod, Martin Harris lived in a circle of admiring incomprehension, except for two physicists who said in hushed tones that Martin was going to break open the big one any day now. Fortunately, he could talk to his colleagues about their research in a remarkably informed manner, which Bernie appreciated. No one had been more impressed with Bernie's poetry than Martin, and together they would speak of the day when they would both be summoned to an ivy league Elysium.

Pequod was often described as a threshold for Harvard and Yale, and Martin was one of those poised ready for flight. In his rooms in Mollock, a computer whispered ceaselessly and Stefan had complained that Martin's terminals were invading the basements where all his art sale catalogues were stored. Huddled in a chair, Martin ran his hands through scraggled brown hair that looked as if it had been recently chewed. The tension surrounding him had been known to unsettle people who were in the next room, but Bernie was used to him now and despite his occasional twinges of envy, he really liked the mathematician. This afternoon Martin looked on the rag end of exhaustion.

'I thought she was going away with her husband last week and that would give me a break, but no – he went off on his own to a conference at Cancun and she almost moved in with me. I'd always known she was more than a simple nymphomaniac – oh, God, Bernie, she's a siren, a succubus, the kind of woman who keeps a man alive in order to make him suffer longer.'

Bernie shook his head and decided this was not the time to mention Felicity's departure. Somehow, he felt that Martin would not know how to show the right degree of sympathy and concern. Besides, he knew what Martin endured every night with his lover. Once he had almost bumped into her leaving Martin's apartment block, a flash of scarlet lipstick above a sable collar, floating ash-blonde hair shadowing her eyes, and a flood of Tabu perfume. Martin's bedroom always reeked of it, and even his suits seemed redolent of musk, sperm and gardenia.

'She won't be satisfied until she's drained my life. Bernie, sometimes I think it's all a plot by Lenstra or Pollard – they know when I'm finished that quadratics will be like crystal wireless. Maybe they sent her to me – perhaps she's a vampire?'

The vampire's name was never spoken even though the whole campus knew that Lenore Marcus, wife of the chairman of the Board of Governors of Pequod College and president of Conspic Industries was Martin's nightly visitor. And because she was Lenore Marcus she could not be dropped off, pushed out or replaced with some less demanding lover.

Bernie had almost finished dressing and this time found even more to please him in the mirror.

'Oh yes, you can afford to relax and enjoy your libido,' Martin said bitterly. 'You're not being eaten alive every night. I shouldn't imagine Felicity is too demanding.' There was a faint note of enquiry in his voice which Bernie ignored. 'By the way, where is she?'

'She's with Stefan.'

'Don't tell me you invited that old fag to Passover? He'll probably sit there and tell anti-semitic jokes all night.'

'Felicity's moving in with him.'

Martin's head jerked as though somebody had hit him, and his knuckles began to crack feverishly.

'She's not – he couldn't be switching. Not Stefan. Do you mean he's so scared of Aids that he—'

Bernie decided the time had come to take refuge in a cliché that did not invite further questioning.

'Felicity and I have come to the parting of the ways.'

'I thought – we all imagined you'd get married – or something like that.'

'I simply couldn't go on living like this. Bernie waved around him and Martin frowned.

'It doesn't look too bad to me, Bernie. I must say I've seen it look a lot worse.'

'The only reason there's a semblance of order here is because I've been cleaning for the last half hour.'

Martin was silent, but now he was twitching as though trying to shake something from the back of his neck.

'Was she – in bed – was it all right, Bernie? She hadn't gone cold on sex, had she, Bernie?'

'Sex had nothing to do with our parting, Martin. It was just that we'd outgrown each other. Now, can we go? My parents want us early because of Grandmother.'

Martin seemed on the verge of tears, 'I don't understand, Bernie. You had everything.'

'I know,' Bernie said. 'Now, we must go, Martin.'

'You're not being eaten alive every night. You're not possessed by a cannibal. Bernie—'

Bernie was at the door when Martin unzipped.

'Look at that,' he said almost weeping. 'I'm in agony.'

Crouched in a web of scratches, Bernie's penis looked as if it had been pinked by a fastidious dressmaker or nibbled by a horde of famished mice. His shorts were flecked with blood.

'Buy her dinner before she comes next time. Crissake, Martin, we're late!'

CHAPTER TWO

Stefan discreetly wiped the stain where Felicity had casually placed her coffee mug on his Italian mosaic table, and began to think furiously. He could never understand why Felicity had fallen in love with a randy little wretch like Bernie Lefkowitz, but amatory relationships between members of the opposite sex were always a mystery to him.

'I really thought Bernie and I had something going,' Felicity said forlornly. 'But everything changed when he got tenure.'

'Oh no, my dear, it was all the brouhaha over those ridiculous poems.'

'I don't know, Stef, I thought they were rather fun.'

'Anything said about Bernie Lofkowitz's occasional verse would have to begin with a qualification.'

As he spoke, his Ariel mind was flashing across the campus, darting from one apartment to another, checking to see who was on leave or who had suddenly decided to move to a suburb where the neighbours kept regular hours and wore three-piece suits to work in the morning. There had to be a vacant apartment somewhere in the building or over in Mollock, a mock-Gothic complex with adjoining wings of terrace houses. One of the great attractions for faculty at Pequod was the subsidized housing first established by Baldwin Marcus who believed passionately in company towns. Only his dream of building a company store next to the science building remained unfulfilled. Nobody was on leave except – the Trugood-Wangs – and Wang was on study leave in China and introducing his New England wife to his Shantung relations, and, what was more to the point, he was coming up for tenure next semester and Stefan was chairing the appointments and promotions committee. Chip Wang and his wife never wore shoes in the house and a faint aroma of furniture polish was always drifting from their screened windows, but Stefan and the head of campus housing were old friends, and Felicity could not remain here. He watched mesmerized as a rose satin scuff dropped from her foot and walked out of sight under his sofa. He thought it would do no harm to move Felicity over to the Trugood-Wangs' house immediately.

'I think I should go back to England now, Stef. Whenever I start feeling at home here something happens and I know they're not really people, they're all disguised Martians with green sucker pads talking about traumas and regressive expectations and parameters of localized aspiration.'

'The superficialities of an apparently similar language can be deceptive, Felicity, We opened the door to the sociologists here and we've had to live with their garbage ever since.'

Stefan de Mornay winced as he recalled the debris that frequently spilled from the apartment across the hall. He must find a solution to this problem immediately, and Stefan did not have the reputation of being the best politician on campus for nothing. His reach extended from the janitors to the President and beyond to Pequod's local patrons. If you wanted your office painted, a student scholarship or a new course approved, Stefan knew how to get it. Now, while his handsome, lined face seemed fraught with concern for Felicity, he was juggling several contradictory desires in his mind. First, he had to get Felicity out of his apartment. He looked around at his icons and Russian silver, and wondered how long it would take Felicity to bring chaos to his little dacha. The icons were all seventeenth-century Stroganovs and every one of them had been smuggled out of the Soviet. It had not been quite so difficult in the '60s before Aeroflot installed X-rays and beady-eyed luggage scanners at their airports: false bottomed suitcases, ingenious shaving kits could all be made to conceal the brilliant small icons. Later, it became much more difficult, and Stefan took to spending his summer vacations in Helsinki where he cruised the waterfront in a lilac sports-coat and cream pants looking like any other old gay waiting for his ship to come in. Stefan's fancy always led him to Russian ships and broad-chested, high-cheeked young sailors who occasionally gave him a parcel wrapped in cheap cloth in return for a large quantity of American dollars.

Stefan saw the world neatly divided into conservers and destroyers, those who pillaged and burned works of art, who made bonfires of paintings and books, who desecrated churches and mosques, and those who painstakingly gathered up the treasures of the past, cleaning and restoring them so that people could grow young contemplating old, forgotten images. When he was an art student in Russia, he walked into St Isaac's Cathedral in St Petersburg and saw what the Soviets had done to profane the sacred, and there, while the Intourist guide harangued him, he made a vow to save what he could of Russia's past. Icons were not simply paintings, they were sacred objects and to deny their sanctity was to betray their function. In the process he had become a world authority on Russian inconography, and a superbly efficient smuggler.

Last summer he had gone to Helsinki as usual and waited for a young Ivan to walk slowly past him, turn, and nod imperceptibly. This Ivan had followed him to his hotel but there was no lusty coupling followed by pleasant bargaining over some small work of art. Instead, Ivan was joined by two dark-jowled KGB thugs who systematically beat Stefan to a pulp. There would be no more trips to Helsinki now, no combination of carnal delights and spiritual pleasure. He looked across to his favourite icon of St Michael and almost wept. His medical bills would keep him a poor man until he died and he would never be able to buy another Stroganov or spend every summer in Europe. Felicity's deep melodious voice called him back.

'I just can't bear it here any longer, Stef.'

'My dear, you have a quest, a goal to reach. Think of Whistler, not of yourself.'

He patted her hand and dabbed the table where sticky rings were beginning to look like an Olympic emblem. Could Felicity's coffee mug be leaking? Second, he could never permit her to leave when she was so close to finding Whistler's lost erotic etchings. Felicity had not come to study Russian iconography with him but to examine the largest collection of art sales catalogues in America. Stefan accepted that Helsinki was now a forbidden city to him and grimaced as he shifted in his chair. It still felt as though the bones of his legs were connected with hot wires, and the ribs on his left side seemed to have a disturbing and agonizing life apart from the rest of his body. However, if he could no longer stroll the waterfronts of Helsinki and Istanbul there were still the catalogues, and as he pored over them he could see the bright enamelled icons passing from one moneyed and unfeeling hand to another. At his death his own icons were to become a special collection in the Pequod College Art Gallery, with one provision: every Lent they would go to the Russian Orthodox cathedral in New York where the faithful could stand and pray to them, and be carried through the incense and images to the feet of God.

'You must stay here, Felicity, and continue the search,' he said firmly.

'Perhaps they don't exist, Stefan. Ruskin probably destroyed all Turner's erotic works, Whistler's mother tore up his drawings of bohemian life in Paris, somebody may have burned the erotica.'

'Ah, but can you be certain of that?'

Stefan's quizzing smile and the eloquent shrug that caused him a flicker of pain had their effect.

'I—'

Felicity faltered, and Stefan knew he had reached her heart. Not the heart that she had given to Bernie Lefkowitz, Stefan sneered inwardly at that, but the heart that belonged to James McNeill Whistler. Art never betrayed or disappointed you, it never came into your bedroom with calloused fists and steel-tipped boots, and when every friendship failed, St Michael's wide gaze would take you to a life beyond the impermanent world.

'My dear, I think you've found the year. All you need now is patience and perseverance. As you know, I've been a fairly successful collector in my time, and I'm beginning to smell a find. I have been reliably informed that some women know they're pregnant when they start smelling coffee or ripe peaches; I know I'm on the verge of a discovery by a distinct prickling in my left ankle.' And heaven knows what else wasn't aching these days he thought as he shifted irritably in his chair. 'Felicity, don't give up now.'

'He'll be leaving now with Martin. Oh, Stef, I even like his parents. His mother is absolutely smashing.'

Myra Lefkowitz never deserved a son like Bernie, Stefan decided as he watched Felicity walk to the window. She was leaning against the frame and looking like an odalisque in her long flowing skirt and sheer blouse. Yes, they both believed in art, and tried to make their lives works of art. Above all, they were conservers. But he could never understand how Felicity could be so feckless with her belongings and her surroundings and so extraordinarily fastidious about her work. She never lost a file card but she would walk down the apartment stairs peeling an orange and dropping the skin behind her.

Felicity managed to glimpse Martin downstairs fidgeting on the snowy path. Just as Betty Levin had done, he stumbled over the banked snow by the walkway and kicked out a ring of keys. The police moped went by and Lorenzo Delgado looked with considerable distaste at Martin whose nightly orgies with Mrs Marcus were known to the whole campus. Bernie drove up just as the keys were put in the safe keeping of the campus police, and Felicity mistily watched them drive off to Cold Spring Harbor and the Passover for which she had especially tinted her hair. As he turned, Bernie almost skidded into the bushes where the remains of Betty Levin were beginning to freeze. He was such a lousy driver, Felicity thought, and remembered the mornings when they had driven down to the shore together, and the time their hands were so busy with each other that they suddenly realized no one was holding the wheel.

Felicity must definitely stay at Pequod, Stefan decided, and he would move her into the Trugood-Wangs' place tonight. He felt a sudden welling of affection for Felicity; it didn't matter that they were of different sex and their personalities were so disparate. They both lived for art. Not art in the way Bernie Lefkowitz exploited it, teaching people to appreciate what they could enjoy perfectly well by themselves. It was

23

hardly necessary to explain why *Hamlet* was a good play or *Pickwick Papers* was a good read. Stefan frequently stated that a great many works of art should be declared out of bounds to scholars for the next fifty years. He had heard and read too much about Beethoven's Ninth, and it was time the Mona Lisa and Macbeth took a long holiday together.

'I must get my Whistlers,' Felicity said abruptly.

'The posters?'

'Yes. Bernie always hated them. He said they were sentimental—'

'Ah, my dear, one day you'll see Bernie unclouded by – sexual delusions.' He found the idea of anyone making love to Bernie Lefkowitz so repellant that he momentarily shuddered and Felicity wondered if he were in pain again. When he was flown back from Helsinki to New York the doctors had jokingly said that it would have been cheaper to post him back in parts.

Stefan could never really interest himself in the young men on campus. There had been a brief flirtation with Tad Buckley in registration, but Tad had left him to live off campus with a local realtor in a Spanish condominium with a jacuzzi and exercise room, and Stefan had not been really sorry. He yearned for the smell of salt and tarry ropes and skin that felt rough and weather-beaten to the touch. Tad had neither excited nor stirred him, and he half sensed that what moved him to passion was not living flesh but the moment when he took a small plastic-wrapped parcel in his hands and felt the icon respond to his trembling fingers. Conservers and destroyers, iconoclasts and iconodules; and he did not simply worship his icons, he loved them with the passion of his whole body. He felt that Felicity shared his passion and he gently took her hand and stroked it.

'Felicity, my dear, I am going to call Melvin Grimes at his home. Melvin has the master keys to every apartment and office on campus. He will send a janitor over here and I shall instruct the janitor to take down the Whistlers, collect your bags, and move everything over to the Trugood-Wangs. If this separation between you and Bernie is permanent, and I hope it is—'

'I still think I love him, Stef.'

'Felicity,' Stefan sighed, 'Bernie is a creep. I know his parents, his mother is a particular friend of mine, and they would both agree that Bernie is less than a moral delinquent but rather more than a wimp.'

'He can be such fun, Stef.'

'A clown can be entertaining too, but I hardly think you'd want to live with one.'

'We enjoyed making love.'

'Felicity – God knows I have not had much experience of heterosexual love but I appreciate its utility in the scheme of human affairs. There must be children.'

24

Felicity began to sob and Stefan let her rest her golden head on his shoulder.

'Seriously, Felicity, I think you should consider what those children would be. Your attitude to motherhood seems a little irresponsible to me. You must visualize the offspring of Bernie Lefkowitz. He is very hairy. Being English, I know how fond you must be of dogs, but do you really want to give birth to something that looks as though it had been rescued from the local pound?'

'Stef, I never told you I liked dogs.'

Stefan put his fingertips together and contemplated the past. 'When I was studying at the Warburg I boarded with a charming couple in Holland Park who lived with labradors. I was expected to share my bed with a snuffling canine of considerable age that was slightly incontinent. The only way I got that dog out of my room was by convincing them that the brute was allergic to me. I imagine you had a dog when you were a little girl, and undoubtedly it was short and dark and very hairy?'

'Stef, I want to have a baby and when I told him – everything started to fall apart. And no, I was never kinky about dogs. We always had budgies and cats and tried to keep the peace between them.'

'A baby – with Bernie Lefkowitz? Felicity, no, you shouldn't even think about it.'

'I'm getting old, Stef.'

'My poor darling girl, of course you should have a baby if that's what you really want, but not Bernie.'

'He's intelligent and sexy and—'

'We must find someone more suitable for you.'

Stefan believed in eugenics and strict marital fidelity for those whose dreary task it was to perpetuate the human species. He frequently maintained to some of his closer friends that the majority of people should marry and be encouraged to have sex once a week under the covers with the light out. But he could not see any breeding potential in Bernie Lefkowitz. Quite cheerfully he would have relegated Bernie to a solitary cage in a zoo.

'There are plenty of eligible young men here at Pequod who would be delighted to give you a baby.'

'Why – why did he take fright when I mentioned it, Stef?'

'Perhaps he thought that he might have to see himself. I adore babies but there are some it's impossible to like: they resemble their parents.'

'I'm sure Bernie's parents want us to get married.'

'My dear, if she could, Myra would marry you herself. She dotes on you.'

'I like her too. At the beginning I thought there would be problems since they were Jewish and I'm C of E.'

'Nobody objects to an Anglican, Felicity. That simply means you have a queen as the head of the church, and I can't see anybody taking exception to that.'

'Why, Stef – why do these men refuse to marry?'

'Because they are moral anarchists. And it's all due to the feminist movement. When women were liberated, they didn't do much for themselves, but they liberated men, and you can see the consequences. A young woman who looks like a Titian madonna can find lovers but not a husband.'

'I really should go back to London.'

Stefan was calling Melvin Grimes and giving him instructions, calmly setting aside some audible complaints about Friday night and overtime.

'It's all arranged, Felicity. You will be in the Trugood-Wang nest this evening.'

'It won't work, Stef. I'll see Bernie every day and—'

'If I know the lascivious predilections of Bernie Lefkowitz, you will see him in the company of some other female tomorrow morning. He has established quite an unsavoury reputation among the more susceptible women on campus. What is most important, we will be working on the catalogues together. Imagine, Felicity, Whistler's lost erotic etchings! They exist, you know they do, and you will be the one to find them.'

Again she was wavering and Stefan became decisive, 'Why don't you pop over to the library for an hour or so and refresh yourself with a few good bibliographies and then go to the Trugood-Wangs – everything there will be ready for you then.'

'I'll go and have a swim. Maybe that will help.'

'A splendid idea. There are sure to be a number of young men at the pool and you can decide which one would make a suitable father.'

'It doesn't work like that, Stef.'

'Then it should. And when it does we may end up with a rational society.'

Felicity left and Stefan plumped up the cushions on his sofa and wiped down his inlaid table with beeswax. He had settled everything very satisfactorily, he thought, and smiled at himself in his bedroom mirror. Suddenly he lurched forward and groaned – the shoulder of his linen cossack shirt was blotched with a spreading yellow stain.

Felicity did not feel the cold as she walked past the science buildings to the gym, for she was numb with misery. She had been in love at least a dozen times since she left home for London, and she had successfully evaded two men desperately anxious to marry her. But one had been an accountant and the other a civil servant like her father and she knew she could endure any kind of man, a liar, a thief, or a junky, but not a bore. Lorenzo Delgado pulled up alongside her on his moped and grinned.

'Hi, Dr Norman. Want a lift anyplace?'

Lorenzo could already feel her breasts against his shoulderblades and was starting to dribble as he spoke.

'Thanks, but I'm going to swim.'

'Wish I could join you,' and he shifted in his seat as he felt his pants tighten. 'By the way, you seen that Dr Levin from the library this evening?'

'Betty Levin?' Felicity could see the dark, intense young woman handing across some books and asking in a small thin voice if she were spending Passover with Bernie's family. 'No, is someone looking for her?'

'Yeah, her mother's been blasting hell out of us for the last hour. I found her keys outside your place and her car's still in the lot so she must have been given a lift, and I wouldn't like to tell you what the traffic's been like on the beltway. Three fatalities in one pile-up. They told her mother that and she started yelling like she was being stuck.'

'I hope she's all right,' Felicity said absently, and walked towards the gym.

All the lights were on and the little people were scampering back and forth like animated dolls. It had taken her some time to lose a tingling sense of apprehension, when she was suddenly surrounded by people whose heads barely reached her shoulder. Everyone seemed to be crowded around one central area of the floor and cheering as a tiny black-haired figure flew high in the air twisting at an improbable angle.

'She's fantastic! She's incredible!' Wendy Forsyth called to her from the crowd but Felicity shrugged and made her way along the wall to the locker rooms. Lester Marcus was jumping up and down in a tailored track suit and, half turning, saw her.

'Dr Norman! You've got to watch this!'

'Sorry,' Felicity said mournfully, 'I'm going to drown myself.'

Lester had not even heard her through the roar of the crowd as the tiny figure was thrown into another twisting arc above their heads, defying space and gravity. Fortunately, Felicity remembered she had left a swimming suit in her locker, and in a moment she was changed and smelling the chlorine of the Olympic pool, dazzling and chemically blue under the fluorescent lights. There was another aroma cutting through the chlorine and Des Freskin gave every impression of being startled by her appearance.

'Felicity. I thought you'd be passing over this evening.' He laughed raucously and she squirmed. Des was obviously sodden with some particularly repellent aftershave lotion and he was flexing his upper arms like a gorilla about to begin his mating ritual.

'I decided to swim.'

'Fine. We can swim laps together.'

'I prefer to swim alone.'

'Sure. I quite understand.' His tone of sympathy did not quite conceal the satisfaction in his freckled face.

Felicity loathed him ever since she had seen him carrying a cage of guinea pigs up to his apartment, and he had obligingly told her what he was going to do with them.

'How about some dinner tomorrow night? It's time you tried my couscous.'

With a garnish of vivisected hamsters, Felicity thought, and shivered.

'Sorry, I'm busy.'

'Sunday then?'

'I shall be consistently busy for a long time, Des.'

He leaned forward and touched her hand, saying in tones of deep commiseration, 'Felicity, I know how you're feeling. I've been dumped a few times myself. I just want you to know that I'm here when you need me. I've got a broad shoulder and it's all yours.'

'Oh, get lost!' she snapped, and walked round to the steps where Elizabeth Crane was just helping Alice Moore out of the pool. Elizabeth and Alice had lived amicably together for the last twenty-six years and everyone said it was the longest and best marriage on campus. They were almost due to retire now and had bought a house on Cape Cod where they planned to fish and write. Felicity had been a favourite of theirs from the beginning and now she saw them glance quickly at each other and whisper something.

'Felicity, dear – we haven't seen you for ages.'

'Nothing but work, Elizabeth. Just one bundle of sales catalogues after another.'

'You'll find your Whistlers, my dear.'

Then they nodded quickly and Alice smiled gently, 'Felicity, we do hope he hasn't hurt you too badly. We didn't know whether we should say anything to you but we do think of you as a friend and – all we can say is that we're very sorry. Bernie's behaved badly and we hope that one day you'll find the right person and she'll make you as happy as Elizabeth has me.

They squeezed each other's hand and Felicity felt stunned. Did everyone at Pequod know that she had broken up with Bernie? Was there some sort of secret radar operating or were the rooms bugged?

'Would you like to have supper with us after your swim, dear?'

'No – no, I think I'll have an early night. I'm moving into the Trugood Wangs' place and there'll be things to do.'

'The Trugood-Wangs? Then you'll be a neighbour.'

The two went off together supporting each other on the wet tiles and

Felicity slid into the water and for a moment thought she would like to drop to the bottom of the pool and stay there. It was like living in a small village where the cottages talked to each other when the people were away, and what you whispered to your lover on the pillow at night was general gossip by morning. The green water closed gently over her head and for a moment she felt like a specimen under glass with the whole college examining her. She broke the surface in a flurry of bubbles, rolled on her back and admired the emerald green of her toe polish igniting sparkles of light in the water.

Bernie's Fiat had stalled twice on the highway and he was now concentrating on the road, listening to the odd rumbles from the motor, and cursing Felicity who had promised to take the car to the garage that week.

'I could never rely on her to do anything. It was like being dragged along in a permanent fog.'

'You should complain,' Martin said bitterly.

Bernie hoped that Martin was not going to continue his monologue about the unspoken Lenore Marcus and her carnivorous habits. He found anyone's sex life except his own rather boring.

'It's women,' Martin said passionately, hunched forward, his head almost touching the windscreen. 'They want to devour us. In her heart every woman is a destroyer of men. You know what they're planning, don't you, Bernie? One day they're going to tie us down, drain our semen, freeze it for future use and then kill the lot of us.'

'Martin, that's sci-fi. You—'

'If I weren't factoring myself ragged, I tell you what I'd do. Bernie—'

Martin had moved over and was almost sitting in his lap in excitement. Bernie pushed him back.

'Cool it, Martin.'

'No, it's something you should write about, Martin. You're a literary scholar and you have plenty of free time.'

'More time than you? I'd put my teaching load against yours any day.'

'Dracula was a woman.'

'Come off it, Martin. Count Dracula?'

'Look at the suffix – it's a feminine ending. An historian in Boston, Raymond McGill, has written a book called *Dracula was a Woman*. I wrote him a letter telling him I thought it was a great work. You should read it, Bernie. If the vampire were a man it would be Draculo. McGill doesn't take it far enough, that's his weakness. Messalina, Caligula, Torquemada – they were all women!'

'Hitler?'

'Did he ever marry? And wouldn't you agree that the whole area of his sex life is a mystery to this day?'

'One of the sociologists might buy it as a theory, Martin. But your timing's wrong. Everything in scholarship is timing. Can you imagine selling that to an academic journal these days? There is a women's movement, you know, and it's one that I happen to sympathize with.'

Martin crouched back muttering to himself and Bernie suddenly realized why he liked the mathematician so much. Certainly he was a genius, but he was also a little mad and it was his madness that Bernie could understand and patronize.

'Martin, you're transferring your anger about this present relationship to all women. I could do the same with Felicity but I—'

'No, you couldn't. You have never known the quintessential female – the harpy, the siren, the succubus.'

'Martin, you must be reasonable—'

Bernie tried to think about Betty Levin. He had been on the point of dating her when he met Felicity. Betty had distinct possibilities, he thought, and tried to deflect Martin from his tirade.

'What do you think of Betty Levin?'

Martin replied instantly as though he had been cataloguing her assets over a long period.

'She has those narrow high breasts that I like and a very tight ass. She could really move on the sack.'

'Yes, she'll be calling me tonight when I get back. I'm definitely going to give her the green light.'

Instantly he saw Felicity wrapped in a dark green shawl and her deep laugh echoed in his head.

'Betty Levin and I are going to be an item,' he said firmly.

'I said you were lucky, Bernie. You've got it made. You're free.'

'Give Lenore – give her the push, Martin. All you have to do is open the door and shove her through it.'

'You make it sound so easy, Bernie. But it's not. Remember who she is.'

'So what? You've got tenure.'

'She can break me.'

'Well, she's eating you alive now. What's the difference?'

'Bernie, I'm short-listed for Harvard and MIT. Both positions will be vacant there in three years' time. I can't move out and get another job now. I'm waiting—'

Bernie wished he too could say he were short-listed but consoled himself with the thought that mathematicians were always in greater demand than literary scholars. Besides, it was only a question of time, and when his book was published and he completed the sequel to *Absence and Omission*, he too would be leaving Pequod for – where?

Sometimes he would wake up during the night and introduce himself to a group of admiring colleagues at a convention, 'Yes, it's a chair at Berkeley – or Harvard – or Yale – or Stanford – or Cornell.' And as he murmured the names he saw himself in a book-lined study where some delectable graduate student was slowly unbuttoning her blouse saying, 'I've always worshipped your mind, Professor Lefkowitz; please let me worship your body.' And every time the girls had been different, some plump and giggling, others tall and languid with the promise of hidden fire. Only lately, every time he entered that book-lined study, Felicity was there waiting for him, one bare leg over the arm of his favourite chair and generally a small mound of fruit peel at her feet.

'You know what Harvard's like, Bernie. They let you find out on the grapevine that you've been short-listed so you won't make a move for the next three years. Then, if you're still hot, they hire you.'

'You'll be hot, Martin.'

'What if there's a sudden scandal – something – God knows what that bitch might cook up about me.'

'If I knew her I might be able to help you, but she barely nods at me.'

Lenore Marcus specialized in remoteness whenever she had to meet faculty. The pale, painted face looked as though she had hired a mask for the occasion and then taken the night off to amuse herself somewhere else. Lester Marcus bobbed up and down at her elbow noisily greeting any gymnasts who were present and doing his best to ignore the academics, while Lenore appeared oblivious of everyone.

'I've been in trouble like this before,' Martin moaned, 'I had to leave UCLA in a hurry. I always told people that I left to come here for more money. The truth is, they threw me out.'

'Martin, you have to keep to the rules. Never, never screw the under-graduates. Keep to the graduates and the faculty. God knows there are enough of them and they're always willing.'

He decided to sound a little surprised when Betty called and he definitely would not suggest her moving in with him until he had taken his time and looked around campus. This was not going to be a rushed relationship.

'I really liked California, but it was the students, Bernie. Yes, you're right. The Dean said I had deflowered the freshman year – those were his words. But it wasn't my fault! They hounded me – no matter where I went there would be one of them waiting for me. And not just one – sometimes three or four – the Dean said the parents were complaining, but nobody considered what it was doing to my health, and to my work. I was down to ninety-eight pounds.'

'Maybe Lenore will get tired of you.'

'She says she'll ruin me first and then kill me if I ever try to leave her.'

31

'Nothing lasts forever,' Bernie said sententiously and began to wonder what Felicity was doing now. 'Stefan won't put up with her. He won't share that little museum of his with her.'

'He's got enough room,' Martin said.

One continuing complaint about Stefan de Mornay was that many years ago, when Sufferin was being renovated, he had persuaded the President to let him have two apartments. The adjoining wall had been removed and Stefan now enjoyed a palatial residence with a small gallery for his icons overlooking the shaded walkways to the meadow assiduously cultivated by the Botany department. Married couples were on a waiting list for the Mollock terraces while singles often had to make do with a shared apartment in Sufferin. And all the time Stefan de Mornay had two apartments with the best view on campus for which he paid one rent simply because he had become a confidant of the old President's secretary and knew who had accompanied him to a conference in Des Moines.

'They say the old fag spends all his time overseas knocking off Russian sailors.'

'Not any longer. He almost died last year, Martin.'

'He's probably got AIDS as well. Maybe—' and Martin began to lick his lips, 'Do you think he's decided to switch and Felicity will—'

'Martin, let's talk about something besides Felicity and your sex life. Let's talk about my poetry.'

The lights of Cold Spring Harbor were directly ahead of them and they took the winding side street that led up to his parents' house with its wide verandas overlooking the bay. Bernie could see the familiar faces already and the conversation littering the room like damp confetti. His father would be supercilious and his mother sarcastic and – then he paused and a thread of cold wound itself into a knot in his stomach. He would be arriving without Felicity, and he felt sure that if the car had run off the road and he'd been rushed half-dead to hospital but Felicity had arrived safely, his mother would have been delighted. Damn! Why did she have to pick this evening to walk out? He began to rehearse excuses and told Martin not to mention Felicity's name.

'Why?'

'Because my mother hates me and loves her.'

'She can't. Your mother's Jewish, isn't she? She's got to hate a shiksa.'

'You don't know what my mother is like, Martin. She is not the typical Jewish mother. I would say that on the whole she would rather commit a crime than a cliché.'

The coldness in his stomach froze to a twisting crystal of pain and he bent over the wheel.

'Oh, God, Martin, this is going to be a terrible night. I wish I were back on campus talking to Betty. Now that's a woman who would never give you any trouble. Betty is – she's balanced. I am going to have a really great relationship with her.'

CHAPTER THREE

Felicity was swimming lazily next to the wall, feeling the tension leave her with every stroke, listening to the susurrus of water in her ears until it seemed as though she had dissolved into the shining glitter falling from her arms, and the liquid, shifting lights at the bottom of the pool. Blue slipping through crystal to green, even the bodies passing her in the next lane were like azure fish and the air above her a floating shimmer of blue. Whistler's favourite colour, and that room at Princes' Gate where the blue began with the Chinese porcelain and then spread out until blue and gold were spun together. Frederick Leyland's house in London, and while he was in the country or in Liverpool, Whistler had taken his house and his wife and changed them forever. A simple commission to touch up the flowers on the leather wall, and over the weeks the whole room became his canvas. That had been the hardest choice for the room was lined with Spanish leather embossed with the arms of Catherine of Aragon that had hung in a Tudor house in Norfolk for centuries. Some of the flowers were red and Whistler decided that they clashed with his painting, *The Princess in the Land of Porcelain*, so he began to paint over them, and the red flowers became blue, and then the blue spread out until it was as if the sky had come down and covered the flowers. Whistler was delighted for he had created the room of his imagination and his mistress, Frances Leyland, would join him there and . . .

Felicity had strayed into the next lane and bumped a thrashing body which grunted in annoyance as she apologized and tried to concentrate on the line of dark tiles beneath her. Whistler had created a work of art, but he had also destroyed the leather which was another great work of art, and when he presented Leyland with a bill for two thousand guineas, Leyland refused to pay and the two men quarrelled violently. Systematically, Leyland set about reducing Whistler to bankruptcy. He never divorced his wife, but they lived apart, and Leyland took to dining alone in the blue Peacock Room at Princes' Gate. Sombrely, the melancholy man drank his soup, staring at the princess who had betrayed him, surrounded by Whistler's world of blue and gold.

One etching of a nude, called *Venus*, was an indication of Whistler's taste, but it was all that was known to exist. Felicity often wondered if he had drawn Frances Leyland as Goya had painted his mistress, the duchess of Alba, but his estate had been left to his sister-in-law, Rosalind Birnie-Philip, and she was a woman of impeccable rectitude. If there had been anything questionable or suggestive in Whistler's estate she would most certainly have destroyed it, just as Ruskin disposed of Turner's erotica and Mrs Richard Burton spent a week feeding a bonfire with her late husband's notes for the *Arabian Nights* and a collection of Persian miniatures.

One evening last year Felicity had finished a lecture on Whistler to a women's guild meeting in Battersea and, when she was swallowing down her tea and wondering if she could just catch the train and make her connection to Kentish Town, a portly woman said matter of factly that she had a letter by that painter, Whistler. Carefully, she put down her tea and prepared to listen, as the woman said she was sure it was by Whistler and would it have any value or was it only his paintings that were worth anything these days?

The letter arrived two days later and Felicity's heart fell, for it was not Whistler's hand, and seemed to be a list of complaints from Miss Birnie-Philip to Lady Haden, Whistler's half-sister. The difficulties with solicitors and bills which had to be paid and three lines: 'I have still not located those *objectionable* plates yet, I know he had them as late as four years ago when Edward Kennedy was here. Would it be possible to question your husband, with the *utmost discretion*, considering the delicacy of this matter, and enquire if he has *any* knowledge of them! They *must* be destroyed.' Edward Kennedy was a dealer in New York and Whistler's close friend. It all seemed so slight, like the sound of a voice on the very edge of hearing, but she began to hunt through sales catalogues, and at the London auction of a small gallery in 1926 she found one item: 'Assorted plates, figures, allegorical, erotic, Haden?' Sir Francis Seymour Haden was Whistler's brother-in-law and they detested each other. Was it possible that Whistler had etched some very lewd pictures and mischievously put Haden's signature to them? After all, when they had been friends and worked together, Whistler always signed Haden's plates for him because Haden couldn't write his name backwards. She wrote to Stefan de Mornay and he immediately offered her a teaching fellowship at Pequod College and now she could not count the hours she had spent poring over Stefan's collection of catalogues looking for anything by Seymour Haden. After three months she had located another sale from Sotheby's in London which included 'plates by Francis Haden', and that was 1957.

The voice was like a muffled buffeting at her ear and she ignored it.

The pool did not close until ten and she knew it had barely been nine when she arrived. The voice became a shout and she glanced across the pool to see if anyone was drowning, but it was empty. She was the only person swimming. At the wall she was just about to turn when someone grabbed her wrist and she found herself hoisted bodily out of the water.

'Get out of the pool!'

It was Chuck Stimson the lifeguard and swimcoach and he seemed – Felicity shook her head because she had forgotten her goggles and the chlorine was still stinging her eyes – yes, he seemed about to explode in some kind of seizure. Moreover, she did not particularly care to be manhandled in that fashion.

'I am perfectly capable of climbing out or using the steps, Chuck.'

'The pool! You're polluting the pool!'

He was unquestionably mad, probably high on coke or dead drunk, but she was not going to take any more insults or abuse this evening. Resolutely she stepped forward, prepared to push him into the pool, when she saw where he was pointing and suddenly faltered—

'Oh, my God!'

Down the length of the pool and spreading out across the surface was a yellow stream.

'It's my hair. I didn't have time to rinse my hair before I came.'

'I don't care what it is – it's what people think it is that matters. Look—'

One middle-aged biologist was hurrying out holding his nose and gasping and two students on the other side were pointing disgustedly at the water.

'I shall catch the first plane back to London tomorrow morning. This place is driving me insane.'

'My dear!' Stefan was at the door waving to her, 'Everything's ready for you at the Trugood-Wangs'.'

'It's no use, Stef.' Crying, she tottered towards him and almost fell on the wet tiles.

'First thing tomorrow morning we go through those French catalogues. Felicity, we're so close—'

Chuck was grumbling that the pool would have to be closed and purified and that would take at least three days and there was a swim meet the following night and—

Stefan walked slowly to the edge of the pool and extended his polished mahogany cane over the surface of the water.

'Vanish!' he said, and instantly the pool was clear and the chemical blue shone antiseptically clear in the lights.

They walked slowly up to the Mollock terraces, stepping to the side of the road as Chief Flyte hurtled past at the wheel of a campus police car.

36

There seemed to be a small crowd outside Sufferin but Felicity was too miserable even to mention it to Stefan who was leaning heavily on her arm and complaining about the cold. She wondered bitterly how Bernie would explain her absence to his mother.

Myra Lefkowitz walked slowly round the Seder table frowning as she checked the place cards for Bernie's deadbeat academic friends and those relations who could be trusted with her mother-in-law. The old bag was short-sighted but she could still count and unless there were a dozen or more for Passover she would put on a turn and ask Josh if he had lost his money again. She paused and smiled as she read Felicity's name aloud like a charm. Instantly turreted castles, Rolls Royces, tiaras, titles and pure vowels fell into her head and she thanked God that for once something good had happened in her life. She still could not believe that Bernie was responsible for Felicity but it only convinced her that God could bless you in the most unexpected ways.

They would all be arriving soon, academics were never late for a free dinner, and everything would begin to turn pleasantly around Felicity. The only flaw Myra could find in Felicity was that she had fallen in love with Bernie instead of someone tall and blond like Seth – but Seth was dead. Myra had learned to live with that particular grief adding it to all the other sorrows in her life. She could see herself now when this house was being built – Josh had walked over to talk to the architect and little Seth was standing on a pile of timber, his fair hair blowing about his head, waving a small American flag and shouting that he was king of the castle. Two rangy women came purposefully down from the next house and began to talk. The said they'd heard some Jews were building here – people called Lefkowitz – and was it miraculously possible that they'd just sold? Myra smiled radiantly, but not effusively, and explained who they were and instantly the two women were gasping like dying fish, 'You couldn't be! But—' They started from Myra to Seth to Josh who was six feet two and blatantly Nordic in his L.L. Bean loafers, and began to babble apologies. As Myra had said in the car that evening on their way back to Manhattan, she was proud to be Jewish, but she had no intention of being ethnic. She ran a kosher home and kept two cuisinarts in the kitchen, but she had found her own people, and she intended to remain with them.

It had not been easy to establish themselves at Cold Spring Harbor, but Seth had helped by making friends with all the local children when they came down to spend weekends, and later he was elected captain of the junior sailing club. Myra shut her eyes and reminded herself that her first-born was dead and all she had now was Bernie. The thought of that made her open her eyes and check the place cards again. She could hear her mother-in-law clattering around upstairs as Bonny got her

ready for dinner. It was too bad that Bonny had declined an invitation to the Seder – she seemed the only person these days who could keep Rosa in order, but Bonny was leaving for a long weekend with her boyfriend in the Village and that meant she and Josh would have to look after the old horror on their own.

What kind of performance would she put on tonight? Fortunately Bernie's friends would be so busy pigging out and arguing with the family and each other that with a little luck Rosa could rave on like a radio in an empty room. She knew she could count on the Frauenfelders to fight and that would give her two brothers and their wives something more exciting to talk about on the way home than anything Josh's mother had done. The difficulty these days was that one never knew what particular turn would take Rosa's fancy. There was her sudden refusal to speak English, cackling away in Yiddish, but that was generally when they were down at the marina and the dockside was gentile to the horizon. More likely she would harangue everyone in sight about politics.

Myra cringed suddenly as she remembered last election day. Cautiously, she insisted on taking Rosa down to the polling booth in the early afternoon when the fewest possible residents of Cold Spring Harbor would be voting. Instead, there was a sudden rush of women who had just had a DAR luncheon meeting at the country club and decided to leave when the lecturer on 'Old Savannah – Sunlight and Shadows', had started to throw up over the peppermint chip ice-cream they had especially ordered for him. Myra liked every one of them: weathered, bleached, suntanned women who had sailboats in their faces and wore faded denim bermuda shorts in summer, standing with lean, jutting hips as if they had just completed a successful two hundred and fifty yard drive down the fairway. None of them had a weight problem. Myra was deeply grateful that she had finally been allowed into their tennis club, and regularly played bridge now at Fiona Cadwallader's where only her name set her apart from the brisk, energetic women slapping down the cards as if they were errant husbands.

The Daughters of the American Revolution parked their Volvos and Mercedes alongside Myra's silver Porsche with its Reagan-Bush stickers and loped in to vote, hooting greetings to her as they came and jeering at a solitary young man in frayed tweeds handing out Democratic flyers. The next instant the curtain was jerked back and a malevolent, blotched old woman yelled at her, 'Where's Angela Davis on the board? I can't find Angela. Where's the Communist ticket?'

It had taken a great many murmured explanations of senility and incipient Alzheimer's disease to smooth over that little fracas. So, she would place Rosa next to Josh, where he could keep an eye on her and

those six million dollars which no one had ever expected Rosa to inherit. Long ago, when they lived on 72nd East and Joshua was still with Fenster, Merton and Wheelwright, Rosa was just another widow in Poughkeepsie, busy with Hadassah and decently thankful when her family invited her to dinner. In those days she had walked around the apartment fingering the drapes, marvelling at the paintings, criticizing the cooking and crocheting impossible yarmulkas in iridescent acrylic for the boys. Everything had been so good then – Myra felt her eyes burn and start to prickle – she had even trained herself to ignore Bernie. Suddenly, out of nowhere, Rosa's cousin died in South Africa and left her seventeen thousand dollars. Joshua immediately investigated an excellent annuity fund that would have helped pay for her retirement in Hebron Village, a beautifully managed home for senior citizens in Patterson, New Jersey, and not more than an hour and twenty minutes drive from Manhattan.

Instead of listening to her son who was regarded as one of the city's best tax shelter experts, she discussed the whole question of investment with an old yenta on the next floor, Hannah Greenblatt, whose late husband had been an insurance salesman in Brooklyn Heights. Naturally, Hiram Greenblatt was a brilliant money maven who had passed on nothing except his insurance policy and a reputation for cheapness to his widow. Hannah told Rosa to invest the whole seventeen thousand dollars in a little company that no one had heard of called IBM, and of course, she wouldn't listen to Josh because Hannah died immediately afterwards and how could Rosa betray her oldest and best friend? And now that stock had doubled and quadrupled and doubled again until Rosa's stock was worth closer to seven than six million dollars.

She should have been in a retirement home years ago: instead they had built an apartment on the top floor which ruined the architectural balance of the house, and hired a daily nurse to look after her. At least once a week she rewrote her will leaving it to Sanctuary and ACLU or the People's Party of America when she suspected the ACLU of being too conservative. Josh cheerfully advised her about every new will and spent hours discussing different legacies with her, secure in the knowledge that he had taken out an incompetency order against her several years before. Nonetheless, incompetency orders could always be challenged, and Rosa had to be watched.

A car pulled into the driveway and Myra called Josh in the voice she reserved for imminent disasters that the family was arriving. It was only her brother Ben with his fat wife who never talked about anything except her sabra relations in Israel and the latest Pridikin recipe for turnip and cucumber casserole. Of course, Bernie would be late, but when had

Bernie ever done anything to please her except – and for Felicity's sake she could almost begin to like her second-born son. She still remembered the shock when a small brown object had been put in her arms and she saw that the baby had a fuzz of black hair. He was obviously a throwback to the rest of the family – her brothers, Ben and Tobias, were both dark – she alone had been the golden girl of the family. From the day that people began noticing her resemblance to Grace Kelly she determined that even if it took her the rest of her life she was going to find her real people. She did not have to wait so long. In school she recognized them: tall, freckled girls who were learning to speak between closed teeth like their mothers, who rode at weekends and dreamed of entering their ponies in the Devon horse show. They were her friends, not the Jewish set who did so well in science and contrived to come first in everything from candle-making to trigonometry. They were like Bernie who won every academic prize at school and who refused to kick a football and who used the baseball bat she bought him to prop open the window, while Seth had a cabinet full of cups and trophies by the time he was twelve. Myra shook her head and drew back her lips, she must not give anyone the impression that she was not enjoying her own Passover.

Ben's wife, Lurlene, was trying to chat with Rosa in fluent Yiddish, but Rosa stared balefully past her towards the door and refused to answer. Bonny had propped her up with pillows in a swivel chair and left with a warm greeting to Ben and his wife.

'I wouldn't want to stay either,' Rosa said and proceeded to ignore Lurlene who had just produced the latest satchel of photos from her family.

Bernie came in a little behind Martin and tried to move across the room to his father. Not that he expected any sympathy or protection from him but he could already see his mother looking past them to the door.

'Martin dear, lovely to see you.' Myra approved of Martin Harris, for he was a reconstructed Horowitz, and there had been a time when she and Josh had planned to become Mr and Mrs Lefton. That was before Josh had been chosen as the first Jewish associate in Fenster, Merton and Wheelwright, and long before the great crash.

Bernie was trying to sidle past and muttered something about Felicity to his mother who gently pushed Martin into the room with one hand and grabbed Bernie's sleeve with the other.

'I do think you could have waited for Felicity. She's not in the car, is she?'

Bernie felt a new ice age closing in around him and tried to look nonchalant.

'Bernie, I hope you didn't leave Felicity to park the car?'

'She couldn't come.'

'Why couldn't she come?'

'Because—'

'Is she ill? Oh my God, Felicity's not ill, is she?'

'We've decided – we've split.'

Bernie had never heard that note of concern in his mother's voice for him and now he watched with something like pleasure as the fright in his mother's face changed to cold fury.

'I want to make sure I'm understanding you correctly, Bernie. Have you quarrelled with Felicity?'

And she made this sound as though Bernie had just burned the American flag on his grandfather's grave.

'We have come to a parting of the ways.'

Bernie tried to escape as the Frauenfelders came in with their son and heir walking purposefully ahead of them in his prayer shawl. The young rabbi from Yeshiva who was related to Lurlene stopped to chat to Myra who greeted them all through clenched and smiling teeth, but she did not release Bernie's arm.

'Mother, I think we should discuss this later.'

'I want to know now.'

'I wasn't ready for a permanent commitment.'

'You are thirty-four years old, Bernie. Thirty-four! You are not Peter Pan in a high chair!'

'Felicity and I are incompatible.'

'In what way, Bernie? Tell me very slowly because I want to understand this.'

His father came over, tall with silver-rinsed hair, still tanned and athletic at sixty-two. Like everyone else he had felt the air vibrating around Bernie and Myra, and now he smoothly told Myra it was time to begin the service. When Myra gritted the news to him about Felicity he looked down at Bernie and said despairingly that he couldn't blame her for showing good taste.

'No, Josh, you weren't listening. *He*, Bernie, has just dumped Felicity.'

Josh looked at his second-born son with disbelief. 'You – you ditched her?'

'I couldn't live with her.'

'Why, Bernie, why?' his mother said. 'That angel was prepared to accept the fact that she was too good for you. You knew that your father and I adored her. I want to know the truth. And don't lie to me because I've had to live with your lies ever since you could talk!'

'She's a slob – I was living in such dreck that I thought I was going to drown in garbage.'

The whole room was still and even Rosa was leaning so far forward that Lurlene thought she would fall out of her chair.

Myra suddenly began to scream and it wasn't Fiona Cadwallader's measured monosyllables but her own dead mother shrieking from one end of the little house in Brooklyn Heights to the other.

'Did you expect Felicity to be your maid? Did you think you had a schwarzer who was going to pick up after you? Felicity was like my daughter. The daughter I should have had—'

'Instead of me, mother. Sorry, but I'm not going to have a sex change to please you, and retroactive abortion is illegal.'

'This kind of behaviour is entirely inappropriate for the occasion,' Josh said icily. 'This is a family occasion and we are all going to have a happy and rewarding Passover.'

Chip Frauenfelder had arrived looking like one of the living dead, but now he came out of the bathroom, rubbing his nose and beaming.

'I really dig Passover here, Myra. It's like being with family.'

'Oh sure,' his wife said and pushed back the hair which fell below her waist. 'If your family should only talk to you.'

Myra felt a sudden urge to tear her clothes and scream and scream until God listened to her. But she restrained herself and told the maid to remove a chair and one table setting – an empty chair would remind her of Felicity, and Seth too.

The four questions had been asked and young Daniel Frauenfelder had received his gift of a modem for his computer. The young rabbi who was still waiting for a pulpit decided it was time to move it along, for Daniel had insisted on replying in Hebrew and at rather greater length than he thought necessary.

'I think we can skip from here to page fourteen, everyone.'

The pages rustled, the knives and forks clashed, and suddenly Daniel was in front of the rabbi, his eyes blazing.

'Hillul ha-shem! You are profaning the holy word of God!'

'Sit down, Daniel,' his mother said. 'Chip, make him sit down!'

Chip had obviously taken up residence in a more pleasant place and stirred his wine with a sprig of parsley.

'The curse of Sodom and Gomorrah will be upon you all,' Daniel said, and proceeded to pray.

'Will you quit davening!' his mother screamed. 'For crissake will you look at that kid!'

'It's prepubescent aggression, Sally. Revolt is natural at his age.' Tob, Myra's younger brother, was a psychiatrist who had just married his fourth wife, a veterinarian with a practice in Deal.

'You call that revolt! Crissake, we were revolutionaries, Chip!' She nudged her husband who would have slid gently from his chair if he had not been blocked by Lurlene's bulk.

'I was marching against Vietnam at his age! I never screwed anyone unless he was a Weatherman or an SDS. Chip, remember how we marched!'

Chip smiled and nodded, and Rosa suddenly stood up and shouted.

'I was Rosa Luxembourg's best friend!'

'No, mother,' Josh said calmly. 'Your aunt once met Rosa Luxembourg, and you were named for your aunt.'

'I was her best friend, I tell you!'

'Right on, bubba!' Sally yelled, and the rabbi sat down and began to help himself to some more horseradish.

'I was her friend, I tell you! Down with the running dogs of capitalism!'

'That's more like it!' Sally pounded the table.

'Da-da-da-dee-bom,' Chip sang absently.

'You could not have been Rosa Luxembourg's friend, mother.' Josh pushed her firmly back against her pillows. 'Rosa Luxembourg was murdered in January 1919. It is not possible for you to have been her friend.'

'I should have died with her,' Rosa said, and saluted with her clenched fist.

It was just as she expected, Myra thought, and wondered what Fiona was doing this evening. Probably she was having a quiet supper with her husband, and maybe some friends had dropped in and they were sitting talking in monosyllables about sailing or the stock market. It was their calm she envied: voices were never raised, no one ever shouted, nobody even sounded excited except at a boat race. Ben and Tob were now arguing about some property they owned, Sally was screeching at Daniel who had begun to daven in a shrill falsetto, her mother-in-law was singing the International, and Bernie was obviously being propositioned by Tob's new wife. If only Felicity had been here, it would have been different – they would all have been watching her, and listening to her, and trying to be a little better than their own Godawful selves.

Bernie forced himself to eat and ignore his new aunt who was breathing heavily in his ear.

'I don't know why I married a man so much older than myself, Bernie. It must have been a kind of madness.'

'Sure,' Bernie said, and tried not to think about Felicity. He would keep Betty Levin in his mind, and rehearsed the exact inflexion with which he would accept her invitation. He hoped she was going to cook dinner for him and not try anything cheap like inviting him to her parents. No, it would definitely be too soon for the parent bit. It seemed that he had accepted another invitation that evening but he couldn't remember who it was. Clearly, Felicity had affected his memory – there had been a time when he had total recall – now, his mind was like a sieve.

'I hear you're a poet,' Sonya said, 'I wish you'd recite some to me now.'

'It's not meant to be recited. I'm not that kind of poet. The reader writes the poem.'

'I'm sure you're a wonderful poet – in every way, Bernie. Do you believe in fate? I do, but of course, I'm a Pisces and we're very intuitive. I believed I married Tob for a purpose and that purpose—'

Josh stood up and motioned to the rabbi, 'I want some order and silence here. We are going to proceed with the service,' and he pulled the rabbi to his feet.

It was the voice he used in district court when addressing the IRS on behalf of a client, and there was a momentary lull. Even Daniel, mumbling under his breath, went back to his chair, deftly avoiding a swinging backhand from his mother. There were no more scenes except when Rosa suddenly pointed to Bernie and said she was going to cut him out of her will unless he made it up with Felicity.

Just before they left, Josh took Bernie aside, and told him that he had disappointed his parents for they had both looked forward to welcoming Felicity as one of the family. That would be a change, Bernie thought. They had certainly never made him too welcome.

'I sincerely hope this is only a temporary separation. It is just a misunderstanding, isn't it?'

'No, father, it is a permanent and irrevocable parting.'

'Bernie – your mother and I have been through a great deal of pain in our lives.'

'Whose pain was that? Did I cause it? Was I responsible? I am not going to be made the victim of my parents' guilt.'

Josh raised his hand magisterially, 'I am not saying it was your fault, Bernie.'

'I would think that in any normal family there would be a little qvelling going on for me. After all, I am a tenured associate professor with a book in press, and a volume of poetry that has been acclaimed by—'

'Poetry! You call that con job poetry? I'd put it in the pet rock and canned air category.'

That really stung Bernie, for he knew it was pointless to give his father a quick lecture on modern structuralist theory and reception responses. His poetry was minimalist, consisting of a single, occasionally two, but never more than three words on blank pages. The most admired was the poem entitled 'Give', which had the article 'the' in the very centre of the page. He swallowed his anger and belched because the gefilte fish was beginning to give him indigestion as usual.

'Now Felicity is really doing something worthwhile. If she locates those lost Whistler etchings she is going to be on top of a gold mine. Do you know what Whistlers are bringing these days at Sotheby's?'

Josh had always appreciated art as one of the best tax shelters available. When Felicity told him about the Whistler etchings he immediately checked with his dealer in New York and found that Whistlers were now going through the roof saleswise – like around $20,000 for one in good condition. His affection for Felicity was now based on solid commercial respect.

'Felicity and I are no longer an item. Keep in touch, father.'

He said goodnight perfunctorily to the family and left with Martin.

'Stuck up little prick,' Ben said, and Myra did not disagree.

Tob was prepared to give a neo-Freudian explanation for Bernie's failings but Myra's head was throbbing and all she wanted was to see everyone go so that she could scream quietly. Naturally, Rosa did not want to go to bed and Josh had to sit and discuss disinheriting Bernie, which was remarkable since she had never even mentioned him in any of her previous wills.

It was bitterly cold on the veranda but Myra went out and tried to draw the frozen landscape into her burning head. All the lights around her shone tranquil and untroubled: the Cadwalladers up on the hill, the Winston-Grays next door, and the cluster of lights down to the left. One of those lights was La Palette where she had experienced the greatest joy since Seth took Tiggy Mortimer to the prom. She had never considered dining at La Palette until Felicity came and then, after some thought, she asked Bonny to make the booking.

Antoine Guérard had reigned over a devoted clientele on Fifth Avenue for twenty years and there was lamentation in the land of *haute cuisine* when he decided to move his restaurant to Cold Spring Harbor. From the very first, he made it clear that he did not welcome any but the very best people to enjoy the best food in Long Island. Myra was afraid to call when she heard chilling stories of people turned away at the door and politely insulted on the phone. If anyone were going to be rebuffed she preferred it should be Bonny. The maid was away and Myra did not trust her own cooking and they both wanted so much to meet Bernie's English girlfriend, particularly since Stefan de Mornay had told her that she was far too good for Bernie.

Felicity came and she could admit to herself even now that it was a great shock – not a disappointment exactly, but it was startling. Myra was expecting Princess Diana with a PhD from London University: when she spoke to Felicity on the phone she had almost swooned at the sound of her deep, musical voice. Then they met and she could see Josh reacting as though he had suddenly developed round heels. Felicity arrived with pearls twined in her hair, and she wasn't wearing a dress, or even a dressy pantsuit. She had wrapped and pinned herself in six large Liberty scarves which dipped and flowed around her and disconcertingly, when she moved suddenly, her body was clearly visible through a great many unexpected chinks. And it was also apparent that her breasts weren't confined by a brassière. Around her waist she had looped and tied a tarnished gold cord which looked as though it had once held back an old cinema curtain, and the ends of the cord were bound around three peacock feathers which almost swept the ground as she walked.

When they edged into La Palette, and Josh announced the Lefkowitz party, Myra knew that they were on the brink of the most hideous social debacle. Over in the corner the Taylor-Greens were forking their way through dinner; just near them the Cadwalladers were reading the menu. And the head waiter was disclaiming all knowledge of the booking as Josh began to snarl at her under his breath. All she could think of was to try and say they had mistaken the night and escape, but Felicity was walking around the room examining the paintings. Guérard prided himself as a collector of modern art and some of his prized possessions and latest acquisitions always decorated the walls of his restaurant. Everyone had stopped eating and was staring at Felicity who pleasantly told Fred Cadwallader to move his chair so she could look at a particular painting more closely. Josh was already backing through the door when Felicity suddenly pointed at the painting and cried, 'Oh dear heaven! The Kandinsky – it's upside down!' She swung round and addressed the whole room which now resembled one enormous gaping mouth, 'I've heard of people hanging Stellas upside down, but not Kandinsky. I don't know how you can eat with that ghastly gaffe on the wall! You must all be feeling terribly queasy.'

Guérard came out himself and demanded to know what Felicity was talking about, for the Kandinsky had been hung by his New York dealer. Myra immediately introduced Felicity as Dr Norman from the Courtauld Institute in London, England, and Guérard wavered. Felicity pushed a few more people aside, took down the Kandinsky and put it back. Immediately, Goldie Van der Klonk stood up and said she would have noticed it if she had not been wearing new contacts. Goldie was on the board of the Pequod College Art Gallery and prided herself on her knowledge of modern art, and her descent from one of those Dutch settlers who bought New York from the Indians.

'I tell you, my dealer hung it himself!' Guérard shouted.

'My dear good man,' Felicity said in perfect French, 'Votre toile, c'est de la merde.'

It was astounding how many people at La Palette that night understood French. It certainly was not necessary for Fred Cadwallader to translate what Felicity had said to the whole room.

And when Guérard was told his Kandinsky was fake he suddenly realized why the price had been so reasonable. The whole room was now applauding Felicity as she proceeded to walk round and look at the other paintings, announcing that the Corot was also a fake and the Utrillo very dubious. Since Guérard had both of them on approval too, he was delighted. Here was a gun he could hold to his dealer's avaricious bald head, and apologies would not be enough; he was going to exact a reduced commission on his next purchase. Instantly, more chairs were pushed back and Felicity was guided to a table in the very centre of the room.

Guérard had insisted on serving them himself, begging Felicity to taste his sauce mimosa and surreptitiously discussing current art prices with her in French. Myra sat there in such bliss that she felt orgasmic, and what was even better she could see Josh experiencing the same ιeeling when Guérard produced liqueurs on the house. They seldom made love these days, but that night in the middle of the restaurant it was as if they were coupling with passion on a bed of roses. All around them the most exclusive group of people in Cold Spring Harbor was marvelling at Felicity.

'Oh yes,' Myra told her friends languidly at bridge the next day. 'It's very serious so far as Bernie's concerned. And Josh and I simply adore her – she's a perfect darling. They haven't fixed a date yet, but I imagine it will be sometime in the spring . . . '

The whole of Cold Spring Harbor had been at her feet, thanks to Felicity. Immediately, she gave a number of parties, inviting everyone she knew, even those people who had previously only nodded distantly to her on the golf course or down at the marina, and watched them all gather round Felicity to pay homage. When they asked Felicity about her home, she laughed and said her parents had retired to a squalid little dump in Chester, and everyone knew about British understatement and proceeded to build moats and towers for her in their imagination. As usual, Fred Cadwallader insisted on the last word at the golf club when he announced that Felicity was obviously related to the royals:

'It's the name – a dead give away – I don't need a degree in history from Princeton to remember all that stuff about King Norman and the conquest of Britain.'

The lights around the harbour were like yahrzeit candles lit for the dead, and the brighter glow of La Palette was for her own death. She began to shiver convulsively and pushed back the sliding door. If she caught pneumonia and died that night it would be a blessing from God – she could not live without Felicity.

*

All the way back to Pequod, Martin tried to reassure Bernie about his poetry, but Bernie was in a savage mood.

'If the old fart knew anything about modern poetry, I wouldn't mind.'

'What do you expect from a lawyer, Bernie? Where are my parents when I want to talk about my work? My mother's on her fourth marriage to some jerk in Spain, and my father's designing swimming pools for rich Arabs in Riyadh.'

'At least they are not being destructive about it. My God, I've had some of my best students come to me and give me the poems they've written from *Absence and Omission* – one of them told me she'd written it on her left breast over her heart.'

'I like big boobs,' Martin said reflectively.

'I built a whole criticism course on those poems!'

They saw the crowd around the main entrance to Sufferin and the flashing lights of the police cars. Not the campus squad cars but the local police and an ambulance and something wrapped on a stretcher being lifted into the back.

CHAPTER FOUR

Lester Marcus was standing in front of the open fireplace in his study, his head barely reaching the mantelpiece. After Lieutenant Poldowski of the county police had finished questioning them all, Marcus promptly ordered the dishevelled group from Sufferin over to his mansion for drinks and some very serious discussion. Bernie could not take his eyes off Martin who was hunched over in a wing chair holding one knee so tightly to his chin that his knuckles were like white marbles. The Lieutenant had asked him if he had seen anything suspicious that evening and Bernie replied that nothing unusual had happened. He could feel Cissie leaning against him on the sofa and tried to edge away from her, but he was wedged into a corner and there were no other seats near him. Poldowski's interrogation had shaken him.

He was not used to being questioned, to being treated like a troubled adolescent who needed humouring. 'Nothing, Dr Lefkowitz, you're absolutely certain that you saw nothing in the least unusual? Think carefully now. The slightest detail could be of importance to us.' It was impertinent for this laconic, smiling man to assume that a tenured professor of English did not have sufficient intelligence to be able to assess the relative importance of events. Especially when he knew who had killed Betty Levin. He looked over at Martin and felt as though he were suddenly falling down an elevator shaft. Martin, staring into space, was a rapist and a murderer, but he had not told Lieutenant Poldowski this. He thought of Betty Levin who would have phoned him by now if – but Martin had cut and hacked her to death.

Jaime Garland filled his glass with neat whisky and stood alongside Lester Marcus who never seemed disturbed when he had to stand with the back of his head on his shoulderblades in order to speak to people.

'This – this appalling disaster must affect all of us,' the President said.

'There's a maniac at large,' Lester barked, and glared at the small group of assembled faculty. 'It was a member of the library staff this evening; what if the next victim is one of the gymnasts? We not only have our own athletes here, we also have visiting teams. If one of those gymnasts is attacked it will mean national press releases.'

'Christ,' the President drank and groaned.

'What disturbs me,' Lester said, 'is that this Lieutenant Poldowski seems to think it could be a member of the Pequod family.'

'Not faculty?' Bernie said weakly.

'That's what he told me,' Des Freskin said belligerently. 'I felt like telling him to shove it.'

'Well, you're quite handy with knives, aren't you?' Bernie replied, and wondered if Des had already managed to date Felicity.

'There is no point to this bickering,' the President intoned. 'In my opinion, and I do not think that my view is unreasonable, or ill-advised in the light of past experience – which has seldom proved inadequate to the situation in hand, and moreover it is a point I have raised before – this crime is the work of some homicidal maniac from Hempstead or Hicksville, or even New York.'

'I'll buy that,' Chief Flyte said, for he was still smarting from some of Poldowski's questions. 'You can't expect me to protect the whole campus from what's out there.' And he waved in a general direction.

'However, I want you all to keep one most important fact in mind,' the President said. 'Rape is not good for enrolment.'

'We're going to have to help police the campus ourselves,' Des Freskin said.

'Oh sure,' a pallid young political scientist squeaked. 'Posses and vigilantes and fascist death squads.'

'If Betty Levin had been carrying a gun this evening we might have had one dead rapist instead of one dead librarian. Think of that when you feel a fit of the pinkoliberals coming on,' Des jeered, and wondered if he had renewed his membership in the National Rifle Association.

President Garland was about to call for order when silence was imposed by the sudden appearance of Lenore Marcus. She glided into the room in a silk robe so pale it looked as though her skin were floating from her body in luminous streamers. Without speaking she walked to the bar and poured herself a large brandy. Her hair was straight and seemed enamelled to her head in one sweeping platinum fold. Lester murmured something as she passed but she ignored him and everyone else, sauntering across the room as if it were empty. Almost at the door she saw Martin, and for one long moment she stared at him and smiled. Bernie thought he heard the whisper of a laugh from her, but he could not be sure. Martin did not look at her, and she shrugged very slightly and disappeared leaving a drift of gardenia in the air.

Her smile struck Bernie like a blow. Never had he seen such a combination of malice, cruelty and triumph in a human face. Martin was still gazing across his knee at the far wall as though trying to read the titles of the leather-bound books. Was this why he had killed Betty Levin – had she driven him beyond madness to murder? And why had it been Betty Levin of all the women on campus? Why couldn't it have been some anonymous woman – not the woman he'd been thinking of sleeping with ever since Felicity had left. Damn Felicity again! If she had not chosen this particular night to walk out on him, he would not have been thinking about Betty, and if Betty had not been in his mind there would not be this aching emptiness in his groin as though everything there had suddenly shrivelled. He must protect Martin, because he knew now why he had committed murder.

As they all left, Cissie asked Bernie for a lift back to campus but he pushed her in the direction of the political scientist.

'We do have a date for tomorrow night, don't we, Bernie?' Cissie said plaintively.

'Oh sure.' He had completely forgotten her and tried to sound enthusiastic.

'We have to console each other, Bernie. I know how fond she was of you and I – Betty was one of my dearest and best friends. I think it would be very therapeutic if we could just hold on to each other and talk about her, don't you?'

Cissie did not want to be callous, but every day she remembered that the last census had revealed that there were two women of her age to every eligible man on Long Island, and since you could count on half of those men being gay, that made the odds even worse. Bernie was everything a woman could ask for: young, tenured, intelligent, and it was common knowledge that his family was loaded. She sat back with some satisfaction while the political scientist ground the gears of his VW and vilified Des Freskin and all the other neo-fascists on campus.

Bernie had assured Lieutenant Poldowski that he had neither seen anything suspicious nor suspected anyone. However, he could not remain silent now. Martin was about to climb out of the Fiat without speaking, but Bernie grabbed his elbow.

'Listen, we have to talk.'

'Bernie, I'm exhausted.'

'So am I . . . And let's not ask how Betty Levin is feeling now, or where she is, because I don't really believe in an afterlife, do you?'

'The world is full of crazies. Why should Pequod be spared its share.'

'Did you kill her?'

Bernie could not read his friend's expression. It was a baffling progression of different passions from anger to something like pride.

'Oh my God, Martin—'

'You really think I could murder a woman, like that?'

'Did you do it?'

'No,' Martin said quietly. 'No, I didn't. But I can understand it. Oh yes, Bernie. I feel for the rapist.'

'You're out of your skull.'

'Is justifiable homicide necessarily insane?'

'Martin, give it to me straight. Did you murder Betty Levin?'

Martin was silent for a time, then he turned and looked directly at Bernie. His face was twisted in torment.

'Did you see Lenore this evening?'

'Yes, I saw her smile at you. Martin, I'm sorry – she's obviously giving you a hard time.' Even as he spoke Bernie realized how lamentably inadequate his words were, but he stumbled on, 'This murder – Betty Levin – you knew her.'

'I did not murder Betty Levin! I am not a rapist. Oh, believe me, Bernie, I wouldn't do it by ones. If I only had the power I'd kill the whole lot of them.'

'Martin, you need help.'

'All I can say is this – somebody has the right idea. But he has no brains, no real courage.'

'Lieutenant Poldowski asked me if I knew anything—'

'Fine, tell him about Lenore Marcus and what she's doing to my life.'

'You know I couldn't do that.'

'Then believe me that I wouldn't kill one woman when what I want to do is destroy them all!'

Bernie tried to sleep that night but he kept feeling the space beside him in the bed. Just to reach out and touch Felicity had once given him a quiet rapture, her skin like warm silk and the softness of it folded around his body. He tried to think about Cissie Curlewis, but even though he knew she would be available now if he cared to call her, he felt spent and decided that her slightly jutting teeth and round darting eyes were not exactly a turn on. He half dozed and woke with a wrenching pain, for it seemed that he had rolled over to embrace Felicity, or was it Cissie, and what he had in his arms was a bleeding corpse.

Stefan de Mornay tactfully explained to Felicity that the Trugood-Wangs were noted for their tidiness and, indeed, even though they had been away for over a week, there was only the faintest shadow of dust on the furniture. Felicity was standing in front of an ornamental china cupboard full of jarringly decorated ginger jars in plastic freezer bags.

'Stef, what do imagine is inside them? Shrunken heads?'

'My dear, it is not our taste,' and he flinched as he saw a dazzling embroidered panel of peonies in varying shades of heliotrope across the sofa. 'However, I have a feeling that the Trugood-Wangs worship every revolting knicknack here.'

'Oh, I'm sure they do,' and Felicity imagined their morning prayers conducted with Pledge to the music of a vacuum cleaner.

'I shall live out of my suitcases, and if I drape a sheet over those jars, I won't have to look at them.'

'That's my dear good girl.'

He gave her a kiss on the cheek and left, humming a melody from the *Nutcracker Suite*, and he was so pleased with himself that he was about to do a small pirouette, but decided against it when his ankle creaked ominously. The lights of Elizabeth Crane and Alice Moore's house were still on and he tapped their window with his cane. It would not hurt at all, he thought, if they called on Felicity regularly to make sure she was not leaving coffee stains on the furniture. It was from them he heard about Betty Levin. People who destroyed works of art and common murderers were of the same order, he said, and begged them to warn Felicity to be careful when she walked around the campus after dark.

Before breakfast the next morning they were on Felicity's doorstep with a pot of coffee and some hot rolls. And then she heard about Betty Levin.

'Poor woman – I often spoke to her in the library. I think she was very keen on Bernie. She always asked me about him in an odd sort of voice.'

'We must all be on our guard, Felicity. I wish you had someone to stay with you here.'

Stealthily, Alice was picking up some scattered clothes and folding them neatly, and as Elizabeth talked she sidled into the next room and made the bed. They not only liked Felicity, they were devoted to Stefan and remembered the time long ago when he first came to Pequod and they had just decided to live together. There were outraged cries from some members of the board, and the words 'moral turpitude' had been spoken, but he defended them and ever since they had known peace. Within a month of his arrival Stefan had appointed himself art adviser and interior decorator to the Cadwalladers, and since Fiona and Fred Cadwallader were both on the board at that time and did not believe in lesbianism on practical grounds – 'What the hell are they supposed to do without the right tools?' Fred had stated – and since no one cared to enlighten him, Elizabeth and Alice had lived happily ever after. They now found it slightly distasteful to be continually hailed by the gay caucus as role models, but it was preferable to the early ostracism.

Elizabeth was still baffled by Felicity's quest, for she was prudish by nature and disliked the present fashion for discussing sex publicly. She had become a geologist because, as she frequently observed, there was no messy sex about rocks.

'When you say erotic, Felicity, you don't mean – vulgar, do you? I really find it hard to believe that the man who could paint his mother with such affection could ever—' and she coughed delicately.

'Elizabeth – they wouldn't be – dirty – if that's what you mean. Good heavens, I often lie awake at night and picture them in my mind. Whatever Whistler lacked, it was not grace and wit. Even when he painted Leyland and himself as quarrelling peacocks, they had an elegant vitality. The truly erotic is never – dirty.'

'Then why do people pay such huge prices for it? Why do they steal it?'

'Steal?'

'My dear, when we first set up house together, we bought a set of cocoa mugs with some very tasteful nudes on them. Women, naturally. I can't bear the thought of a naked man with all that – untidiness between his legs. Well, every single one of those mugs vanished. And when I say vanished I really mean stolen. We had students in for supper, a few of our colleagues who would associate with us, and the mugs disappeared.'

Felicity did not seem to be listening, and Elizabeth apologized for boring her with domestic trifles.

'Oh no, please, what you've just said is fascinating. People steal paintings, but I always thought that copper plates would be safe because Whistler put Seymour Haden's signature on them. And who cares about Haden these days? But of course, if they were classified as erotic . . . '

'I wouldn't put it past some depraved individual to steal them, Felicity.'

Felicity began to laugh and leaned over and hugged Elizabeth. 'Oh, my dear, you've just made my work here a thousand times easier.'

'I really don't understand. As a geologist I use a spectroscope to examine—'

'The single word 'erotic' would be enough to attract a certain kind of collector. Do you mind if I rush? I have to talk to Stefan about this.'

She was gone and Alice came out of the bedroom shaking her head.

'We are going to have a job on our hands, my dear. It really looked as though she'd had a pillow fight in there.'

'And she flew out of here without locking the door. We must make a point of checking every day.'

Alice sighed, for she knew that the cleaning would be left to her since Elizabeth didn't know one end of a broom from the other.

Bernie was walking across the English Hall when he saw Felicity running towards him, and instantly he knew that she had been looking for him and was probably going to have hysterics in the middle of campus. He decided to play it very cool indeed; an assurance that they would always be friends but not lovers, and a brief reference to it all having been fun, but now it was time to adjust to a changed relationship. Felicity ran past him, a long, knitted scarf trailing behind her, and she did not even seem to be aware that he was standing there. It wasn't as if she had cut him, it was worse than that. She hadn't seen him.

Fortunately, he was teaching Thackeray that morning and he was able to be brilliantly sarcastic at the expense of Amelia and Dobbin. The students were entranced, hanging on every word, as he paced the floor delivering one scintillating piece of invective after another. At the end of the lecture there was a scattering of applause and he felt considerably better. In the front row, Deb Turner looked swooningly at her best friend, Muffin Winston, and said, 'Awesome.' 'The greatest,' Muffin breathed, and Bernie gave them a smile indicating a nice compromise between deprecation and approval.

It was quite true what Martin had said to him – he had everything, and he was going to make the most of it. The thought of Martin made him feel uneasy, but he told himself that by speaking as bluntly as he had, Martin would probably think twice before he attacked another woman. That is – if he had committed murder. Somehow he could not see Martin as a killer. But what if Martin's prick were examined for scars and they were found to be an exact match for Lenore's front teeth? Should that be his decision or was it Lieutenant Poldowski's job. No, damn it! He was not going to hand over his best frend to a bumbling county cop. As for Felicity, he looked across the campus and it seemed that attractive young women were blossoming everywhere like crocus in the snow. Most of those who passed him were students, but there were others. He waved to Melba Tunstall in chemistry, and she made a series of semaphore gestures which he interpreted as meaning that she was late for class but that she would call him. He did indeed have everything, and it was all comfortably between his legs and his ears.

Felicity found Stefan in the gallery where an exhibit of watercolour crayons was just being mounted.

'I must say they don't really speak to me, Felicity. They seem more like the promises of paintings than actual works of art.' Then he paused and frowned. 'Why aren't you down with the catalogues?'

'Stef, I had an idea that could save weeks and months of work.'

'Nothing can substitute for the meticulous examination of sales catalogues, Felicity. I appreciate that—'

'The last date was 1957 – perhaps we should ckeck for any thefts of art works.'

'My dear, paintings are stolen every day of the week.'

'But Interpol has registers of stolen works. And since copper plates are an odd sort of item it's unlikely they would be lumped together with sketches or paintings.'

'Yes – and insurance companies keep moderately accurate records, too.'

'Let's start by asking if any Haden plates have been stolen.'

55

'Felicity, if it were known that they were by Whistler, there would be some reason to steal them, but Haden – who is Seymour Haden?'

'Actually, there is a market for his stuff today. But I know now that it's not etchings I'm looking for, but plates. And who buys copper plates? However, if they're listed as erotic—'

'Ah—' Stefan pursed his lips as every aberration from Kraft-Ebbing flooded his mind.

'That word alone is enough to attract a certain kind of thief.'

Stefan frowned. The greatest works of art, he knew, could not be protected from the contaminating gaze of the grubby spirit.

'Did I tell you when I first saw the *Mona Lisa*,' he said thoughtfully.

'Stef – this is important.'

'I was very young then, not yet twenty. And we had just liberated Paris. My very special friend was Desmond Whittaker – you must know Desmond, he retired from the Metropolitan some years ago. Desmond and I decided that we had to celebrate in some of the lesser known bistros of the city. Desmond is a good deal older than I and he knew every corner of Paris; but it was my first time. Somehow we picked up a little British sailor, nice little Cockney, and, early in the morning, boozy and bleary eyed, we said we could not leave Paris until we had seen the *Mona Lisa*. Only then would we really know that the forces of darkness had been driven back and civilization restored to the world. Felicity, the Louvre was not open yet, but Desmond knew several of the staff, and we staggered in and stood in front of her. Desmond began to cry and I was speechless. We could feel the calm beauty of that figure conquering the brutality and horror of the world, but our little friend put his head on one side and said, "Funny look she's got on 'er face, 'asn't she? As though someone's doin' 'er a kindness from behind." '

'Stef, please, be serious,' Felicity laughed.

'No, you don't see my point. Desmond and I were weeping in front of a masterpiece, but our little friend was enchanted by the *Mona Lisa* too. He thought it was quite one of the dirtiest pictures he'd ever seen, and he wouldn't have half minded taking it back for the messroom.'

'That's what I've been trying to say, Stef. If there is a record of any Haden plates having been stolen—'

'Do you know how many collectors of pornography there must be?'

'Thousands, I'm sure. But these would not be cheap.'

'I accept that. Well, my dear, why are you standing there? I have a list of insurance companies. You must write to them all immediately.'

'Why not get in touch with Interpol?'

'The less dealings you have with the police, the better,' Stefan said sourly, remembering the occasion when he had been questioned about certain icons he had gallantly rescued from a shady antique collector in

Vienna. He sensed that Felicity would be very busy indeed for the rest of the day, and he could slip away and have lunch with Myra Lefkowitz at La Palette. Stefan knew the social register by heart, and he cultivated its members assiduously. Not that Myra would ever be cited in that register, but she had been accepted by people like the Cadwalladers and the Van der Klonks and she was very generous. Moreover, he enjoyed good food, and he had never fallen into the egregiously bad habit of eating at home.

The *riz de veau financier* was a masterpiece, and the tart of wild strawberries set him quoting Pushkin. He could have wished for a more vivacious luncheon companion but he both admired and liked Myra, and it was obvious that she was holding back tears with considerable difficulty.

'Why – why did he let her go, Stef? You said yourself she was too good for him.'

'When I saw them together, I always thought of Beauty and the Beast. Except that the beast was a disguised prince and Bernie is a conniving little peasant at heart.'

'We must get them together again. I daren't talk to Felicity. I thought about sending her flowers or—'

'Do, Myra. Flowers would be delightful.'

'And a little note – "Felicity, darling, I shall always think of you as my daughter". You don't think that's too much, do you?'

'Myra, I know she's fond of you.'

'Oh Stef, she means everything to me. If you could have been here the night she hanged Kandinsky—'

'I recall every moment of it, Myra,' he said hastily, for she had told him the story a dozen times over. 'No, I think some flowers would be helpful now, and we'll allow them both a little time to simmer down.'

It was then he told her that Felicity wanted a child and Myra rushed for the powder room and sobbed over the toilet. A grandchild! Felicity's baby in one of those marvellous tall, black English prams with a monogram on the side, and she could hear herself telling Mabel Jackson Warner and Fiona that he really was a marvellous baby, but so fair; they had to be careful about his sunkicks.

She seemed calm when she came back to the table and Stefan marvelled at her self-control. Myra had created herself, and that was what he admired. If you could not be an artist then the very least you should do is make your life a work of art. When he heard people talking about sincerity and 'being yourself', he felt a wave of nausea sweep over him and he had a vision of Darwin rushing past him down the slope of devolution into the primeval ooze. The most important thing was that people should not be themselves. Admittedly, some began with better material than others. Most people were born like lumps of broken cement; others were blocks of Parian marble. But everyone had a duty to improve. Myra was a splendid example. She looked like the sister of at least a dozen women in the restaurant: tall, with blonde hair streaked silver, suntanned and athletic, and a voice pitched so that the timbre was slightly off key. And she had created this from a Jewish girl out of Brooklyn Heights whose father had been a car salesman, just as he had made Stefan de Mornay from Stevie Muchkin whose parents had raised hogs in Iowa. When he looked back to his childhood now it was as if he were turning the pages of an old and forgotten book of nursery tales. He could see the family saying grace before dinner with their trotters on the table, and the hairy snouts all pointed in his direction and grunting that he was the first Muchkin ever to complain about having to clean out a pig-pen. He had run away and joined the army when he was barely seventeen. Stefan de Mornay had been born in graduate school and groomed in the museums and art galleries of Europe, and the only legacy from the Muchkins was an allergy to pork in all forms from bacon to chops. As he whimsically told the Lefkowitzes, he had a kosher stomach.

'Do you think there's any hope at all, Stef?'

'I see it as a lovers' tiff, Myra. But,' and he hesitated, as he really did not care for Bernie, 'For your sake, and because I know it's what you and Josh want, I shall play go-between.'

'There is always a gift for the matchmaker, Stef.'

'You have already been more than generous in gifts for the gallery.' He sighed, 'I only wish that muscled little dwarf Lester Marcus were Jewish and then he might have some appreciation for art. What I dream of is a Russian room in the gallery, because I cannot live forever, and I want my icons to be properly housed. But Marcus puts all his cash into that wretched gymnastic training programme—'

'You can always count on us for a donation.'

'My dear,' and he patted her hand, 'I know I can, and if you could, you would give more.'

'Things have been a little difficult since the crash.'

'I understand perfectly, my dear.'

Stefan, like everyone else, knew in general terms what had happened at Fenster, Merton and Wheelwright, and when he had been asked for details by people like the Cadwalladers and the Coffin-Abernechies, he always said it was the most blatant and iniquitous case of anti-semitism since the pogroms in the Ukraine. Josh, he would say in measured tones, had been made the scapegoat for the financial ineptitude of two of the senior partners. To save the reputation of the firm, he had been sacrificed. And although Fred Cadwallader seemed to have a different version, Stefan told the story so well that he was believed.

Myra dropped Stefan off behind the gallery because she did not want to run into Bernie, and she wanted to select the flowers herself from the florist. Not one of those chintzy little arrangements stuck in a plastic bowl, but an armful of gorgeous and expensive blossoms that Felicity could arrange herself.

The cellophane-wrapped box was on the kitchen table when Felicity came home that evening, and she began laughing with joy because she was sure that Bernie had sent them. They were from his mother and she sat down and cried. Suddenly she was alone, and everything around her was unfamiliar and disapproving. For months now she had been used to someone being there when she came back from teaching or poring over catalogues until her eyes glazed. They cooked together, or Bernie would suggest a restaurant in New York and then they would drive to the Village. When he knew she loved opera he bought season tickets to the Metropolitan for her and they sat by the fountain in Lincoln Center watching the moon and the city lights. He seemed as interested in her search for the Whistlers as she was, and often he would come down to the basement, take a bundle of catalogues and help her. Once, they had even made love among the catalogues . . .

If they were so happy together why couldn't they take the next step and marry and have a family? It was rubbish to say that it was her sloppiness that had parted them. She looked around her and saw the tea towel folded precisely over the rack by the sink, and in the next room the bed was made with her slippers beside it. Everything had been so confused last night, and in the morning she heard about Betty Levin and police were all over the campus asking questions. Had she done all this herself? She shrugged and decided she must have reverted to her boarding school days when pimply faced prefects exacted fines and penalties for beds without hospital corners and untidy lockers. The bemusement changed to anger when she saw her coffee mug rinsed and on the shelf – surely Bernie could not have had such an impact on her that subconsciously she was turning into a drudge just to please him?

Wendy Forsyth was calling to her outside the door and Felicity kicked off her shoes and let her in. Of all the resident feminists, Wendy was the one she liked most, if only because she had a sense of humour and didn't mind laughing at herself occasionally.

'You should have heard him at the women's meeting this afternoon, Felicity.'

'Bernie?'

'Quite the little leader. He wants some of the male faculty to form posses and patrol the campus at night.'

'Seems reasonable.'

'Bernie says they should dress as women – and act as decoys.'

'You mean, the police think there'll be another attack?'

'Betty was murdered by a maniac. Probably it's a serial killer, and he'll be looking for another victim.'

'I am going to be careful, Wendy.'

'Careful isn't enough, we've got to catch the bastard. And from what the police are saying it could be a student, or a member of the faculty.'

'You mean—'

'Every man on campus is a suspect.'

'Surely not Stefan de Mornay, or—'

'Well, not Stef. He can hardly get up the stairs, but as for the rest . . . '

'None of them seems capable of – murder.'

'We have a pretty good personality profile for killers like this.'

Wendy was a social psychologist so Felicity knew it was pointless to argue with her.

'What I really came to talk to you about was a different kind of protection.'

Felicity remembered an old shillelagh her father had inherited from a distant cousin in Ireland, and wondered if she should keep something like that in her bag.

'You need a diaphragm.'

Felicity felt the room shifting slightly—

'I'm sorry, I must have missed something in between, Wendy.'

'You've broken up with Bernie, but I don't imagine you're going to live as a celibate for the rest of your life?'

'Well, I hadn't really—'

'No, of course not. And you've been on the pill, haven't you?'

'Yes.'

'How convenient it is for men when women are prepared to be poisoned for them. I'll make an appointment at the clinic for you tomorrow morning. Dr Wesker will measure you and then you can throw away those little hormonal time bombs.'

'Wendy, I appreciate you're my friend, and it's difficult for me to say this, but I'm not used to discussing my sex life as though it were last week's groceries.'

'We've all been aware of your cultural inhibitions, Felicity.'

'Perhaps inhibitions are not such a bad thing, really.'

'It's going to take time before your consciousness is raised. But we're all here to help you.'

The phone rang and it was the Frauenfelders inviting her for dinner.

Wendy shrugged when Felicity accepted. 'Well, he does have the best supply of coke on campus – if you're into drugs.'

'I'm not sure I'm into anything,' Felicity said wearily. 'I would just like to spend one day here without feeling as though I'm being dragged through a seminar in hygiene. You all talk so much about sex,' she said, and wanted to add that she thought that talk was all most of them did.

Cissie Curlewis was not the most boring woman Bernie knew, but she was the most irritating. Bernie prided himself on being able to please women, and not by any show of male authority, but simply by considering their interests and feelings. He knew a great deal more about Whistler than most art critics because he had taken the trouble to read Felicity's articles, and they had been to the Freer in Washington and stood in the Peacock Room, and he had spent some of his time checking sales catalogues for her. But Cissie was a chemist and already making a name for herself in sludge. Over dinner he put his head in his hands and shuddered inwardly, for her teeth and little round eyes began to resemble a rat peering at him from a sewer vent. He coughed over the expensive Californian white Cissie had provided and found his eyes watering. Instantly her arms were round him and he saw flecks of antipasto between her teeth.

'Bernie, I know how you feel. I was so fond of Betty. I spent half an hour today talking to her mother. My God, the way that woman is suffering. But I know you're hurting too, darling. Oh, Bernie, we should comfort each other. Let's go to bed now. We can have dessert later. It's chocolate mocha so it won't spoil.'

'Cissie,' he fumbled for the right words as she reached for his shirt buttons. 'Cissie, this is not the time. I shouldn't have accepted your invitation. We are good friends and I know that you can sympathize with my trauma. But I have to be alone—'

'Bernie, we can be alone together.'

'That's what I'm afraid of,' he said, and left.

Cissie kicked the sofa twice and phoned Michael Dempster. His wife answered so she assumed a professional voice and said the readings were through on the most recent sludge samples if he cared to come over and check them.

Bernie had been half-way through his veal cutlet when Felicity was escorted by Wendy Forsyth to the Frauenfelders' front door. The campus was very still, students were walking in groups, and there were lights strung between the trees. It all looked festive, except for the feeling of apprehension that could be felt like a cold wind.

A glowering Daniel Frauenfelder greeted them at the door in his prayer shawl, and Wendy called for Chip to escort her back to Sufferin. Chip sauntered from the living room, offered her his arm with an Errol Flynn bow and the two left. As they turned the corner, Felicity watched them go and noticed that Chip was barefoot but did not seem to feel the cold, so she shrugged and let Daniel show her into the living room. It was a maze of Mexican artefacts, cross-eyed Aztec gods and straw baskets. She sat down on the torn sofa and Daniel stood in front of her like a small, interrogating angel.

'And what are you going to be when you grow up, Daniel?' Felicity said pleasantly.

The boy was silent.

Felicity gave up trying, 'Now look, you little creep. You know I don't really want to he here, and I'm not enjoying myself in the least, if that's any consolation to you.'

'You're a shiksa.'

'That's quite true, Daniel, but I'm not anti-semitic. In fact, I was rather hoping to marry a Jew.'

'You would have to convert.'

'I was ready to do all that and swim three laps of the mikveh or whatever you call it.'

Daniel seemed to be mellowing slightly and said that he didn't know whether he wanted to be a famous rabbi or a great atomic physicist.

'Whatever you do, I am sure you will do it brilliantly, Daniel. At the moment you're clearly a professional charmer, aren't you?'

Daniel looked as though he was about to hit her when Sally burst into the room scattering dishcloths and groceries.

'Is that kid annoying you?'

'Not in the least, Sally.'

'Well, he does everyone else. For crissake,' Sally screamed, 'will you get that goddam shawl off! And I swear I'm going to burn those yarmulkas!'

'If you yell at me like that, I'll report you,' Daniel bellowed. 'There are laws against child abuse and endangering my civil rights.'

Chip sauntered back into the room with blue feet and Sally threw a box of organic cereal at him.

'Couldn't you keep off the coke for one night, Chip? Do you have to space out every goddam night?'

'My parents,' Daniel said evenly to Felicity, 'are both social delinquents. They are also junkies and blasphemers.'

'I should have drowned you at birth,' Chip said, and handed Felicity a joint.

'I want a little quiet,' Sally shrilled. 'Felicity, I know you must be all broken up over that little jerk, Bernie. But the world hasn't come to an end. Oh, Felicity, have I got a guy for you.'

Chuck Stimson walked in and grinned sheepishly at Felicity.

It was, Felicity thought, quite one of the most unpleasant meals she had ever endured. Chuck was busy apologizing to her for his behaviour at the pool and promising to design a special training programme for her. 'It's the pectoral muscles, Felicity. I have a combination of weights and exercizes that could totally redesign your whole chest area.'

The meal was organic and tasted of earth: Chip insisted they all try his latest liqueur, for he had installed a small distillery in the chemistry lab and kept half the campus supplied with cut-price liqueurs. He regarded this as a distinct come-down from the days in California when he was an associate professor at Berkeley and manufactured his own line of ecstasy pills from an LSD base. People had been known to levitate on Chip's pills and many described the world spread out beneath like a tapestry of strange colours. It was only when there were several fatal injuries as a result of people stepping off roofs and walking out of windows that Chip had been forced to close down and look for another job. At Pequod he never drugged before noon, and students found a remarkably alert and considerate teacher in the mornings. After lunch he handed over the labs to the co-adjutant faculty and retired to his office to dream of the days when he was Lord of Space.

Felicity insisted on leaving at ten and Chuck obviously thought he was being invited back to her place for some preliminary training.

'You can't still be mad at me about your hair, Felicity. I mean, you got to see my point of view. That pool must be kept pure—'

'Goodnight, Chuck.'

He tried to kiss her and she pushed him firmly away and slammed the door on him. Then a thread of fear wound itself around her. The police had said the murderer could be a member of the faculty, or even a student. She had accepted Chuck's offer to see her home, just as Wendy had asked Chip to escort her to Sufferin. Either of them could be the rapist. Every room was full of perfume from Myra's peonies and roses, and Felicity began to cry as she remembered her last birthday when Bernie had given her thirty bunches of violets and an amethyst bracelet. She almost reached out for the phone to call him, but instead she made herself a cup of tea and, again, she was bemused, for it really seemed as though the kitchen floor had cleaned and polished itself.

CHAPTER FIVE

Bernie was still wondering about Martin as he walked to class the next morning – he had woken a little after five from a nightmare in which Martin burst open the door of his study brandishing a blood-stained sword and with the light of murder in his eyes. Bernie tried to reason with him, but Martin kept calling him Bernadette and threatened to cut out his womb. It was impossible to get to sleep again. Even though he tried to compose a few poems in his head and went over the day's lectures, the terror remained with him. The emptiness of his apartment was also beginning to depress him, but he told himself that this time he was not going to rush headlong into another heavy relationship. The walls were now decorated with Robert Motherwell posters, though the tidiness of the room did not reflect someone's orderly spirit, but the absence of any real life. That would all change when someone moved in with him, and he had a sudden and incongruent vision of a Stepford wife. No, he could never be happy with a domestic automaton in frills with a plastic smile and a pneumatic body. No matter what you did and no matter how well you did it, you had to end up talking. The talking was important. He couldn't deny that Felicity was always interesting but – no! – Felicity had been a disaster . . . He slammed the door and walked purposefully to class.

Irritatingly, Felicity was still on his mind when he saw her going in the direction of the art gallery. She looked across at him, smiled, and seemed about to speak. Purposefully, he strode past as though rapt in thoughts too profound to be disturbed by any human consideration, and decided to enjoy his misery for a day or two more at least. Another poem came to him – a blank page with 'alone' in the middle of it. But he discarded the idea as being unambiguous and a little sentimental. A really great poem would undoubtedly result from his parting with Felicity. She would never know it but that one poem would be the quintessential expression of his loss. He tried to remember whether it was Goethe or Schiller who could not write unless inspired by a bundle of old love letters from an unhappy affair.

The news that he was available would already have flown around the campus, and Bernie wondered who would be calling him next. Melba had left a message for him and there was another from a Tig Fletcher whom he vaguely recalled having met at one of the Frauenfelders' parties. If she were a friend of the Frauenfelders she would be very political, and he was not sure he wanted to do a refresher course on Marxist theory at the moment. He was definitely going to take his time and look around.

'He cut me dead!' Felicity was outraged and thumped her box of slides on the table of her office in the gallery.

'My dear, think about art, it is the only refuge from the world.'

'Stefan, I was about to speak to him – and he cut me.'

Stefan de Mornay wriggled uncomfortably because Felicity always seemed to confront him with two contrary choices. He would have given a good deal to please Myra because he knew she could be very generous, and he dreamed of a Russian room in the gallery. But he also felt that Bernie was a jumped up little snit. When he was coming up for tenure Stefan had discussed the whole matter with Wendell Grierson, the chair of the English Department and a noted eighteenth-century scholar. 'I agree that he lacks bottom,' Grierson had said, 'but the President feels that a book in press and all this flap about his poetry warrant tenure.' And since Stefan never queried a presidential decision unless his own interests were affected, he had shrugged and allowed Bernie's tenure to pass without comment.

'Perhaps he didn't see you, my dear?'

'Oh, he saw me all right.'

'Felicity, sublimate! You must practise sublimating. We have more pressing matters on hand. How many letters were sent out yesterday?'

'Exactly four hundred and sixty seven, to every insurance company in England, Europe and America, thanks to the word processor.'

'Now, we must wait. Some will write and others will accept our offer to phone us collect. But in the meantime I shall call up some of my contacts in the art world. And remind me to see that all the burglar alarms are checked in the gallery.'

'The alarms?'

'I was talking to that pleasant fellow, Poldowski, from the county police, and he tells me that this rapist murderer could be a student or a faculty member. And a man who can commit murder is quite capable of attacking paintings. I'm convinced there is a connection between icono-clasm and murder. Do you know how many priceless icons were destroyed when the Bolsheviks came to power? Many of them were torn from the church walls and burned as firewood. We must take every precaution to protect the paintings here – with one exception.'

The exception was an almost life-size painting entitled *La Petite Joyeuse* by a justifiably obscure artist of the late nineteenth century that hung just inside the door to the French room. It was generally concealed by a large stand of decorative ferns and when Felicity peered through the foliage she understood why. The whole centre of the painting was devoted to the lovingly detailed pink bottom of a can-can dancer, surrounded by frills. Black net stockings extended from the frills to red high-heeled shoes, and a simpering face looked coyly over a black satin shoulder. It was, Felicity thought, quite the most vulgar picture she had seen outside of a *Playboy* or *Penthouse* magazine, and when she asked Stefan about it he groaned.

La Petite Joyeuse had been purchased many years ago by Fred Cadwallader's grandfather from the artist himself, a certain Jules Pascin who specialized in salacious nudes. Cadwallader placed it on the mantelpiece in his bedroom and spent many happy hours contemplating its aesthetic qualities. When his wife saw how much it pleased him she gave it to the Pequod art gallery as a bequest when Cadwallader was on a moose-hunting expedition in Maine. And because it was a Cadwallader bequest and the family had never failed to support the gallery, Stefan de Mornay hung it in the darkest corner of the French room, concealed behind a bank of ferns which was only removed when the Cadwalladers arrived to admire their generosity. Stefan sometimes mused about a selective fire in the gallery, or paying a thief to remove it, but Fred Cadwallader seemed as attached to the painting as his grandfather and would often stand in front of it, shaking his head, and saying it should never have been allowed to leave the family. Stefan knew that if thieves did break into the gallery they would make straight for the Monet and the small but elegant Degas.

From his study window, Bernie could see the Lieutenant talking to Lester Marcus. Every few steps Marcus stopped abruptly and gesticulated violently and the tall, slouched figure looked down and nodded. Marcus seemed to be doing all the talking and Bernie had a sudden wild urge to lean out the window and shout to them that Martin Harris was the rapist. And then he saw Martin himself shuffling across the quad, abstractedly tearing his hair with one hand, clutching a box of computer disks in the other, muttering, and apparently oblivious to everything around him. He almost passed between the two men without seeing them, and Poldowski turned slowly and watched him for a few moments, then spoke to Lester Marcus. Did they already know about him? Was Martin a suspect? And still Bernie could not see Martin harming anyone. If he were a homicidal maniac surely Lenore would

have been the first victim, not Betty Levin and those two students whose names he had already forgotten.

He could think of a dozen different students in his own classes who could be responsible. In his seminar on the Victorian novel there were two who had potential rapist written all over them. One of them, Hexter Blaine, lifted weights and dreamed of being offered a football scholarship at some large state university, and there was a pallid youth with acne who was always grovelling round the floor for lost pencils and obviously trying to look up the women students' skirts. Bernie had seen Muffin Winston snarl at him, and once Deb Turner stamped on his hand. The latter breathed him a greeting as he took his place at the head of the table, and he gave them both a circumspect smile. There was no point in encouraging students these days when sexual harassment warnings were posted up in every dormitory and the faculty had been told that in such cases even tenure could be revoked. Harvard or Yale were his holy grails and he was not going to have some nymphomaniacal adolescent blemishing his record.

Bernie could teach *Jane Eyre* with his eyes closed and proceeded to do so, dwelling on the miseries of alienation and isolation in the novel. Suddenly he heard chairs pushed back and a murmur of voices. He looked up and she was there. It was as though she had materialized from some alien planet, a being made of light and air with a shock of shining black hair. A tiny figure in a white body suit that seemed to glow with every movement. As he stared at her transfixed, he could feel a tingling spread from his eyes to every part of his body. She spoke and her voice was high and light and lilting.

'English 304?'

Bernie was barely able to speak and simply nodded.

She looked around at the students, and sat down. But sitting hardly described it, for she seemed to balance for a second and then stretched her legs up on either side of her head. She turned and looked at him through a pair of perfectly shaped thighs.

'I'm Mariana Ashmole.'

'Bernie Lefkowitz,' he said weakly.

'I beg your pardon?' she seemed puzzled.

'Lefkowitz.'

'Oh, an ethnic name,' and smiled sympathetically.

She explained that she was on the gymnastics team and had been appointed as co-instructor for freshman English while she studied for her MA. Pivoting on her buttocks she added briefly that she hadn't had time to finish stretching after her workout, and locked her ankles behind her head. Slowly she brought her legs forward and tucked them under

the table; then she proceeded to take charge of the seminar.

'What we must establish is the correct sexocritical orientation to the text.'

Bernie could only nod as she swung round towards him, and he suddenly realized that he had never interested himself in any of the gymnasts before. There always seemed an invisible barrier between the academic and the gymnastic faculty at Pequod, and Bernie began to wonder why. He had taught some of the gymnasts from time to time and found them a muscled and exhausted little group who tried to huddle in the back of the classroom where they could doze in peace between training sessions. Their unappealing scrubbed little faces were always drowsy and it was difficult to determine their sex. Mariana Ashmole was quite different. Her body seemed electrical, and he could tell that he was not the only one affected. Hexter Blaine was cracking his knuckles and fidgeting while the pallid youth was sitting bolt upright and staring at her.

'It's *Jane Eyre* isn't it? Well, Dr Lefkowitz I know that you must already have identified the vaginal vocabulary?'

Bernie murmured that they were just opening up the text, and Mariana frowned.

'If we are taking a gynocritical approach then I hardly think we want to proceed from a male authoritarian stance.'

Without hesitation Bernie asked if she would care to lead the seminar and she took over, causing a flurry of confusion when she demanded that the pallid youth identify an example of the periodicity of clitoral comma usage. Mariana had casually pushed a folder to Bernie when she began talking and he surreptitiously opened it. She was obviously an early bloomer, admitted to Vassar at fourteen, and graduating with honours from Berkeley when she was nineteen. Adding swiftly under the table with his fingers, Bernie calculated that she was just twenty, already a graduate and was here on a Marcus scholarship. She was not a student at all, not technically a student, since only undergraduates were classified as untouchables by Bernie.

The whole class seemed bemused and when she set the assignment for their next meeting on castration fears in Rochester, everyone scribbled obediently except Deb and Muffin who looked to Bernie for his approval. He nodded, and as they passed by him Deb said audibly, 'Shit! I hope she's not going to give us an encore. That sounded like the crap on the vaginal douche ads.'

He realized he still had Mariana's folder in his hand and as he handed it back to her he said in what he hoped was the voice of authority, 'Perhaps we could discuss this in my study. I may even be able to find you a cup of coffee.'

She laughed and he noticed that her teeth were round and shining like a child's, and the top of her glistening black hair was just below his shoulder. It gave him an indescribable feeling of pleasure to be with a woman that he did not have to look up to.

She refused coffee and he ran down the corridor to fetch her a tall glass of ice water which she swallowed in one gulp and then sat there crunching the ice. Light seemed to be generated by the silken texture of her body-suit as she moved at angles and with a speed that did not seem quite human. He marvelled at her thighs and the precise and enticing triangle above them. Her breasts were no more than the faintest outline and yet she was indisputably and wonderfully feminine. It was almost unbearable to sit there discussing her transcript from Berkeley when what he wanted to do was reach out and run his hand down the length of her amazing body. Her self confidence delighted him and he listened intently while she lectured him on the latest in gynocritics.

'If I were not a man I would describe myself as a fervent feminist, Mariana.'

'Yeah, I've heard you're pretty liberated, Dr Lefkowitz.'

'Bernie, please. I always like my graduate students to use my first name.'

'Bernie, that's kind of cute. I like it.'

'You are in—' and he faltered because he really did not know what gymnasts did apart from putting their bodies in unnatural and painful attitudes. 'You are in a team here?'

'Louise Grunch and I are working out a doubles routine for the Olympics.'

'The Olympics!' He tried to sound amazed and succeeded.

'Gymnastics are awarded to individuals and teams. Louise and I are developing a series of routines together that will qualify as a new programme. You've seen the synchronized swimming?'

'Oh yes, yes – wonderful,' he lied.

'Well, Louise was my spotter when I was in the last Olympics team and we worked together so well that I decided it was time to take the sport a quantum leap forward. We spoke to Lester Marcus in Los Angeles and he offered us both scholarships on the spot.'

'Louise is—'

'Louise is not a brain like me, but she's very muscular and has fantastic co-ordination, so she's doing something in physical education, I think.'

'Ah, yes, very suitable.'

'But I am not only a great athlete, I also have a genius IQ.'

'I'm sure you have.'

'Oh, there's no question about it. I was tested when I was six and

Daddy immediately hired special tutors for me and I went into an accelerated learning programme. I want you to understand that I am only sitting in on your undergraduate seminar because I need a unit of Victorian novel.'

'I hope that I can do everything possible to help you, Mariana. I should add that I always expect my graduate students to be my friends.'

'I like your attitude, Bernie. The teacher who doesn't make every student a learning experience is a dummy in my book,' and she reached out and took his hand in an extraordinarily strong grip. 'Why don't you come down on Friday night and watch Louise and me work out?'

'I couldn't think of anything I'd enjoy more. And, how about having supper with me afterwards?'

'You sure move fast,' she said.

'Is it a deal?'

'Why not? But I warn you, I need a lot of protein after a workout.'

His luck had changed. Bernie could feel it in the warmth of spring sunshine and the Wordsworth memorial bank of daffodils outside English Hall. Even his mail looked interesting: the usual book advertisements and a letter from . . . His heart turned over and he almost collided with Martin Harris on his way to lunch.

'Martin – the Ploughshare Press – it's from them.'

'They publish poetry, don't they?'

'Martin, it's a commercial press. They don't ask for subventions or print on junk paper. They are—'

'Why don't you open it?'

Trembling, he prised open the crisp, antique-finished envelope and read slowly with Martin peering over his shoulder.

'They are interested in my next collection of poems – 'view to publication' in their contemporary poets series. Martin that is simply the greatest!'

Martin seemed genuinely pleased by his success and Bernie crowed all the way to the faculty club. He also told Martin about Mariana Ashmole.

'She is unique, Martin. I've never seen anything like her.'

'A gymnast?' Martin was licking his lips feverishly. 'Can you imagine what their muscle control is like. My God, they could grip you for hours.'

'I didn't think of that,' Bernie said slowly, and almost had an erection on the spot.

'None of this "Darling, I've had enough" stuff. Or, "Get it over with quickly, honey, my legs are aching". Bernie, you know how they exercise. Well, can you imagine what their vaginas are like?'

'I – I hadn't actually thought of that,' Bernie shrugged. 'I mean, I never treat a woman like a sex object. However—'

'What is she like?'

'Tiny, with black hair and huge black eyes. She is the polar opposite to Felicity, and I think that's what I like most about her.'

'I would trade my vampire for Felicity any day,' Martin said wistfully.

'Martin,' again Bernie felt that twinge of suspicion as he looked at his friend, 'if you had a problem – I mean – a real problem, you'd talk to me, wouldn't you? I mean – we are friends—'

'I have only one problem, Bernie. She was there last night and she'll be in my apartment again this evening.' Wearily he said, 'She'll only leave me when she's devoured me like one of those black widow spiders that eats the male after mating.'

'Every man on campus is suspect until this maniac is caught.'

'When – if he gets caught, I'd like to give him a medal,' Martin said savagely.

Nobody could talk like this and be a killer, Bernie thought, as the two found a quiet table in the faculty club. Within minutes Melba and Doris Torno from the German department had joined them and Bernie watched them spar with each other. Melba offered him dinner the following night which he accepted, and Doris promptly said she had arranged a small party for Friday. Bernie firmly declined the latter.

Felicity finished her lecture on Turner and decided she had no appetitie for lunch. No matter what she did, or how she tried to forget him, everything reminded her of Bernie. Des Freskin arrived and suggested pizzas and a movie and she pleaded another engagement. She began to sort slides in a ferociously preoccupied fashion while he sat on the edge of her desk oozing sympathy.

'Heck, I know just what you're going through. I was almost engaged to a girl last year, and she not only ditched me, she joined the Animal Liberation Front, and the next thing my lab was raided. Raided – and I was in the middle of some very heavy research testing the resistance of beagles to carbon monoxide.'

'Des, I'm very, very busy.'

Chuck Stimson elbowed himself into the room and told her he'd just worked out a great training programme for her involving weights. Seeing Des on one end of Felicity's desk he promptly sat himself down on the other and the two snarled at each other like belligerent bookends.

She stood up and pointed to the door, 'Everyone! Out! I want to be left in peace.'

They went off together and she heard Des complaining that it wasn't safe for a man to walk alone around the campus at night. Chief Flyte had hired extra guards and he had twice been asked for his ID on his way back from the lab. They then agreed that Bernie Lefkowitz must have given Felicity a very rough time, and when Chuck said he thought it was time somebody kicked the little fart's arse up to his ears, Des agreed enthusiastically.

It had taken her months to trace the Haden plates to a sale in 1957 and now Felicity wondered if she weren't chasing a phantom. There had been times when the weeks of poring over catalogues had been a pleasure because she could almost feel the presence of Whistler at her side. What if she could take the plates in her hands and then prepare them for printing? She knew the kind of paper she would choose – a thin silky Japanese paper, as translucent as porcelain, with a slightly golden tinge. First the inking, leaving a film of brown ink that she would rub with her palm just as Whistler had done, and finally she would press the dampened paper on to the plate on the etching press. That was the moment when she often caught her breath and almost fainted because it was like the weight of a body being pressed down upon her. There would be a miracle – an etching of infinite subtlety and grace – Whistler's work of art created through the agency of her own hands. That was what she had begun to yearn for when she and Bernie made love. She wanted that love to create a child. In her mind, she knew that her love-making and her search for Whistler's lost erotic etchings had become one, but now she felt that the search and her body were both barren. Hope long-deferred makes the heart sick; the words came back to her with a particular bitterness. Hearts do not ache, but she could feel a dull pain in her chest as though the pump of life had become a cold stone.

The cough, faint and diffident, disturbed her as she methodically sorted through insurance lists during the afternoon. She looked up and Martin was standing at the door, ashen-faced and trembling.

'Oh, hello. Are you the messenger?' she said sourly.

'Felicity,' he seemed on the verge of choking and clutched his throat. 'Well?'

'I – I'm sorry.' And then the words came in a babble. 'If you had been mine I would never have let you go because I could see you made him happy and now he has every woman on campus chasing after him even some gymnast and he'll never be happy again.'

Before she could answer he was gone, and she heard him stumbling down the stairs that led to the main gallery.

Bernie dressed with particular care that Friday night in a dark red Italian jogging suit with matching Nikes and he was just smoothing his hair when Martin knocked and immediately let himself in. They had exchanged keys two years ago so they could use each other's apartment at exam time when frantic students came hammering at the door all hours of the day and night with stories of impending breakdown and possible suicide. Martin shifted uneasily from one foot to the other and said he was at a loose end. One of the computers had developed a glitch and three weeks' factoring had been lost.

It would not look quite so planned, Bernie thought, if he strolled into the gym with a friend, so he promptly invited Martin to come along. He appreciated that Martin had very little social life since Lenore Marcus had decided to make him her nightly companion, and now his friend was clearly distraught about his work. He wished he could have helped him in some way but all he could do was nod sympathetically and uncomprehendingly as Martin tore his hair and spoke about algorithms and linked polyhedrons. Besides, it would do no harm to keep an eye on Martin.

The campus had been quiet since the death of Betty Levin, television crews made a brief appearance and interviewed some women students who all said they were terrified, but so what? There was violence everywhere and why not at Pequod? Lorenzo Delgado was given the job of training some newly recruited campus police and cheerfully calculated what he was making in overtime. Bernie's suggestion that male faculty dress as women and act as decoys was still being debated by the women's studies faculty, where he had the comfortable feeling that when they discussed the male academic most likely to be arrested as a rapist, his name was not even on their list.

The gym was crowded and brilliantly lit around a circle that appeared to be covered with a taut canvas. There were a few faculty members present but he could tell by the sea of heads bobbing around him at shoulder level that he was surrounded by gymnasts.

'Makes you feel like Gulliver among the Lilliputians,' he said easily to Martin who was mumbling something about Verishovsky's theorem. Over by the far wall he saw a tall slender figure in a hooded, black track suit and Bernie recognized Lenore Marcus. She ignored him and stared directly at Martin and smiled. 'My God, she's waiting here for him,' Bernie thought, 'and she doesn't give a damn who sees her.' He felt a sudden twinge of pity for Martin who had moved from Verishovsky to a modular proposition by Igor Lupescu. They were just about to make their way down to some seats at the far corner when Lester Marcus stood on one of the benches and hailed them.

'Over here – perfect view.'

Martin tried to dive in the opposite direction but Bernie had hold of his elbow.

'What are you worried about? Do you think he cares even if he does know?'

'You're right,' Martin said, 'He's probably grateful to me for taking her off his hands. He wouldn't be looking quite so fit if he had to cope with her every night.'

Bernie smiled and thought it would do no harm to let the chairman of the board know that he had just been invited to publish his next volume of poetry with the Ploughshare Press, but Marcus seemed more impressed that the two of them had come to see the gymnastics.

'This college has a great tradition, and that tradition is going to be raised to glory among the stars this evening. I'm glad that you're both aware of the importance of the occasion.'

His seamed face creased into a grimace that could have been a smile and he reached up and slapped Bernie on the back.

'I wish more of the faculty took your interest in what constitutes the heart and purpose of Pequod.'

'Mariana Ashmole invited me to see her routine,' Bernie said nonchalantly.

'The heck she did!' Lester seemed even more impressed. 'She is unquestionably the divine muse of gymnastics. I know as a poet you'll appreciate the point of those words. In my opinion Mariana should have received the gold at the last Olympics but she suffered a pulled muscle just before the floor exercises and she could barely do a flying pirouette. A great, great tragedy. But, like the phoenix, she has vaulted to even more splendid heights and we are going to see history made tonight.'

Martin had buried his head in his hands and Bernie could appreciate the tangle of emotions that must have been tormenting him. He knew from his own despair during the early part of the week what it meant to suffer.

'There they are!' Lester Marcus jumped up on the seat again and began to clap, and instantly the whole gymnasium exploded with shouts and cheers.

She was standing in the white circle, turning and smiling to the audience, arms outflung, her radiant yellow body-suit reflecting the lights as though she had just stepped out of a pool of molten gold. The figure beside her was also in yellow but in some indefinable way she seemed coarser and less brilliant, as if she were Mariana's shadow. The second movement of Tchaikovsky's Third Symphony crashed down from the loudspeakers and Bernie winced, because he had a good ear for music and this sounded as though it were being ground out through steel drums. Then the two figures began to move in unison, bowing to each other, turning in an arabesque with their left feet touching, and at every movement the crowd cheered and stamped. Lester Marcus was on the seat again, stamping out his own enthusiasm, and gradually Bernie caught the excitement as Louise began to throw Mariana high above her head.

It began with Mariana spinning away from her partner, then suddenly reversing and running back to her so quickly that it was like a golden blur of light. She jumped, Louise caught her ankles and flung her up, and in mid-air Mariana twisted and spun and looked as if she were about to fall to the ground at the very moment when Louise miraculously caught her shoulders inches above the canvas. Bernie could not remember quite the same sort of thrill since his grandmother had taken him to Barnum and Bailey's and he'd watched the lions jump through hoops of fire. One incredible throw tossed Mariana so high that for seconds she was flying with arms outstretched, her feet arched behind her, like some fantastic, glittering bird. She began to fall and Louise did not move, she was still, her hands on her thighs, staring out at the audience. Again that terrifying instant, for this time Mariana was hurtling down headfirst, and so quickly that Bernie could not see what had happened, but Louise had caught her by the shoulders and the two were kneeling, facing each other, hands clasped, and smiling like happy children.

Bernie found himself cheering as the two figures turned again and smiled to every side of the gymnasium. Suddenly they had hold of each other's hands and feet, their backs arched inward, and a hoop of gold was rolling faster and faster around the canvas.

'My God, they'll kill themselves,' Bernie cried.

Lester Marcus began shouting, 'Pequod! Pequod! Pequod!' and the crowd yelled with him.

The golden ring was revolving so fast that Bernie could only see a blur of light dazzling and turning. The music crashed to a sudden chord and there were two distinct figures again, bowing and smiling.

Bernie felt quite breathless and realized that Lester had been hammering at him with his fists.

'You have just seen a miracle!' Lester said and wiped his eyes with a silk monogrammed handkerchief.

'I think you're right,' Bernie said weakly. 'But the bruises—' all he could think of was Mariana Ashmole's astonishing body pounded against the floor.

'She won't have a mark on her,' Lester said. 'Principle of physics – you can touch a hot stove without burning so long as you don't hold on to it. Their bodies never touch the floor for more than a split second.'

Bernie turned to Martin for confirmation of this surprising fact and gasped. Martin looked as though he were paralysed, his mouth hanging open, a spurt of saliva at either side, his eyes fixed and staring.

'Martin,' Bernie shook him, wondering if the sight of Lenore had produced this effect, but when he looked across the gym she had vanished. Martin swayed weakly.

'Martin, are you all right?'

'She's—' Martin was staring down at the two gold figures now lost in a cheering crowd.

'What did I tell you? Isn't she fantastic?'

'She's a vision.'

Bernie laughed and said that he was taking her to supper, and he had an idea that after a workout like that she would have a pretty good appetite.

Lester Marcus heard him and told him he was a lucky man, and that if he were younger and not married, he would be down there in the changing room with a dozen of the biggest and most expensive red roses ever grown. Bernie laughed again and thought how pleasant it was to be on such good terms with the chairman of the board.

'You take care of her, Bernard,' Lester frowned, and his eyes disappeared in a web of wrinkles. 'I have been out of my mind since the murder. Don't forget that this campus is being terrorized by some maniac from Hicksville or Hempstead. If anything happens to one of our gymnasts I swear I'll take matters into my own hands and then—'

He was interrupted by Mariana who had pushed her way imperiously through the crowd and was smiling up at Bernie.

'Do we still have a date, Bernie?'

'Why else would I be here?' he smiled.

CHAPTER SIX

While Bernie watched Mariana inhale two large steaks and a bowl of canneloni that would have satisfied a crew of Sicilian roadworkers, the lower depths of Pequod were stirring. There had been a number of faculty complaints about Deborah Turner and Margaret (known as Muffin) Winston. They specialized in failing grades and incompletes, and early in the term Wendy Forsyth had charged into the admissions office demanding to know how either of them had managed to get into a college like Pequod that prided itself on academic standards. It was understood that gymnasts arrived with special exemptions, but Muffin was a fat girl who was trying to develop bulimia so she could gorge and vomit herself into a delectable state of emaciation. Eating was not difficult for her, but she was having problems with the vomiting, and Deborah had twice been charged with smoking pot in the lunchroom.

The admissions officer, a harried women with frayed blonde hair, reminded Wendy that Pequod required students to be in the top five percentile of their high school graduation class before they could even hope to be considered for Pequod; however, there were exceptions.

'Such as?' Wendy had insisted.

'Well, what we're really looking for is an interesting personality profile on the incoming student.'

'What exactly does that mean?'

'Does Daddy have a million bucks?'

Wendy discovered that P.J. Winston was a megamillionaire specializing in takeovers and container companies, while Ed Turner was the Turner of Skyview Land Developments Inc. She shrugged helplessly when the facts of academic enrolment were made clear to her and after they failed her next quiz she promptly advised both young women to drop Sociology and become English majors.

Deb and Muffin shared a large studio apartment in the old dormitory wing on the far side of the campus, and across the hall was a particular friend of theirs, Tobby Martin. Tobby was from a prosperous black family in White Plains and her decision to become a student at Pequod had been the occasion of great rejoicing in admissions. A minority student whose parents did not flinch at the fees and who could not possibly ask for a scholarship because of the family's income, was a rare prize. Tobby was now admitted to Deb's special council.

The pot smoke drifted up and festooned the ceiling in heavy coils and Deb pulled out a yellow pad and frowned.

'If we don't move now that shitty little gymfreak will grab him.'

'I have been crazy about Bernie ever since I took Literary Masterpieces with him. Man! What a hunk! When I look at him his smile makes my ears tickle,' Tobby sighed.

'It's got to be one of us,' Muffin said between mouthfuls of salami and peanut butter pretzels. 'We've loved him longer.'

'He's even stopped and talked to me after class,' Tobby said.

'OK, so you get to give him the invitation, Tobby. He'll trust you.'

Tobby shifted uncomfortably, 'I don't think the naked bit is so cool.'

Deb grinned, 'He either takes one of us or we get him on an S.H. It'll be three against one if he tries to back off, and sexual harassment is heavy duty stuff. You know how the place is jumping over this rape bit? We move in on him before the freaksville does a takeover.'

'He's a neat guy,' Tobby said, and Muffin jeered.

'If he weren't so cool we wouldn't want him. Shit! Can you imagine what Bernie's like in bed? I bet he has the longest, smoothest, coolest dick on campus. I have lain in bed frigging myself wild just thinking of Bernie slowly pulling it out in front of me and—'

More to shut her up than to agree with her, Tobby said she would give him the invitation the following day after Literary Masterpieces.

'Awesome,' Muffin said, and chomped down on two Mars bars.

Approximately three miles to the west of this den of iniquity, in the Trattoria Fiorentina, Mariana declined a second wedge of chocolate cake with double cream and contented herself with a plate of cheese and crackers.

'It's terrible, Bernie. In the middle of my second flying split I suddenly thought of chocolate cake and I almost lost my concentration.'

'I can see why you've achieved so much, Mariana. You must have extraordinary concentration and determination.'

Mariana smiled and Bernie felt that his role as teacher was being radically undermined . . .

'Determination? Determination is nothing,' she scoffed. 'Determination lets you finish a paper on time or get out of bed when you don't feel like it. What I have is – control.'

She drove the prongs of her fork deeply into the table and smiled again.

'You know Zen, of course.'

'Naturally,' and Bernie was grateful that two years ago he had enjoyed a brief affair with an interior decorator who was into the I Ching.

'My whole being has to be concentrated into the defeat of gravity.'

'But you did come down and fortunately your partner caught you.'

'At that moment we were one spirit.'

Her black eyes glittered and held his gaze. The urge to reach across the table and take her was irresistible but he knew instinctively that Mariana Ashmole would have to be enticed into his bed. The trouble was that when she stared at him with wide, unblinking eyes he felt rather like an unworldly rabbit transfixed by the original serpent. Then she laughed and instantly he felt her youth, but there was no vulnerability in her lack of years; everything she said and did seemed fixed by absolute certainties.

'I've asked for you to be my teaching instructor, Bernie.'

He knew she must be attracted to him, but Bernie concealed his delight with a thoughtful nod.

'I have my own theory of language instruction which is based upon the interaction of cognitive-physical responses.

'Ah,' Bernie said.

'Naturally, all gender will be eliminated from speech.'

'Some of the students come from fairly traditional backgrounds and they may find that a trifle difficult.'

'Difficulties are meant to be overcome,' Mariana said, and frowned.

Bernie drove her back to Mollock where she shared an apartment with Louise. He looked up and saw that Martin's light was on and heaved a deep sigh of relief. Lenore would undoubtedly be keeping him occupied for the rest of the night.

'Poor Martin,' Bernie sighed.

'Yes,' Mariana laughed. 'He's our upstairs neighbour.'

'He's having a very hard time,' Bernie said defensively, for it was obvious to him that she knew all about Lenore's nightly visits.

'There is no question about that,' Mariana replied slowly, and this time he found her attitude disturbing, for quite suddenly she doubled over and guffawed.

'Martin is my best friend.'

'I'm sorry, Bernie,' and she wiped her eyes. 'It's just—'

'I quite appreciate why some people would find it entertaining. It happens that he's my friend.'

'I understand, Bernie. Sorry, it was cheap to laugh at him.' She paused and frowned again, 'I never really saw him until I met him this evening with you. He has very spiritual eyes.'

It was the first time she had expressed uncertainty about anything all night and now she was leaning against him and he could feel the taut warmth of her body against his.

'Mariana,' he breathed.

'Bernie, I really dig you.'

She was kissing him with open mouth, her tongue reaching out to touch the back of his throat. Martin was right. She had a muscle control that was unbelievable. The tip of her tongue was feathering delicate strokes across the roof of his mouth and now twining round his own tongue until he began to feel aroused to the point of pain. She leaned back and smiled –

'Oh yes, Bernie, you really turn me on.'

'Let's go back to my place now. Mariana, I'm on fire!'

She suddenly vaulted out of his car and grinned at him through the window.

'Goodnight, Bernie. This needs thought.'

She flew up the front steps of Mollock and gave him one brief wave before disappearing. Bernie fell back exhausted. She could not possibly be a tease – everything about her was so direct that there were times when he felt as though he were falling down a well. No, she simply needed time to think about the time and the place. But of course, he would take care of all that. Perhaps she was a little hesitant since it was their first date, but nothing she said or did showed any degree of hesitation. She talked and ate the way she threw herself high in the air above their heads, twisting and bending as if no power of earth could ever pull her down.

He parked his car by Sufferin where he was accosted by one of the new police guards; but even this rather cretinoid character instantly approved his ID and watched him walk to the main entrance.

This affair was moving faster than most; Bernie could still feel Mariana's excitement when they were kissing. Who taught her to kiss like that? She must be very experienced, he thought with considerable satisfaction. Once, Martin was discussing virgins with him in extraordinary detail and Bernie had replied honestly that, for him, every woman was a virgin since he could never see why he should recognize any other man's rights except his own. It was an attitude that had made it possible for him to have some gratifying affairs with a number of married women.

He looked around his apartment with satisfaction – Mariana would approve of the Robert Motherwell posters, and he thought he knew where he could pick up a couple of Josef Albers, while from a back closet he had retrieved two Picasso vases that looked original from a distance. Flowers, yes; there would be flowers and stark white sheets. He closed his eyes and saw her standing against that circle of canvas surrounded by cheers and applause. It was surprising that she had not already been snatched up by one of the other gymnasts, but he knew that she had not been on campus for long and it was well known that the male gymnasts believed in conserving their energies for the rings and vaulting horse.

Everything had changed for him, and he would not have been surprised to receive an invitation to apply for a position at one of the major ivy league universities. Mariana Ashmole would have moved in here by then – he tried to imagine their love-making and almost ejaculated. She had really set his balls on fire. If there was one thing in his life that Bernie never doubted, it was his ability to please a woman sexually. He never handed a woman a multichoice quiz, or even asked many questions, rather he let a woman take the initiative and then learned from that what really gave her pleasure. And he had discovered that when he was twelve, from his brother's girlfriend. Everyone expected Bernie to grow up in Seth's shadow, Seth the bright, blond, athletic brother; but he had something his brother coveted beyond football letters and swimming cups. It was Bernie who knew how to please women.

He was just twelve when Seth brought home Winkie Tresselmayn, a plumply pink heiress of fifteen, for a weekend of tennis with the family. Late one afternoon, Winkie found Bernie skulking in the summerhouse where he had retreated after being kicked off the court for incompetent play by his brother. Tearfully, he told Winkie that girls scared him, and Winkie, who had a kindly disposition, proceeded to allay his fears. In due course, Bernie made a point of getting to know all Seth's girlfriends, after which he bedded every one of them. This was very convenient when he was still too young for a driver's licence. And when one girl told his parents that she was pregnant she obligingly added that Seth was responsible. Fortunately, their father seemed to regard it more as a tribute to Seth's blossoming manhood than incipient social delinquency, and the whole matter was dealt with by a circumspect gynaecologist. It did, however, take Seth a long time before he learned that pregnancy was not the inevitable result of manual foreplay.

Bernie rolled over on his pillow and smiled: sometimes the anticipation was as great as the fulfilment. With Felicity, what he had hoped for was nothing compared with the actual experience but – he would not think about her. She was his past. His future was glowing like the brilliant spinning hoop that had dazzled him in the gym. He was tenured, he had a book in press, a volume of poetry, and another requested by the Ploughshare Press, he was on friendly terms with Lester Marcus, and everyone at Pequod knew that Jaime Garland was the mouthpiece for Lester Marcus, and now, to crown it all – he had Mariana Ashmole. Her lightning figure flashed into his mind, and he felt again that sharp, probing tongue in his mouth. When he slept he dreamed that she was winding her body round him and reaching zones of ecstasy he never knew he possessed.

Next morning, even the motley crowd in Literary Masterpieces seemed moved by his discussion of *Don Quixote,* and there was a scattering of applause when he finished. If he had not become an academic he would have enjoyed being an actor provided he could write his own lines. A few students gathered round him to praise and question after the lecture and Bernie was in such good humour that he gave them more than the customary ten minutes. At the edge of the group he saw Tobby Martin standing shyly, a little away from the rest. He was quite fond of Tobby, for it was difficult to dislike anyone who sat in the middle of the class with an expression of fervent adoration. Timidly, she handed him an envelope which looked as though it had been hand lettered.

'It's the third-floor party for English, Dr Lefkowitz. You will come, won't you?'

'When is it, Tobby?'

One of the drawbacks to faculty life at Pequod was the feeling on the part of the students that they were all one big happy family with the academics as their surrogate parents. It was an attitude encouraged by the admissions office and deplored by the faculty which resented being disturbed in the early hours of the morning with questions about term papers. Students regularly gave parties to which they invited their professors, and Bernie had no objection to these. You could always arrive early and leave in time to catch a late movie. Besides, if the English faculty were invited it would give him a chance to gloat over his colleagues, and inform Grierson that he was to be published by Plough- share. Genially, he accepted the invitation and asked if it were a formal occasion.

'Oh no,' Tobby said quickly. 'Come as you are. It's in your honour.'

That, Bernie thought, was a tribute to his teaching and his standing in the department. He would not be at all surprised if the students didn't nominate him for the Most Popular Professor of the Year award. It was not something you took very seriously, but it made a useful addition to your curriculum vitae: 'Well, as a matter of fact, they took me quite by surprise, but I daresay the students get up to the same sort of foolishness here at Yale.' Or Harvard – or Stanford – and it would be something that Mariana would appreciate. As a celebrity she knew that popularity had to be earned. He made a point of telling her about it quite casually when he called her that afternoon.

Cissie Curlewis also made a point of telling Felicity about Bernie's new love since there now seemed no hope of his being hers, and Wendy Forsyth warned her to save her diaphragm for a man who knew how to appreciate her. Felicity smiled wanly and said she was too busy with her research to think about anything else. This wasn't true and no one believed her, but letters were beginning to arrive and one of them really excited her. It was a brief note from the Northumberland Gate Insurance

Company in London stating that four plates by Seymour Haden (signed, erotic?) had been reported stolen from Twyford's Antiques in Chelsea in 1979. A claim for six hundred and fifty pounds had been settled in 1981. Felicity read the letter again and walked across to Stefan's office. He was having a bad morning and moaned every time he shifted in his chair. But in front of him he had a number of letters spread out like tarot cards.

'Stefan, can I get you anything?'

'A new skeleton, my dear. I think the weather must be changing because every bone in my body is aching. It's all the steel pins those clever surgeons used to put me together again – they're very effective barometers.'

'Let me get you some aspirin.'

He reached out and patted her hand, 'Oh Felicity, I am so very fond of you. What a pity I'm not young and handsome and then we could have that baby together, couldn't we?'

She laughed and handed him the letter which he read slowly and placed in the middle of the others.

'Come round here, this has the making of an interesting story.'

They were all from insurance companies and they all reported the theft of erotic works of art. One claim for a series of Persian miniatures had been settled for twenty-two thousand dollars.

'What does all this tell you, Felicity?'

'Someone is stealing erotica. But isn't that what we always thought. Isn't it what Elizabeth said when—'

'Oh, Felicity, look for the pattern. The earliest we have here is 1978, and over there is the Atlas Insurance Company investigating the loss of a marble sculpture by Canova—' He snorted, 'A likely Canova, I'm sure.'

'Stef, it does look as though there's been a rash of thefts quite recently. But how does this help me find the Whistlers? Do we advertise? Or let the thief know that he doesn't have a second-rate Victorian etcher but James MacNeill Whistler?'

'My dear, we now find out who has been buying erotic works of art since approximately 1976. My goodness, whoever he is, and I imagine it's a male, he must have a very large if unselective collection. Canova indeed!'

'Yes, Stef, but if he's prepared to buy stolen art works, he'll be doing it secretly and—'

'My dear Felicity, nobody keeps a secret in the art world. And I do have some old and very dear friends. Do you think you could drive me to New York this afternoon. 'I—' he gestured helplessly and his fingers looked as though someone had erratically stitched them to his hands.

'But your three o'clock lecture—'

'I shall cancel it. Better still, let them have another Kenneth Clark movie. Pick me up at one thirty sharp. First I must make a few calls.'

Felicity expected to be given an address in some dilapidated building in the Village where they would have to climb up three flights of stairs to an unpainted door with a fly-blotched card pinned to it. Instead, Stef told her to park on 72nd Street and they walked slowly round into Madison Avenue and to the august premises of Henslow and Macbeth, the most highly esteemed antique dealers in Manhattan. Stef nodded to the uniformed doorman who seemed to know him, and Felicity almost tripped as she saw him call a cab for Woody Allen.

'Oh yes, my dear, all the celebrities come here,' Stef murmured. 'And a great many other people too.'

Felicity had heard of the legendary Archibald Macbeth but she never imagined that she would be sitting in his office admiring his collection of T'ang embroideries and Ch'ien Lung enamels. There was an opulence about the whole shop which made her feel a little uneasy, and she decided that she felt more at home in art galleries which freely admitted the public. Archibald Macbeth reminded her of a richly decorated dragon curled around his treasure horde, mantling his wealth with uniformed guards and burglar alarms. In the gilded elevator and along the panelled corridor, tiny red lights winked unceasingly. She felt sure that if she touched one of the vases or placed a finger tip on the glass-covered embroideries, sirens would suddenly shriek and a crowd of armed police jump out from every cupboard. The sleek and manicured Mr Macbeth seemed already acquainted with Felicity's subject.

'Dr Norman, I make it my business to know who is investigating what. Seymour Haden, isn't it? Odd, I thought you were regarded as a Whistler expert.'

To her surprise, Stefan came straight to the point, leaning over on the head of his cane, and showing his teeth to Macbeth.

'Archie, I'm too old and too sick to fence – and so are you.'

Archie smiled deprecatingly, 'I certainly havn't tangled with the KGB recently.'

'Whistler's erotic etchings.'

'Were there any?'

He turned to Felicity Norman and smirked, 'I'm familiar with art historians in hot pursuit of their obsessions. Last month I had a young fellow in here who was quite convinced he knew where to find a lost da Vinci Madonna.'

Stefan nodded to Felicity and she said firmly, 'They were by Whistler but he chose to give them Seymour Haden's signature. Haden was his brother-in-law.'

'Yes, yes, I know all about Whistler's escapades. I always think Ruskin had justice on his side when he criticized Whistler's technique. Now, please don't misunderstand me. Personally I live in a world of Chinese art, but I can appreciate the general regard for Whistler. After all, how can you criticize a man who was so attached to his mother?'

He chuckled and Felicity was about to respond angrily when Stefan intervened.

'Who is buying erotic art these days, Archie?'

'Who is not?' Archie smirked again, and looped his fingers through his gold watch chain.

'I don't think it's a universal taste, Archie. Somebody is paying such high prices for erotica that our light-fingered friends are abroad and active.'

Archie elevated one shoulder in the faint intimation of a shrug, and looked away.

'Archie, we have known each other for many years now, and we both know more about each other than we would like any one else to know.'

'My God, Stefan, you're not trying to blackmail me, are you? I expected better from you than that.' He waved an admonishing finger and chortled.

'And you will receive better, I assure you. I propose a deal.'

Archie was suddenly intent and leaned across his desk as though preparing to jump it. 'Whistler's erotic etchings. Dear heaven, they would bring hundreds of thousands at Christie's. Perhaps more—'

'I think they were bought by your friend as Haden's.'

'Stefan, if I could help you—'

'You will help me because you know that I have always dealt very fairly with you in the past.'

Archie nodded and Stefan said quietly, 'Who is he?'

'The purchases are always made through an agent.'

'His name?'

'Thomas Kucich.'

'No better than a fence, wouldn't you agree?'

'Stefan, at times he's been very useful to us all.'

'You and I always prefer to deal with principals.'

'Thomas Kucich has bought several Chinese prints from us. He has never questioned the price.' Or the quality, he felt like adding, but he knew that would be understood by Stefan.

Stefan's voice was so soft that Felicity could scarcely hear him, but Archie was watching him with such intentness that he seemed to be lip-reading.

'Archie, you hate mysteries as much as I do. You went to a great deal of trouble to find the purchaser. Who is he?'

'If I knew him—'

There was a long silence between them and Stefan said slowly, 'They are not exactly etchings, Archie. What your collector has unwittingly bought are Whistler's original copper plates. Whoever has them would be able to run off an edition of prints.'

Archie chewed on his upper lip, pulled out a slip of paper and wrote three words. 'That's all I have,' he said. 'I don't know any more than that. I think he's Tunisian, but that is my own supposition.'

Stefan carefully folded the slip of paper and put it in his top pocket. 'When have you ever guessed wrongly, Archie?' he said winningly. 'Your taste is impeccable, your judgement unfailingly correct.'

Not until they were driving back to Long Island did Stefan take out the slip and read what was written there.

'Taraq ben Mollah – now that's someone I've never come across before. But it must be a sign of the times. It used to be Arabs who tried to sell you dirty postcards in Alexandria and Tunis. Now it seems we have an Arab who is buying dirty pictures.'

'Stefan, if he has the kind of money to buy fake Canovas he must be well known.'

'Don't worry, my dear, we shall find him. But we must walk very carefully now.'

'Stefan, did you – I don't like to question you – but, did you mean what you said when you promised Macbeth the prints?'

'Ah, how delightful. Haydn's *Mass in Time of War*,' he reached over and turned up the radio. 'A pity it's so seldom played. Brahms seems to be out of favour with the Bartok and Berg crew.'

'Did you mean—?'

He sighed contentedly and closed his eyes murmuring, 'Do you remember the words of Anatole France – another artist under a temporary cloud these days – 'In place of presents, give promises, they cost less and count far more. Who gives more than he who gives hope?''

Everything seemed to be radiating light in her apartment when she returned, but she was now convinced that the Mollock terraces had room service like a motel. If only she could tell Bernie how close she was to holding the plates in her hands. It was like a physical sensation: she held out her hands in front of her and felt the weight of them.

Wendy Forsyth rapped at her window and within seconds Felicity had blurted out the news.

Even the imperturbable sociologist was impressed. 'You've actually got a name?'

'If I could only pick up a Tunisian phone directory or—'

'Do you know anybody at your embassy in Washington?'

'As a matter of fact the second secretary is an old friend of mine.'

'Call her—'

'Him.'

'It would be. Ask him to get in touch with his counterpart in the Tunisian embassy. All those diplomatic types know each other.'

'How much should I tell him?'

'Nothing. Why should you? Just let him know you want to get a line on this character because you think he may be willing to provide a scholarship – anything like that.'

Felicity was grateful that Wendy did not ask her for any details. Instead, as she phoned Algie Mortimer long distance, Wendy regaled her with the latest scandal about Bernie. She was glad she could only hear bits and pieces as Algie promised to blitz Washington for any information about Taraq ben Mollah. He promised that he would call her back within twenty-four hours, and when was she coming down to Washington?

Bernie could almost believe that Mariana was infatuated with him. There were moments when she actually seemed to be listening to him in his Victorian seminar, and when they said goodnight she wound her legs around him and kissed him with a protracted and passionate intensity. She would engage in every kind of oral sex until he felt himself breaking into pieces from the baffled ecstasy her tongue woke in him, but she would not let him respond. He fondled every part of her body until he was almost crying with his hunger to know her, but just as he was about to take her on the seat of the car, anywhere, she would twist away from him with extraordinary dexterity and vanish up the steps to Mollock or into the gym. Twice he had been down to the gym to work out, more from a desperate need to expend energy than to exercise, and found himself in the company of Chuck Stimson or Des Freskin who rippled their biceps in front of him and lifted weights that would have broken a coal-miner's back. The two had become quite friendly since they had each decided to move in on Felicity. Bernie was beginning to feel physically ragged from sexual frustration, a sensation that was so new to him he thought at first he was coming down with some virus.

He spent a great deal of his time watching Mariana go through her routines with Louise, a lowering, stolid young woman, who had now taken to greeting him laconically when he took his place in the stands beside Lester Marcus. Nothing quenched the latter's enthusiasm for the gymnasts' routine, but even though Bernie had taken the trouble to learn the difference between a glide kip and a penny drop, he felt himself on the edge of bored irritation. His first visit to the circus had been an intoxicating thrill from beginning to end, but when his grandmother offered to take him again the following year, he had preferred to see a show at the Museum of Modern Art. He tried to throw himself into the frantic excitement as Mariana spun above their heads, but he knew that all he wanted was to impale that brilliant, twisting small figure on his aching penis. As he watched her make that same giddy fall to earth he could think of nothing but filling her body with his own flesh, and he sat there gnawing at his knuckles.

'Don't let it get to you, Bernard,' Lester slapped him on the knee. 'She won't fall – Louise is like a rock – and Mariana is probably the greatest aerial gymnast of all time.'

The frenzy of frustration that was tearing at him was not helped by Martin who came to see Mariana as often as he did. Martin sat there enthralled, and over lunch the next day he would question Bernie feverishly about what sex had been like with Mariana. He tried to be understanding with Martin, but the continual interrogations about his non-existent sex life were infuriating. Only the occasional glimpse of Lenore Marcus on the opposite side of the gym made him appreciate what inspired Martin's anguished questions. Bernie resolved that either Mariana slept with him or he would drop her after giving her a lecture on the anti-social and dehumanizing effects of teasing.

It was their fourth date and after she had swallowed her third lamb chop Bernie determined to make a direct proposition.

'Mariana, I want to sleep with you.'

'No you don't. You want to fuck me,' she laughed, and her small round teeth seemed transparent in the muted rose lights of the Trattoria Fiorentina.

'My God, Mariana! You don't know how much! I've been having wet dreams because of you.'

She laughed and then instantly became serious, 'Bernie, you know that I'm crazy about you.'

'Then why—' his voice was almost cracking and he reached over and took both her hands, 'why have you been tormenting me?'

'Bernie, if you want to I can let you touch me.'

'Do you think I'm satisfied with you jerking me off in the car? I'm not a school kid.' He felt like saying that he never had been a fan of mutual masturbation since he had always found women responded to more advanced and satisfying forms of love-making.

She spoke firmly as though he had not spoken, 'But I can't permit you to penetrate any orifice.'

'What?' He sat there stunned.

'Bernie, it's quite simple. The totality of my psychic space is one with the totality of my physical space, both generating an auric energy.'

'I don't understand,' he said weakly.

'It's quite simple,' she said patiently. 'An invasion of one space is an invasion of the other leading to the inevitable decay of the auric force. That's logical, isn't it?'

'The force?'

'Psychic energy manifesting itself as material force! Is that clear anough for you?'

'No,' he said honestly.

CHAPTER SEVEN

Algie called Felicity the following afternoon and seemed to think that all his sleuthing should be rewarded by her taking the next train down to Washington for a long weekend with him. 'I couldn't get much out of Yusuf over at the Tunisian Embassy except that your Mr ben Mollah is an international financier with residences here, there and everywhere. So, I got in touch with a few chaps at the State Department and they gave me a bead on the character. He is filthily rich but he's something of an invalid so he dosses down in a villa in Lausanne, the Villa Francesca. You should be able to reach him there, old girl. Now, when do I see you?'

Felicity made a vague date for the end of term and rushed off to see Stefan. She expected him to share her excitement but instead he frowned and said pettishly, 'My dear, I hope this young fellow has been discreet.'

'Stef, he's a diplomat.'

'These days that could mean he knows how to stamp passports and very little else. You're quite sure you were circumspect?'

'I let him think I wanted to wangle a grant or a scholarship out of ben Mollah.'

Stefan still seemed troubled, 'I wish you'd let me find out about our collector of erotica. Well,' and he brightened up considerably, 'at least we have an address. Felicity, when can you leave?'

'I suppose I'll have to wait until the end of the term.'

'Rubbish! You must go now. I can hire someone to finish your British painters series. I may even give the remaining lectures myself.'

'Stefan – how do I get to Lausanne?'

'My dear girl, by plane to Geneva of course. We're not talking about Mongolia or Kazakhstan.'

She sat, disconsolate. 'Stef, I don't have any money'.

'I see.'

'I was so miserable last week I bought a pair of boots on sale—'

The boots were dark green suede with gold frogging down the sides and Stefan had admired them enormously.

'I shall have to find the money for you, my dear.'

'Stefan, could you?'

'I certainly haven't a penny left in my budget, so I shall have to make an appeal elsewhere—'

'Would the President help?'

'I don't want to bother the President about this. In fact, the fewer people who know about your trip the better. Let them believe that you have fled home to England to escape the misery of seeing that hairy little snit every day. By the way, I saw Bernie this morning on the stairs and he's looking poorly. Nothing to alarm you, my dear, simply the effect of a solitary life.'

This could have been confirmed by Cissie Curlewis who frequently stood on her toilet with a stethoscope applied to the ceiling. All she heard were Bernie's disconsolate footsteps and the regular noises of scrubbing and general house-cleaning.

'And now,' Stefan continued, 'let me tell you how I think Mr ben Mollah should be approached. In the meantime, you must have a bag packed ready to leave on the instant we can arrange a flight for you.'

He invited himself to dinner with Josh and Myra Lefkowitz and drove slowly down to Cold Spring Harbor. Every turn of the wheel sent a jarring pain down his arms, but he pursed his lips and thought of St Michael. If only the KGB thugs had not been quite so efficient about breaking his hands. Long before he lost consciousness they stamped methodically on his fingers, cursing him and shouting that they would like to cut off the hands of every thief who stole Soviet art treasures. If only he could add one more Stroganov to his collection, and he began to paint the icon in his imagination and almost missed the turning to the Lefkowitz house.

Rosa had been more than usually difficult and even Bonny Wintergreen was muttering that the old bitch should be locked up in the nearest institution. These days their only relief came when she was dropped off at the Har Zion synagogue in Hicksville for a session with the local chapter of Hadassah. Josh was sure that she'd found a nest of decayed Bolsheviks there who were happy to play canasta with her and plot the next revolution. In between she was making life hell for everyone at home. Before she left for her Hadassah meetings she would insist on six different changes before finally deciding what to wear and then, weighted down with baroque pearls and rouged like a circus clown, she would order Bonny to drive her to Hicksville where an old caretaker graciously escorted her from the car and into the synagogue. After that Bonnie could count on at least four hours of peace. This evening Rosa made a brief appearance at dinner and seemed in an unusually good mood which Myra attributed to Stefan. Rosa seemed convinced that Stefan de Mornay shared all her political views.

'I've left everything to you, Professor de Mornay,' she said amiably.

'Mrs Lefkowitz, you're too kind,' Stefan murmured.

'And it's for the Rosa Luxembourg room in that museum of yours. I was Rosa Luxembourg's best friend, you know. Without me she would never have written the Communist Manifesto.'

'An enchanting document, Mrs Lefkowitz.'

'It's all going to you, Professor,' and she snarled at Josh and Myra. 'My family won't get a dime out of me.'

She stamped up to bed and Myra sighed heavily. Josh squeezed her hand, 'It won't be for very much longer, Myra. Think of the money.'

'I do, Josh.'

They were both still recovering from the affair of the mezuzah. Myra arrived home the day before and saw that their old mezuzah, no larger than a small battery, had been taken down from the door jamb and in its place there was a twelve inch gold cylinder studded with semi-precious stones. Rosa opened the door and said it was her gift to the family. The soul of tact, Myra said that she thought it was perfectly divine but an alarming enticement to thieves. 'Touch it,' Rosa barked. Myra did and nothing happened. 'Really touch it!' Rosa persisted. Myra tugged at the mezuzah and all the burglar alarms went off inside the house. It had taken two days of shrieking to get the damn thing down and their old one replaced. Rosa was still in a filthy mood which she had expressed by simpering at Stefan and snarling at them. Added to this was the latest news about Bernie.

'Is it really true, Stef? A gymnast?'

'I fear so, but we are all of the opinion that this is just a passing infatuation.'

'It's more than that,' Myra gritted through her teeth. 'I heard it from Fiona yesterday. Bernie's been taking her to that Italian restaurant with the spotty tablecloths, the one that should have been cited years ago.' She made a mental note to phone the council health inspector next day.

It had been more than a passing remark from Fiona over bridge. By the way everyone paused to listen to her answer, Myra could feel the chill winding itself around her like the white mist that climbed out of the harbour to shroud the houses at nightfall. Dodie Steegmuller had smiled thinly across the room at her and Myra realized they must all know that Felicity was no longer part of her life. And how could she go on saying that Bernie and Felicity had just had a lovers' tiff when he was obviously in such hot pursuit of some rubber-jointed gymnast? She had not heard from Bernie since passover, and now the reality of her loss was an iron cage around her. Her first-born dead, and the moment Bernie seemed about to become a true son to her, he disappointed her again. If only it had been Bernie and not Seth – she had almost lost the thread of what

Stefan was saying about Felicity.

'I am telling you in the most absolute and complete confidence.'

As a tax lawyer Josh merely nodded, for in his time he had heard more confessions than most priests.

'We have located the Whistler etchings.'

'And—'

'I would go with Felicity if I could, but every morning I wonder if I can survive until evening. I either live like a drugged automaton, or else I endure pain that is sometimes excruciating.'

'You're sending Felicity away?' Myra said shrilly, and immediately lowered her voice to a measured drawl. 'I was hoping that she would make it up with Bernie.'

'I have a little scheme that will accomplish that,' Stefan lied, for he didn't have the faintest notion how sending Felicity to Lausanne would bring her back to Bernie in Pequod. However, he lowered his eyes and tried to look omniscient. Since he had been practising this expression for many years, he was moderately successful now. 'When she has the Whistlers, Bernie will be a changed man.'

'I won't have Felicity leaving now!' Myra said, and wished she could keep her voice down.

'Could you – give us some idea what you have in mind?' Josh said cautiously.

'None. I can tell you nothing except that if Felicity is out of the way – preferably in Lausanne – you will find Bernie waiting for her with open arms when she returns.'

'It doesn't make sense to me,' Myra said doggedly.

'Trust me,' Stefan said, and raised his eyes to some power above them all.

'How much will it cost to trust you, Stefan?' Josh replied, after a moment's pause.

'I have calculated her expenses to the last cent. Fortunately, Felicity is not extravagant. Two and a half thousand dollars will cover it handsomely. I would give her the money myself, but at the moment, I am in debt to a great many excellent New York surgeons and anaesthsiologists.'

'You have medical insurance from Pequod,' Josh said sharply.

'Which pays eighty per cent of all major medical expenses up to and including one hundred thousand. Would you like me to tell you what it cost to stitch and pin me together again?'

The discussion about doctors' bills seemed to convince Josh, for he had once had several surgeons as clients.

'I think I could manage that if it can be written off as a donation to the college.'

92

'To the art gallery, which will guarantee your tax credits, Josh.'

'No! Josh, I forbid you!' Myra screamed, and slapped her hand on the table.

'Myra – the neighbours! The Cadwalladers are entertaining this evening. I saw the cars.'

Immediately Myra was calm, pushing back her straight silver-blond hair and clenching her teeth.

'Nothing either of you have said makes any sense to me. I want Felicity here where Bernie can see her and realize what he's lost.'

Stefan sighed gustily and said sweetly, 'Absence makes the heart grow fonder, Myra.'

'I've never believed that, Stef. Absence puts someone else on your side of the bed.'

'Myra, I beg you to believe that I want nothing more than your happiness.'

Myra began to cry softly, 'I can't bear to lose Felicity, not after Seth—'

'Myra!' Josh's voice was sharp and she shuddered as though he had hit her, and was silent.

Josh nodded to Stefan. 'I'll give you the cheque now.'

Stefan got up slowly and said, 'Myra, I give you my word that those two young people will come together again. And I must add that Felicity deserves someone far better than Bernie.'

'We all know that,' Myra said through her tears.

Josh lay awake listening to all the sounds a house makes during the night. His mother was snoring upstairs, Myra kept tossing and moaning in her sleep, the heating came on, and he heard the pipes creak in response, and somewhere on the roof a loose tile was clattering in the wind. He would get himself a beer despite everything his doctor said about keeping his weight down to save his heart. It was the first time Myra had spoken Seth's name aloud in years and the sound of it had shaken him.

The kitchen was full of the faint humming of machines as he sat at the table, drinking from the can the way he used to before he became one of New York's best known tax attorneys. Perhaps he had been a fool to hand over a cheque like that, but Stefan was right, he had faith in the old gay. He tried to crush the can the way his father did, for his trust had been misplaced once before. Never with Myra. When he first saw her at Newport he couldn't believe the tall, brown, long-legged blonde wasn't some classy shiksa from one of the local mansions. Then he saw the little golden chai at her neck and he immediately got himself introduced.

Later, Myra told him that she had been walking around him for the last two days waiting for him to see her, and she admitted his being Jewish had been just as much of a surprise to her. He had been divorced for almost a year and she was just surfacing after her second marriage had gone down the drain. Exactly three days later, when they looked at each other naked in her bedroom mirror, it was as if they were brother and sister, with their long brown bodies and fair hair.

He wasn't too bad now for a man who often felt closer to seventy than sixty: he still enjoyed a little sex now and then with Myra. God knows he had been tempted a thousand times; even Bonny had suggested that he might like a massage in the privacy of his office, but he had never been unfaithful to Myra. Everything had blossomed for him after their marriage. He was an associate with Jacobson, Melton, Cohen and Dienster, and already he had a number of very good clients. It was the 1960s and every New York law firm was being assailed with charges of restricted hiring and told by the bar association to open its ranks to minorities. Reluctantly, Jacobson hired a woman, and three months later a black with a BCL from Oxford. But word was out that Merton, Fenster and Wheelwright, undoubtedly the bastion of legal Waspdom in Manhattan, was looking for a Jew.

At first nobody could believe the news. The firm was established in the eighteenth century and had continued in an unbroken line of Harvard Mertons and Yale Fensters to the present day. Their clients came from the same background: bankers and corporate managers, old estates and family trusts where the money had been piled up from generation to generation like a rich manure. Now John Merton and Randolph Fenster were faced with a crisis that could not be ignored.

'We've got to bend a little,' Merton growled.

'You don't give in to revolutionaries,' Fenster replied. 'You put them all up against the nearest wall and shoot them.'

'In 1776 my family were Royalists to a man, loyal to their sovereign, but they had enough sense to bankroll Washington on the side, so when the Republic was established the Mertons were on top.'

Fenster was all for telling the bar association where to go, but he seldom let anger direct his actions. He fulminated for a few minutes, blowing out his white moustache like the sails on a Yankee clipper, and then subsided. 'I won't have a woman in here,' he said.

'Did I suggest that?'

'No, but I'm saying it.'

Merton frowned, 'We have to make a choice between Yids, niggers and women.'

'Dear God in heaven,' Fenster groaned.

'I say a Yid. I've met a few that I could tolerate.'

'A young one that we can kick out as soon as all this equal hiring rubbish is over.'

'A sop to the radicals – what else?'

Myra encouraged Josh to apply, and at first he was reluctant. He knew he was being considered as a partner by his own firm, and he was well aware of the risks involved in jumping from one uncertainty to another. Myra was insistent, and he still remembered her that morning, laying out his charcoal suit and blindingly white shirt and telling him over and over that he was going to lead them into their promised land.

When Josh walked in, Merton was startled, and promptly nudged Fenster who was settling himself down to doze after interviewing a succession of bright young Jewish attorneys.

'My God, do they all have to wear their brains around their necks like sandwich boards?' Fenster had rumbled and prepared to sleep through the next three interviews. He was always bad tempered when his naps were disturbed. 'What the Hades—' and his mouth fell open.

They were both entranced by Joshua Lefkowitz, and kept looking up from the resumé to the man – tall, sitting easily, a little reserved, and obviously more eager to talk about his squash than his prizes in law school. But John Merton had built his reputation for sagacity by acting as though he stood alone in a world of liars and cheats, so he asked Josh to step outside for a few brief minutes.

'He's a ring-in, Randolph.'

'He looks damn good to me, John. None of this flashy nonsense. He—'

'He's not Jewish.'

'What do you mean – not Jewish. Ever met anybody called Lefkowitz who wasn't Jewish?'

Neither of them had met anyone called Lefkowitz before, but that did not deter John Merton who began to rap his pince-nez on the desk. 'I say he's a fraud.'

'Ever met a Joshua who wasn't Jewish?'

'My great uncle was called Joshua, and Joshua Merton came over on the *Mayflower*.'

'Today – today, keep to the present.'

'Randolph, how many applications a year do we receive from young attorneys?'

'Hundreds. Never look at them. Leave all that to the secretaries.'

'Quite so. I wouldn't put it past some bright young Baptist to try and pass himself off as a Jew. Never cared for Baptists,' he added thoughtfully. 'Tricky devils, Baptists.'

They exchanged a long and significant stare and called Josh back into the office where they genially invited him to lunch at the Century Club. Randolph wasn't sure that any of his own clubs were accepting Jews.

The three of them sat examining the menu and then they asked Joshua to make his choice. The menu was depressing and Joshua settled on a shrimp cocktail and a salad.

'No, no, my boy, you can't have that! Merton said.

'Soup,' Fenster said. 'You can't have a good meal without soup.'

'And after that we'll try the Irish stew. And waiter—'

The ancient waiter creaked over and Merton demanded a large jug of water and a bottle of claret.

Half-way through the meal, Josh felt as if he were going to burst, but the two old men kept filling his glass and Fenster said, 'Water, you must drink a lot of water, my boy. If you don't you'll have collapsed kidneys by the time you're forty.'

Josh managed to swallow his fruit custard and suddenly stood up and said he had to use the bathroom.

'Time we all had a leak,' Merton said, and they raced for the wash-room.

Josh unzippered and stood with eyes closed in that blissful moment of release. On either side of him Merton and Fenster bent over and looked closely, Merton even put on his pince-nez, and then they nodded to each other and smiled.

Those had been glorious years and eventually Josh was made a full partner of Merton, Fenster, and Wheelwright. They had an apartment in Manhattan and two sons, only one of whom was a disappointment. Josh brought his old clients with him and added others, including a group of rich Syrian Jews, and for all of them he built tax shelters of extraordinary grace and ingenuity that rose up more elegantly from a tax return than Shelley's pleasure dome, and stood more firmly against investigation than a bomb shelter.

Seth had finished law at Harvard and gone to Washington for a year of general experience. Bernie was insisting on his right to become a scholar and not a lawyer because, in Josh's opinion, he disliked getting up early in the morning and enjoyed reading novels. Everything seemed blessed around them and then – the crash came. This time Josh did succeed in crumpling the can and he put his head on his arms. Sixteen of his clients were investigated by an IRS that was armed with detailed blueprints of those elegant tax shelters. Brutally, they all came tumbling down in District Court and there was no defence. Four of his clients went to prison, including Ezra Masoon, the patriarch of the Syrian Jews. Josh was in fear for his life. He resigned from the firm to the execrations of his other partners, and planned to leave the country. Above all others he feared the vengeance of Ezra Masoon, but Ezra came to see him just before he was taken off to a correctional institution in Connecticut. The old Syrian put his hand on Josh's shoulder, 'You have suffered more than any of us. You have lost more than any of us. Try to live your life as though this has been a bad dream.'

They sold the apartment and retired to their summer house at Cold

Spring Harbor and gradually he had been able to build up a business again, opening a small office, generally calling on his clients in their own homes. As long as they were imprisoned, he visited Ezra and his other clients every week, often travelling half-way across the country to see them, and when they were released they remained his friends. 'It was not because of Joshua Lefkowitz's lack of legal skill that they were in prison,' Ezra said. 'It was a calamity from God and must be accepted as Job did his tribulations.' But how could one really hope to live after that kind of disaster? Fenster and Merton had blamed him for the crash and wanted to sue him for damages, his name was tarnished forever in New York, and there was even talk of having him disbarred. Clubs shut their doors to him, Myra was in daily analysis with an unsympathetic shrink. Again, and this time from prison, Ezra saved him by saying that Merton, Fenster and Wheelwright had made Josh a scapegoat for their own breach of confidence. The story was believed by some who maintained that John Merton had made a deal with the IRS that saved his own clients at the expense of Josh Lefkowitz's Jewish clients. It wasn't the truth, but it was credible enough to save Josh from investigation by the ethics committee of the bar association. Life had never been the same . . .

Myra reached over and stroked his head. 'Josh, I'm sorry. I didn't mean to shriek like that at dinner. Please, come back to bed.'

'If only Bernie—'

'We can expect nothing from Bernie.'

'I thought he'd changed when he brought Felicity home, Myra. He seemed different when he was with her.'

'Maybe Stefan does have something up his sleeve, Josh. He's a remarkable man. I want to believe him. I have to believe something.'

'I'm too old to believe in miracles, Myra.'

'Perhaps we should try praying.'

Rosa had a nightmare upstairs and began screaming that the bourgeois fascist pigs were invading, and Josh went up to try and calm her.

'Bernie, why? Why?' Myra moaned and beat her fists together as she heard Josh trying to reason calmly with his mother. It was, she thought bitterly, as though she had lost both her sons.

Bernie's anguish was now a torment of the mind as well as the body. He could not sleep that night and decided to scrub the kitchen and the bathroom in order to touch base with reality. Mariana was a virgin and she intended to remain one because of something she called the auric force. When he pressed her for explanations she told him patiently that she practised a form of energy containment that was maintained by physical movement: what Carlos Castanedas had accomplished with drugs she could generate from the nerve centres of her own body. 'When

I throw myself into the air, I throw my head first,' she said at dinner, and Bernie suddenly felt that if he didn't fill his lungs with cold air he would faint.

He wanted to hammer on the walls, to stamp and yell, but he knew if he did that, the whole of Sufferin would come beating on his door threatening to report him to Melvin Grimes. Nothing had ever affected him like this. He knew she was hot for him, he could feel it in her kisses, and yet she refused him because of – of the auric force. If only there were no ideas in the world, and only feelings! But that sounded like something Felicity would say and he thrust her out of his mind. He wanted Mariana Ashmole, he lusted for her with a need that was fast becoming a frenzy. Perhaps composing a poem would help, but his mind was fixed on Mariana and all he could see were the black eyes and the body twisting and turning in the light above his head. He must have her!

She was in his office waiting for him next morning, standing by the wall with one leg extended above her head. Slowly she turned and stretched the other leg and all Bernie could see was the delicate triangle that shone for him now like a lodestone.

'Bernie, you're late.'

'Late?' he said hoarsely.

'My class.'

'It's not till eleven. Are we still reading *Jane Eyre*?'

He had never felt uneasy with students before but now, with Mariana in the seminar, he knew his role as teacher had been snatched from him.

'*My* class – my freshman English class. You have to write a report on it for Professor Grierson. Oh Bernie—' She stood in front of him and slowly extended one leg until it was on the back of his chair and level with his shoulder, 'You will be amazed at what I've accomplished with those students.'

'Really?'

He could scarcely breathe for his nose was between her legs, but just as he was about to lean forward and kiss her with all his pent-up hunger, she pivoted and now she had her left foot on the back of her head.

'Your class – when is it, Mariana? Did I get a notice from Grierson. I can't remember anything.' What he wanted to do was scream that he was losing his mind, that his penis had become a burning rod, his balls like red hot coals. One leg was now forming a square to her body like a compass, and she smiled at him again.

'Bernie, two o'clock, room 37. I must explain my method to you first. As you know, I am a feminist.'

'Yes, I know,' he groaned.

'And you do seem to be aware of some of the more conservative feminist criticism.'

'Yes – Mariana, I want you!'

'Please, let me finish,' she said sharply. 'We can discuss sex later. That's your problem, Bernie, you have no control.'

'I want to fuck you, Mariana! If I don't I'll go crazy.'

'I doubt it. But you must appreciate my method before you attend my class. Now, Showalter, Moers, Gilbert and Gubar have a reputation in some circles, but I regard them as essentially obstructive.'

He felt like weeping and rocked back and forth in his chair.

'Obstructive because they have taken criticism to a certain point and then put up a brick wall. Criticism cannot be enunciated, it must be demonstrated.'

'Mariana,' he moaned.

Slowly she bent forward and balanced on her hands, 'Language is action, language is dynamic auric force.'

'Oh God, not the force,' he whimpered.

'So my classes are very physical, and mind expanding. You will be amazed what happens when I teach freshman English.'

'Mariana!' He looked down at her face and up at the soles of her feet, 'Mariana, I don't know how you can say you want to teach English.'

'I am teaching it, Bernie, and quite brilliantly. And don't think I am going to be another unpublished academic. I am recording my insights and at the end of the year I shall hire someone to type them up and – Bernie,' she gave him a brilliant smile, 'you could be a great help with that.'

'How can you practise celibacy and hope to teach literature?'

'I don't see any dislocation of natural function between the two.'

She rolled over and seemed to split in half with her legs outstretched on either side.

'Love! Love is what literature is all about. Wanting it and getting it, Mariana. 'Come live with me and be my love . . . My love is like a red, red rose that's newly sprung in June . . . She walks in beauty like the night of cloudless climes and starry skies; and all that's best of dark and bright meet in her aspect and her eyes . . . For God's sake hold your tongue, and let me love . . . To love, It is to be all made of sighs and tears; it is to be all made of fantasy, all made of passion, and all made of wishes; all adoration, duty, and observance; all humbleness, patience, and impatience; all purity, all trial.' How can you ever understand what you're reading about until you've experienced it?'

She sat there for a moment, then slowly curled forward and did a backflip. He wondered if she had heard him.

'How can you even know what virginity is until you've known sexuality? Mariana – you talk about experiencing language – and you sound as though you're making a bunch of freshman kids experience physical action. Surely you should be experiencing your own body first?'

'Bernie,' she said patiently, 'have you ever heard of imaginative identification?'

'But you have just based your whole theory upon lived experience.'

Clearly, she disliked argument and sat down. For the first time with her Bernie felt sure of himself, but Mariana was merely resting between exercises and began to rotate her ankles.

'Mariana, there's no logic between what you say and what you do.'

'How dare you accuse me of being illogical!' She stood up abruptly and almost stamped her foot.

'Physical experience is the heart and soul of your theory, but you won't experience love!'

'I have to keep the auric force in balance.'

'And nothing must penetrate your orifices.'

'Precisely.'

'You eat, don't you? What happens to your orificial mouth when you push two steaks and a mound of pasta down it?'

'I'll see you in room 37 at two o'clock,' she said sharply. 'And you'll have to teach *Jane Eyre* without me this morning. I have better things to do than listen to your – your—' It was obvious she could not find any handy pejorative to describe Bernie's views and flung herself out the door, almost knocking Martin down.

'What's going on? Have you scored yet?' he said breathlessly.

'Were you outside there, listening?'

Martin blushed and tried to speak but all he could do was flail his arms.

'I'm sick of you following me around, Martin. I'm starting to feel like a rat in a Skinner box being watched by a bunch of myopic psychologists.'

Martin babbled and tried to back into a corner of the study, knocking over a pile of books.

'It's—' how could Bernie explain his plight to anyone, even to Martin, his best friend. Martin's insatiable sexual curiosity had once amused him, and for a time it had alarmed him; now it was infuriating. 'She is a virgin, a radical celibate, and it has something to do with the auric force.'

'A virgin?' Martin said hoarsely.

'I presume you're acquainted with the term?' His studied calm broke and he shouted, 'I'm going berserk! My God, I've never met a woman in my life before I couldn't get. All I had to do with most of them was stand still and wait for them to grab me by the balls. I am in agony, Martin.'

'She's done this to you?'

Bernie could not understand what Martin meant, but there was a note in his voice that sent a sudden chill through him. The campus was more relaxed, students could be seen at night walking singly between the buildings, but the police were still on overtime, and Lieutenant Poldowski seemed to have become a member of the faculty. Wherever he went Bernie would catch a glimpse of the tall, slouched figure chatting to a janitor or a group of students. Bernie suddenly realized that whenever he had seen Poldowski, Martin had been with him. Was it possible that Martin was suspected and being followed by the Lieutenant?

'Martin, this is just taking longer than usual,' he tried to sound casual and failed.

'First they drive us mad, then they destroy us.'

'Martin, I'm horny as hell, that's all. Do you think I could switch with you for one night? The way I feel now I know I could really satisfy Lenore.'

'I – I can't go on living like this, Bernie.'

Martin seemed on the verge of tears when Muffin put her head around the door and said, 'You haven't forgotten the English party have you, Dr Lefkowitz?'

CHAPTER EIGHT

A little before nine that morning the phone rang twice and Felicity rushed to answer it. She half expected it to be Bernie, or Stef telling her that there was no money for a trip to Switzerland, but a man's voice said, 'Felicity Norman?' She replied that it was, and then there was heavy breathing.

'Oh push off!' she shouted, and slammed the receiver down with such force that it cracked.

'Why must people buy such chintzy phones?' she asked herself, glaring at the fragments of the ornately decorated gilt telephone that Phyllis Trugood's aunt had bought as a wedding present in a San Francisco boutique.

'A man must be desperate to make an obscene phone call before nine in the morning,' she told Alice and Elizabeth when they arrived a few minutes later with a pot of coffee and hot rolls.

Alice sidled into the bedroom with a duster and a can of polish and Felicity said absently, 'Elizabeth, is Alice well? She looks a little peaky to me. She hasn't been overworking, has she?'

They heard a short laugh from the bedroom, but Felicity was busy picking up little pieces of phone from the floor.

'Do you know, for one mad moment I thought it might be Bernie.'

Elizabeth too was looking at the phone and wringing her hands. 'Oh dear! Oh dear! I can't imagine what Phyllis will say about this when she gets back. She's so particular, and Wang's worse.'

'I'll pick one up somewhere for them, Elizabeth. What was it supposed to be? A genuine reproduction restoration telephone? I imagine there are thousands of them in every K-mart.'

'Felicity, I don't like the sound of this anonymous caller. You should speak to the police about it.'

'He certainly knew my name——'

'And where to find you.'

'I'll speak to Stefan about it this morning. With a little bit of luck and a plane ticket I'll be on my way to Switzerland tomorrow morning.'

'Oh dear heaven,' Elizabeth murmured. 'The Trugood Wangs asked us to keep an eye on their house. What can we say to them?'

From Felicity's office in the gallery she could look across a broad flagstone square to a corner of Botany meadow dazzling now with wild tulips and daffodils. Beyond it and out of sight to the left was Sufferin, but Bernie would have left for his office in English Hall by now. She knew Stefan always chose that way to walk from his apartment, but this morning he was late. Two phone calls distracted her, one from Des and the other from Chuck inviting her to a swim meet. She told both of them that she was going back to England and at the other end of the line she heard Des curse Bernie before smashing down his own phone.

Chuck seemed to take it more calmly and offered to drive her to the airport. The problem was that she didn't have the price of a cab fare to New York until her next pay cheque arrived, and she began to wonder seriously now if Stefan had been able to find the money for her journey. On the wall opposite her desk she had hung a photo of Poynter's pencil sketch of the young Whistler wearing a broad brimmed painter's hat and loose cravat. The alert sardonic eyes met hers and she said softly, 'I'm very close to them now, Jimmy. You never really wanted them destroyed, did you?' And it seemed to her that the half smile became a conspiratorial grin.

Felicity heard Stefan cry out from somewhere in the gallery, followed by a muffled thump that sounded as though he had collapsed. She almost jumped across her desk and bounded down the corridor, then from the landing she saw him swaying below her and holding on to the rail. He was gasping and clutching his chest.

'Stef! Stef! Are you all right?'

His face was ashen and he sagged down in a crumpled heap on the step, pulled out an embroidered handkerchief and wiped his mouth.

'Stef, wait here and I'll call for a doctor.'

Suddenly he began to laugh and rocked from side to side, waving the handkerchief over his head.

'Bottoms has gone!'

'What?'

'She's gone, Felicity! Gone at last! I walked past the fern bank just now and saw that some of the maidenhairs had been disturbed. When I looked behind, the wall was empty. Bottoms has been taken from us. *La Petite Joyeuse* has been stolen!'

'Some of the students must have borrowed her for a lark.'

'No – Oh dear, no – this is a very professional job. The whole burglar alarm system has been tampered with. The switchboard is dead. Whoever has done this must have known the key.'

'But you change it every week, Stef.'

'A most professional job. Well, my dear, she's gone. We must inform the police later today—'

'Later? I'll call now!'

'Felicity dear, please, let's give the thief time to get Bottoms away. We'll discover her absence after lunch. Oh, and why aren't you packing?'

She was so bewildered that abruptly she sat down next to him on the step.

'I have a cheque for two and a half thousand dollars for you. Now, that should see you safely to Lausanne and back. It's an expensive place but there's one restaurant you simply mustn't miss.'

Groaning, he stood up and tucked the handkerchief back into the pocket of his alpine jacket.

'You see, I even dressed for the occasion. Oh, what a pity I'm not well enough to go with you.'

He seemed to have forgotten all about *La Petite Joyeuse Perdue* and told Felicity that there were a great many things she needed to know before she approached Mr Taraq ben Mollah.

Felicity thought she should phone first, or at least send a letter, but Stefan had other ideas.

'Felicity, my child, I shall give you the necessary introductions and all the authority you need to negotiate with this rogue, but the element of surprise is essential. You see, what you must do is first accuse him of theft, and then show him how you can save him from criminal prosecution.'

'Stef—' there was one question Felicity knew she must ask him, but she hesitated.

He was obviously expecting it and fell into an attitude of deep umbrage, 'No, I did not steal the painting. No, I have not the faintest idea who has taken it. But if it is a student prank as you suggest, I hope the students responsible have enough sense to burn the bloody thing so we can collect the insurance.

The Victorian seminar was restive and it was clear that everyone except Muffin and Deb now regarded Bernie as the substitute teacher for Mariana Ashmole. Even the pallid youth seemed dedicated to clitoral comma usage and there was a distinct atmosphere of torpid boredom when Bernie tried to discuss some recent theories of narratology. He dismissed the seminar before the hour and as they shuffled out, Muffin smiled at him and said, 'We've been cooking up a real storm for tonight, Dr Lefkowitz.'

Bernie assured her that he had never forgotten a students' English party, but his anxiety was now so acute that he felt incapable of putting two coherent sentences together. It was as if Mariana were tumbling and turning inside his head. Sometimes he would see her whole, sometimes it would be the taut muscles of her thighs, or an eye glittering through a tangle of black hair, and always the lodestone of her pelvis with every crease and curve accentuated by her body suit. He had no idea what he ate for lunch or whether he had indeed eaten, but at two o'clock he was in room 37, mesmerized by the vision of Mariana Ashmole on the platform. It was the first time he had ever seen her in a dress, and it was obvious that she regarded this as a formal occasion.

He slipped into a seat at the side of the wall, pulled out a yellow pad, and tried to look professorial. The dress was made of red jersey that seemed reluctant to leave the warmth of her body, and again he had to fight back the impulse to lunge forward and take here there – in front of the students – anywhere. Carefully, he placed his briefcase on his lap and glanced sideways to see if any of the students had witnessed his agitation. They were all intent on Mariana.

She turned slowly, arms outstretched, as she did in the gym before she began her routine. There was a hushed anticipation in the classroom that Bernie had never felt before.

'Repeat after me – "language is power!" '

They responded in unison and Bernie felt a twinge of apprehension, for there was a suppressed excitement crackling through the room that made his skin prickle.

'Today,' she smiled brilliantly at him and then radiated to the students, 'today is very special because this is a demonstration class for Dr Lefkowitz who is my supervisor in the English Department.'

A few students shifted and looked at him, and Bernie nodded in their direction, but most were still staring at Mariana.

'Verbs! Today we are going to consider verbs and dangling participles.'

There was a ripple of anticipation and Bernie's bewilderment grew as the boy in front of him wriggled nervously and a girl began to jiggle in her seat.

Mariana swung round to the blackboard and wrote in bold letters: 'The horses race madly across the campus'.

She pointed to the class, 'Everyone recognize the verb?'

Strangely, there was silence, and Bernie wondered if she had been given a class of remedial English by mistake.

Mariana did not seem disturbed. She leaned forward as though about to dive into their midst and whispered, 'What is the word that is moving all the other words in the sentence? Those horses have to be moved—'

She began to prance across the platform and Bernie had the sudden vision of a circus horse with a scarlet saddle.

Now she had spun around and her voice was a shout, 'All right, everyone, demonstration time! Nouns and verbs in pairs, and remember verbs must push nouns. Those horses can't move unless you make them move. We need strong verbs to make nouns work!'

Instantly there was a rush of movement as some students grabbed hold of the backs of the desks while others hung on to the seats.

'Now, push!' Mariana shouted, lunging and twisting. 'What you must feel is the physical sensation of language!'

Bernie crouched back against the wall as chairs rocketed past him and crashed into each other.

Mariana ran into the middle of the mêlée encouraging the fainthearted to push harder, stepping over fallen bodies, jumping over broken desks. This continued for some minutes and then she flew back to the board, wrote a sentence, turned and shouted, 'A dangling participle! What you are going to feel now is the positive pain when a participle is wrongly given the power of a preposition or an adverb. Sentences on your chairs – now!' Those who were still standing climbed on to the seats of their desks, and Mariana shouted, 'Everyone! Dangle those participles! Once you've felt it, you'll never dangle another!'

Some nouns were still pushing verbs around the class, others had climbed on top of the desks and were yanking sentences up by their armpits, or, in one screaming case, by the neck. Bernie found himself crouched against the wall and wondering if he could reach the door before he was trampled.

Mariana stood in the middle of the platform and her voice rang out high and clear, 'Language is a physical force! You must feel it to know it!'

Grierson had not been sympathetic afterwards, even though Mariana was defiant in defence of her method, 'Surely, Professor Grierson, a broken chair is a small price to pay for effective communication?'

'Three students in the infirmary, Miss Ashmole?'

Bernie tried to catch her eye, but she was not intimidated by Grierson's bleak gaze.

'Professor Grierson, before a gymnast reaches any degree of skill there are bruises and broken bones. My collar bone was fractured sixteen times before I learned to penny drop. Those students actually experienced language this afternoon.'

'There are other methods, Miss Ashmole, and I hope, Dr Lefkowitz, that you will take the time and trouble to acquaint your young colleague with them.'

Bernie backed out the door apologizing profusely and Mariana pushed past him snorting indignantly. He knew when Grierson was in a rage and he was not going to inflame him with unnecessary explanations. This evening at the English party there would be time to explain that Mariana was attempting an experimental mode which would never be repeated again in any Pequod classroom.

'The stupid old shit! Doesn't he realize what I'm doing for these students?'

'Mariana, he has a point. Consider the wear and tear on the furniture – and the students.'

'Pain is an essential part of learning.'

'The parents may not think so.'

Quite suddenly she looked up at him and frowned, 'When do you want to fuck?'

He could not believe he'd heard her, and stumbled.

'Bernie, watch your feet. You always seem to be falling over yourself. I asked you a question.'

'Mariana – do you mean—?'

'What you said this morning made sense. And I am always in total acceptance of logic.'

'Come live with me and be my love,' Bernie breathed, and tried to kiss her.

Effortlessly, she pushed him away and said, 'Not that junk. The eating bit. I really bought that.'

They were standing on the steps of English Hall and on either side the daffodils bent their heads and glowed. Bernie felt such an explosion of joy that the whole spring morning seemed to have been suddenly poured into his head.

'Mariana – when?' was all he could say.

'Well, definitely not tonight. The Californians are going to be performing this evening, and there'll be a reception for them afterwards at Lester's place. You'll come, won't you?'

'Afterwards – Mariana, I'm dying for you.'

'Tomorrow night,' she said firmly. 'I'll cut practice early and we can fuck.'

'If I can live till then.'

She looked up at him and her smile made him want to cry with delight, 'Bernie, it's going to be the first time for me, and I know it will be a real happening.'

'Mariana, it'll be whatever you want—'

'After all, I am an exceptional woman, and when I surrender my virginity – Bernie—' she seemed to have a doubt.

Bernie assured her that the auric force would remain intact, that quite possibly it would be strengthened in the same way that food sustained it. Mariana smiled again, 'Because it is the first time for me, stars will nova, suns will burn to ultimate heat and explode in the sky. Showers of meteors will surround us and we'll be transported in time across strange galaxies of infinite wonder and majestic beauty.'

It was as if he had suddenly stepped into an icy puddle. Bernie faltered and tried to laugh, 'I – well, Mariana, I've never had any complaints. Mariana, it's never a good idea to expect miracles the first time—'

'What other people have experienced is not what I shall experience, Bernie. For me, it will be heaven, a return to a primordial state of grace in a paradise of unearthly rapture. It is,' she said emphatically, 'going to be one hell of a trip.'

She stood on her toes, kissed him passionately and ran off in the direction of the gym. The red jersey skirt seemed to drag at her legs so she hitched it up to her thighs and flew across the ground.

Bernie was still standing there when Sally Frauenfelder rattled up to him clanking Indian beads and bracelets.

'Where is he? Where is the bastard?'

'Who?' Bernie said absently.

'Chip. He's got the furniture.'

'I haven't the faintest idea, Sally.'

She was gone and Bernie remained among the daffodils feeling as though he had just been buried. A familiar voice was in his ear and he realized that Martin was at his side and in the distance he could see Lieutenant Poldowski.

'Bernie, are you sick or something? You look as though something's hit you.'

Bernie did not answer and Martin began to shuffle nervously, 'Is it a new poem? It's – it's not Mariana, is it?'

It was as if he were listening to another Bernie Lefkowitz, as though the real Bernie Lefkowitz were standing with Lieutenant Poldowski watching a man of medium height with white scrolled black hair answer Martin Harris on the steps of English Hall.

'I have a date with her – tomorrow night.'

'You mean – you're finally going to score with her?'

'Yes,' and he heard his own voice like the echo of another.

'Oh, my God!' Martin covered his face with his hands and began to sob, and Bernie suddenly became himself again.

'Martin, what did I say?'

'Nothing – nothing at all.' Martin shook himself like a wet dog and said he'd struck nothing but glitches in his computer all day, and Lenore wanted to tattoo his balls.

'You're kidding?'

'She's insane, Bernie. I – I know what it's going to be like for you and Mariana. But I – I—' he broke down again and Martin took his arm and tried to move him out of the doorway.

'You've got to get rid of her, Martin.'

'How? Just tell me how?'

'I – I'll think of something.'

'Perhaps I should throw up academic life altogether. I could get a job as a computer analyst. I can't bear my life here any longer.'

'Hold on, Martin. Something will come to me.'

'It's so easy for you, Bernie. You get it all.'

For a moment Bernie felt like agreeing, but he could still hear Mariana's voice and once again he had the jolting sensation of time coming to an end for him. He laughed shakily. No woman had ever complained about him sexually. That one area of his life was more than successful, it was a triumphal progress from one bed to the next. Once he had dreamed that he was clad in armour and striding through ranks of adoring women with an outstretched sword in his hand. He knew what that meant as soon as he woke and thought how pleasantly the unconscious could confirm the realities of one's everyday life. Mariana was an enthusiast, that was all, and once he had her in bed it would be quite different. He looked up at the sky dappled with docile white clouds, and laughed.

Felicity thought a great deal before she decided to call on Bernie that evening and say goodbye. She had heard about his infatuation with Mariana Ashmole and seriously wondered about his sanity. Mariana Ashmole struck her as a manic little creature who seemed to spend more time doing somersaults in mid-air than a frantic frog, but then she could never see why so much effort should be expended on such grotesquely unnatural actions as trying to put your right foot behind your left ear while standing on a narrow board.

Bernie's apartment astounded her and she wondered if it was the same place where she had lived so blissfully with him. It looked surgically clean, the cushions on the sofa set at precise angles, a table glistening with fresh wax.

'It took me some time to get it back into shape,' Bernie said defensively.

'Bernie—'

She hardly knew what to say for it was obvious he was dressed to go out, in a modish velour jogging suit.

'I hear you're leaving us,' he said brightly.

'Yes, yes, I am, and I thought I should say goodbye, Bernie.' Whatever happened she was not going to cry.

'Felicity, we had a lot of fun, but times change – we have to change with them.'

He had said this so many times before to so many different women that the words came easily to him and had a ring of practised sincerity.

'I've seen Mariana Ashmole.'

'Felicity, Mariana and I were made for each other.'

'Yes, well, I hope you'll be happy.'

'I always am when I'm with the right woman. But, as you know, nothing lasts for very long with me. I admit it – I just don't have staying power when it comes to sexual relationships.'

'That could be a definition of immaturity, Bernie.'

'So what's wrong with immaturity? I have no complaints. Blessed are the young in heart.'

Felicity shrugged, for she knew it was hopeless to try and argue with him, and pointless now as well.

'Be happy, Felicity.'

'I'll try,' she said, and wondered when she had ever felt quite so miserable.

'If you don't mind, I have to dash off to an English party. Look, I hate to rush you – there's so much I'd love to discuss with you, but this is one of those student affairs, and I gave them my word I'd be there.'

'All I really wanted to do was say goodbye.'

Felicity could feel him edging her towards the door and she turned and ran.

Bernie sighed and wondered why he had ever been so crazy about this tall, yellow-haired and slightly overweight woman. He half closed his eyes and Mariana jumped into his head and slowly and enticingly did the splits. Tomorrow night those legs would be around his hips and he would be inside her, taking possession of a body that seemed beyond the pull of earth and gravity. He decided to spend three quarters of an hour at the party and no longer; just time enough to inform Grierson of Mariana Ashmole's special status at Pequod as a star gymnast, and mention that his next collection of poems would be published by the Ploughshare Press.

Lorenzo Delgado had begun his evening round and was chugging by the meadow when he saw Felicity hurrying along the main walkway with her head down.

'You shouldn't be here alone, Dr Norman. Can I give you a lift anywhere?' Lorenzo still lived in hope of getting Felicity on the back of his moped.

Felicity was crying and pulled a scarf up around her face, saying that she was just going back to the terraces to finish packing. Reluctantly, Lorenzo drove off, and Felicity looked mistily around her and wondered when she would ever see Pequod again.

It had not been easy to see and talk to Bernie again, especially when he was so changed. There was an air of haggard excitement about him, dark hollows under his eyes, and an edge to his voice that she had never heard before. She wondered if he had taken to coking up with Chip Frauenfelder and his little circle of potheads. Why had she ever loved this man, and why, she wondered, did she still love him? It was painfully obvious that he couldn't spare a few minutes to wish her good luck on her journey – he hadn't bothered to ask whether she was going back to England, or whether she was off in search of the Whistler etchings. He hadn't even mentioned Whistler, and she knew with an aching certainty that she had completely fallen out of Bernie's life. Well, there were other men in the world, she thought dismally. Felicity enjoyed loving and being loved and a single bed held no particular charm for her. She wouldn't have described herself as sex starved but she was beginning to feel the need of a little scrooming. Instead of slamming the phone down on her mysterious caller that morning she should have asked him round for a quick klorg on the mattress. But that might have thrown him into shock for the rest of his life. Perhaps she should go round to the gym and see what Chuck was doing this evening, but, when she saw a stream of tiny figures scampering towards the gym, she decided to rinse her hair and finish packing instead.

It was clear to Bernie that elaborate preparations had been made for the party. Muffin, Deb and Tobby were wearing draped sheets with wreaths of purloined daffodils in their hair.

'Sorry, you didn't tell me it was a costume party, Deb. I would have worn something more suitable.' Bernie said pleasantly.

'Oh no, Dr Lefkowitz, you look just great,' Deb breathed.

'Am I the first?' Bernie wondered if he had possibly arrived too early. 'You said seven, didn't you?'

'Yes,' Tobby squeaked.

'Seven thirty,' Deb interjected quickly.

'Well, what shall we talk about?' Bernie said easily, trying not to glance at his watch in the dimly lit room.

'Have some dolmades,' Muffin said, brushing crumbs from her lips, and proffering a platter of dingily damp little bundles.

'Now how did you know I liked Greek food,' Bernie said, and almost choked. 'What's in them?'

'Oh, the usual stuff,' Muffin said casually.

'I've made them myself,' Bernie said. 'And these seem to have a very peculiar flavour. Not bad, mind you, but different.'

It was difficult to pull one apart in that light and examine it, but it had the flavour of stale cornflakes laced with salami, and the vine leaf was tougher and more aromatic than anything he had ever tasted before.

'Where did you get the vine leaves, Muffin?'

'I couldn't find any so I used ivy leaves, they're the same shape.'

'I see. Ingenious.' Bernie could feel the dolmades fighting its way into his gut and wondered if he could get to the bathroom and vomit before it passed beyond hope of recall. There was something disturbing about these three white robed figures and the absence of any other member of the department. Grierson always arrived before everyone else and left early at any of these affairs, and Wilson Trench, the American specialist, was the same. Bernie realized that he was quite alone with three young women who were slowly circling round him like Indians in an old Western.

'I just remembered I'm expecting a call from my publisher at seven thirty,' Bernie said brightly. 'I'll dash off and come back here later – when everyone else has arrived.'

He groped for the door but Muffin shoved past him and locked it.

Bruce Springsteen's voice filled the room and the air began to vibrate to hard rock.

'This is for you—' Deb yelled.

'Turn it down! He can't hear you,' Muffin shouted.

'This is not funny, and I'm leaving,' Bernie said angrily.

'Bernie – Bernie – this is all for you,' Deb wailed.

They pushed him into a chair and he sat there gripping the arms as the three of them dropped their sheets and began to dance. White, bulging beige, and black swaying and jiving together and now they were singing down Bruce Springsteen.

'Bernie! Take one of us! You gotta take one of us!'

He had fallen for a caper so old that it had gone out of style with bloomers and tight lacing. He, Bernie Lefkowitz, who knew every student wile, who always prided himself on never crossing the line between student adoration and student sex, was now being attacked by three naked sophomores. 'Yes, Dr Lefkowitz, we find your publishing record outstanding, but is it true that there was a little problem with the female students at Pequod? Here at Harvard we really don't encourage that sort of behaviour.' He was not going to have that kind of blot on his vitae!

'Bernie, we're hot for you! Only for you!'

He pushed past them and they began to scream.

'Don't let him go!'

'I don't think this is so cool,' Tobby wailed. 'If my mother finds out about this she'll kill me!'

'Get his pants,' Deb ordered.

He tried to fight them off but the three of them were on top of him and dragging at his pants.

'Now,' said Deb, 'let's grab some gear and get to hell out of here.'

Bernie heard them moving around him but the room was now in darkness and one of them had turned the recorder up to full blast. The sound was beating at his head as he tried to fumble around the walls. A door opened and slammed and he realized he was alone. He fell over the recorder and Springsteen was silent, then by groping his way across the floor he found the light switch. There was no phone and something was beginning to throb in his stomach. What he had to do was get out of here quickly and back to Sufferin before those little harpies roused the whole campus. If he could get back quickly and grab another suit he could stroll over to the gym and if anyone questioned him, he would state that those young ghouls had stolen his pants. 'Yes, I noticed they were gone from my locker when I was working out last week. Perhaps I dropped them. I know I had to wear my sweatpants back to Sufferin.' That's what the three of them had yet to discover. He was so far ahead of these nymphomaniacal airheaded sophomores, that he would be back in his apartment before they even started to think sexual harassment. The window was ajar and he slid it open and climbed swiftly down the ivy. Fortunately, everyone seemed to be in the gym this evening and the campus was quiet with only an occasional gust of wind along the walkways. He felt it against his legs and crept along close to the buildings.

Tobby was beginning to whimper, 'This is for the shits. Listen, you guys, I'm going back to give Bernie his pants.'

'No! If you want to chicken out, go ahead. We are going to hang these on the notice board in the cafeteria.' And Deb swung Bernie's pants above her head.

Tobby tried to grab them but they pushed her away and jeered.

'You are nothing but a niggerfink, Tobby!'

She became very angry then and swung a punch at Muffin who yelled hysterically and began to run as fast as her fat legs could carry her. Deb danced ahead brandishing the pants and shouting, 'Try and get them, niggerfink!'

'I am going to split on the two of you. I am going to tell Bernie the truth,' Tobby shouted.

Raging, she swung round and headed for the dorm. Deb and Muffin were shrieking with laughter and for a moment she thought of following them and beating them both into the ground, but she remembered Bernie and began to jog back towards the dorm.

The hands were at Tobby's throat before she could scream, and someone was kicking her legs out from under her and cursing her. If she had not been so angry she would never have reacted so quickly, but Tobby was furious and jerked forward and twisted sideways in one desperate movement. She saw and felt the knife in the same instant and screamed. The man was on top of her but she rolled and something seemed to grate against the bone of her shoulder. Mumbling obscenities, the man tried to slash her into silence but Tobby screamed, and screamed again.

Lorenzo Delgado was adjusting his earphones otherwise he might not have heard her, but Tobby's voice carried, and Delgado blew the moped's siren and put the machine into top gear. When he turned the corner he saw a body lying by the walkway and glimpsed a figure disappearing into the darkness.

Felicity had every intention of packing methodically but after she had tinted her hair and decided to scrub the yellow stain from the bath in the morning, a feeling of despairing fatigue came over her. Listlessly, she threw clothes into the long duffle bag she used for travelling and when Wendy phoned her to come over for a farewell drink, she made an excuse and refused. But Wendy was insistent and, reluctantly, Felicity pulled a cloak over her damp hair, and walked round to the Mollock apartments. As she passed by Elizabeth and Alice's window she saw that they were entertaining Stefan to supper.

Wendy had prepared a meal and insisted that Felicity eat with her, and it was while they were having their coffee that they heard the police siren wail across the campus.

'God, I hope that maniac's not at large again,' Wendy said anxiously.

'I rather think he phoned me early this morning,' Felicity said, and told Wendy about her caller.

'You should have reported it immediately to the police.'

'I suppose so, but I had so many other things to do and it just slipped my mind.'

Wendy gave her details of some of the latest research on rape which made her feel slightly queasy, and grateful that she would be on her way to Switzerland next day.

'Forget him,' Wendy said firmly.

'That's what everyone tells me, Wendy, but I can't. If I could explain what I feel about Bernie rationally, then perhaps I could put him out of my mind. But somehow, in a way I can't explain, Bernie satisfied something in me and now – what I feel is the loss.'

Wendy promptly told her of three excellent books on the subject of female obsession and Felicity said she really did have to get some sleep and finish packing.

The lights of a police car flashed in the distance as Felicity opened her door. She knew immediately that someone else was in the room with her and reached for the light. Her outstretched arm was knocked aside and a man was grappling with her. Felicity too began to scream and kicked and bit what felt like a hand at her throat. China crashed around her and suddenly she had the feeling that the man was not trying to rape her, he was trying to get away from her. She fell back and the man lunged for the door almost knocking down Stefan and his two dinner companions.

CHAPTER NINE

The whole apartment was a shambles with drawers pulled out and the contents of Felicity's duffle bag scattered across the room. Elizabeth ran next door to call the police, while Alice and Felicity helped Stefan into a chair. It had been a difficult evening for him trying to placate the two women, assuring them that Felicity would be gone in the morning and there would no longer be any need for daily housecleaning. 'I have never known anybody so messy, so completely unaware of what has to be done to keep a home in order,' Alice had wailed, and Stefan promised them both that Felicity would not be returning to the Trugood-Wang residence after her trip to Switzerland. He was not certain where he could put her without damaging some old and very good friendships on campus, be he was prepared to consider that problem when it became urgent.

Felicity was still puzzled by the intruder's behaviour, 'I don't think he was trying to attack me, Stef.'

'My dear, I hope you're not trying to make excuses for a homicidal rapist.'

'I'm not – it's just that I think he was trying to get away.'

'Of course he was. Listen to the police sirens out there. If you were this criminal wouldn't you want to escape?'

'But why would he want to hide here? In my house?'

'Did you leave the door unlocked?'

'I – I'm not sure.'

'Now Felicity, the reason you gave me a spare key to Bernie's apartment was because you were always forgetting yours.'

Alice said sharply, 'You never locked the door behind you, Felicity. When I came in here to clean I always found it unlocked and once it was wide open.'

Felicity was bewildered, 'Alice, you mean, you have been doing everything here—'

Alice began to sniffle, 'Yes, and you never noticed. Never saw what I had done for you.'

115

'Oh God, Alice, I'm so sorry. I thought these terraces must have room service.'

'Room service!' Alice snorted.

'I am grateful. I'm sorry – I don't know why I'm such a slob. Bernie said that was why he couldn't live with me, but I simply don't see what is around me. When I'm thinking about Whistler I'm living in the Peacock Room or at Speke Hall, and my head is light years away from where my body is supposed to be.'

'One day you will have to learn that you live here – in this world, and not in some dream of art.' Alice growled.

Elizabeth trotted in and gasped, 'There's been another murder! It's one of the students. The policeman on the switch wouldn't give me any details, but that Lieutenant Poldowski is coming over here immediately.'

It was confirmation of what Stefan had thought from the first. Somewhere across the campus the murderer had committed his crime and then looked for a hiding place, and, quite possibly, Felicity had left her door open and he had slipped inside.

'You say that you struggled with him, Felicity?'

'I fought like hell.'

It was the extent of the damage that Stefan found perplexing – Felicity was standing on the broken pieces of twenty-seven ginger gars still in their plastic bags. The sofa had been ripped and food from the refrigerator was spilling from the shelves.

'Could he have been looking for something here?'

'A disguise,' Elizabeth said.

'In the fridge?' Alice retorted.

'Ah well,' Stefan sighed. 'We must wait for that excellent fellow, Lieutenant Poldowski, to enlighten us. And we must spare a thought for the absent Trugood-Wangs. I propose that they be told their vacant house was burgled while they were in China. There is no reason why they should ever discover that someone was living here.'

'Stefan,' Elizabeth said sharply, 'is that quite honest?'

'If the house was burgled in their absence then they will be able to make a claim upon the insurance for all this. I'll have a word with Melvin Grimes – he's very helpful in these matters.'

And Stefan had already decided that Melvin would forget that anyone had been given the key to the Trugood-Wangs' small home. That afternoon Stefan had called the gallery's own insurance company and told a sympathetic young woman that a priceless French painting had been stolen from the gallery. To his amazement, she accepted a valuation of two hundred and fifty thousand dollars without a murmur, and Stefan wished he had doubled the amount. It was Fred Cadwallader who insisted that a private reward of five thousand dollars should be given to anybody who knew of the present whereabouts of *La Petite Joyeuse*. He seemed distraught by the theft and stalked up and down the gallery for almost an hour, lamenting the day when the Cadwallader estate had relinquished such a treasure.

Stefan sighed, and hoped that the Trugood-Wangs had indeed taken out insurance on their household goods. But knowing them as he did, he was sure that every bill had been paid before they left for China, and that every ginger jar was described and itemized on an insurance inventory.

Tobby was barely conscious when they lifted her into the ambulance, but everyone heard her whispering Bernie's name over and over again. Jaime Garland was frantic, demanding that the police do something immediately to save his college from imminent destruction.

Anger contorted Lester Marcus's face into masks of terrifying rage, 'This fiend knows the Californian teams are here this evening. He knows that we have a group of international gymnasts as our guests.'

'Happily, the doctor says Tobby will live,' Jaime said in a voice of studied calm. 'In this hour of grievous trouble we must consider what effect this will have on the college. One rape can be explained away, but habitual rape eats into the very fabric and substance of college life, and many people, quite without reason, I might add, begin seriously to question the moral standards and physical safety of the institution in question.'

'This maniac is after our gymnasts, I tell you. Last time, when that Betty Levin was murdered, we had the first appearance on campus of Mariana Ashmole and Louise Grunch; tonight, there's a standing room audience in the gym with two Olympic judges on the bench. I tell you, this fiend won't rest until he's killed a gymnast. And I want him caught now!'

Lester Marcus was dancing in a frenzy and his voice broke on a shriek of fury.

Lorenzo Delgado had never enjoyed himself quite so much. He had discovered Tobby Martin and actually caught a glimpse of her assailant. Even Lieutenant Poldowski praised him for having tried to catch the rapist and for then attending to the victim. Tobby had been slashed across the shoulders, but the knife had been wielded with such force that the bones of her upper arms were chipped and splintered. Now, everyone was out in pursuit of the maniac, and Lorenzo Delgado was chafing to get in on the chase again. All he had seen was the bent figure of a man wearing a jogging suit and a ski helmet, running along the wall at an incredible speed. Nothing else had been visible.

Lieutenant Poldowski received the message on his car radio about an intruder at Felicity's house and drove round there with one of the county police.

'It will be my sad duty to inform Tobby Martin's parents,' Jaime said dolefully, aware that any more incidents like this might force him to leave Pequod. And where does a college president go who has a reputation of not being able to curb incidents of rape on his campus? Jaime Garland had once been a medieval historian, but now he wasn't really sure he knew the differences between a manor and a glebe, and he had forgotten everything he had ever known about Hugh Bigod's eyre and gavelkind tenure. That was the hard truth: presidents are not tenured, and when they are cast aside in a storm of scandal they are like beached whales.

Lieutenant Poldowski scratched his thinning grey hair as he looked around him at the chaos of broken china and tumbled furniture.

'And you still think he was trying to escape, Dr Norman?'

'Lieutenant, I know it may sound a little odd to you, but I am quite certain that he had no intention of raping me. He – he wasn't touching the places you'd expect . . . if you know what I mean.'

'You can't be certain of that,' Elizabeth said.

'I just felt it.'

Lieutenant Poldowski sighed, for he was learning that academics seemed quite incapable of giving straight answers to anything. He was tired of listening to theories and opinions when all he wanted to know was who had seen what, where, and the approximate time.

'And you had a threatening phone call this morning, Dr Norman?'

'Someone who knew my name and then engaged in some heavy breathing.'

'I see.'

'It's possible the rapist could run across the campus and hide in here, but it would have taken time to do all this.' He gestured at the wreckage.

'Oh no,' Alice said thinly. 'It doesn't take some people any time at all to change an orderly environment into a trash heap.'

Felicity murmured that she was very sorry for all the trouble she had caused, and Alice began to look mollified.

'Lieutenant Poldowski, Dr Norman is booked on a flight to Switzerland early tomorrow morning,' Stefan said anxiously. 'It's a matter of important research. She will be able to leave, won't she?'

Poldowski stared at Stefan for a moment and said slowly, 'We may be dealing with two unrelated incidents this evening. Didn't you say that a painting had been stolen from the gallery today?'

'Today, last night, we can't be certain.' Stefan sketched uncertainty with his hand.

'Yes, I've been getting calls about it from a Fred Cadwallader. He seems to think I should use every man I've got to try and find this painting.'

'When you have rape and murder on your hands?' Stefan smiled deprecatingly. 'I feel the loss of that painting more acutely than anyone, but human life comes first.'

Poldowski wondered why Stefan seemed quite so cheerful, but the old man had puzzled him from the first.

'I think you can make your flight tomorrow, Dr Norman. You're quite sure you didn't see the intruder?'

'No, but he's tall. I could tell that when I was wrestling with him, and I bit his hand.'

'Well, if we find someone with teeth marks, I'll let you know. How long do you plan to be away?'

'I haven't the faintest idea, Lieutenant, but I hope to be staying at the Villa Francesca in Lausanne, care of a Mr Taraq ben Mollah.'

Bernie heard the wailing of the police sirens as he crawled through the azaleas along the science walkway. If he cut across Botany Meadow he would be able to reach Sufferin within minutes, but there would not be any protecting shadows. Four paths led across the meadow and since the murder of Betty Levin the whole area was out of bounds after dark. Still, he had been lucky so far. Twice, county police cars had careened past him, and he thought he glimpsed an ambulance when he was crossing Aristotle Square. Obviously, there was some trouble on the campus, but that would occupy everyone's attention and give him time to reach his apartment and change. The dolmades had become a throbbing ulcer in his stomach, but when he stopped once and tried to vomit, all he could manage were a few dry retchings. He was still so angry that he barely noticed the cold even though his feet were numb and he was stumbling.

The meadow was ahead of him and beyond it he could see the welcoming lights of Sufferin. How he would make those students pay if they tried to bring any charges against him! Deb and Muffin both deserved to fail, and he would see to it that they collected straight Fs on every paper they presented to him. It wouldn't hurt to talk to some of the women counsellors either; they might persuade the little harpies to transfer to reform school.

Bernie had one leg over the gate to Botany Meadow when he heard a shout and a torch shone in his face.

'Stop! Hold it right there or I'll blow you away!'

Lorenzo Delgado's night was made. Not only had he discovered the victim, but now he had the murderer in his gunsight.

'Get down there real slow, keep your hands up, and walk towards me.'

Bernie felt his stomach give a sudden churning thump as the

dolmades joined forces with terror. He must remain calm and think of something to satisfy Lorenzo.

'Well, it's good to see you, Lorenzo. Perhaps you can give me a lift back to Sufferin? I – lost my pants.'

'Put out your hands – real slow now – and don't try anything clever.'

Bernie extended his hands and Lorenzo snapped on a set of handcuffs.

'Now, just a minute, Officer Delgado, I think you're overstepping the bounds of your authority here. I'm Dr Lefkowitz—'

'I know who you are, you – you're a motherfucking rapist and murderer.'

'You must be insane!'

'I am going to call the Chief right now and if you move an inch I'll shoot you through the balls. Oh boy,' he said to himself, 'this is going to be one up the ass of those county cops. Who is the first on the scene of the crime and then apprehends the criminal – Lorenzo Delgado.'

Chief Flyte told Lorenzo to take Bernie to the campus police station where he would join them within minutes. The chief realized at once what an opportunity this was to reinstate himself with President Garland and Lester Marcus, especially the latter who had told him more than once that if there weren't some startling improvements in campus safety, Pequod would be looking for a new police chief.

Lorenzo was puzzled at first as to how to get Bernie to the police station, because he certainly wasn't going to have a homicidal rapist on the back of his moped and breathing down his neck. But there was a length of rope in the satchel and he tied one length around Bernie's waist and told him to run behind.

'This is an infringement of my civil rights,' Bernie screamed, and Lorenzo punched him in the jaw.

'If you say I hit you, I shall swear you fell over and hit yourself. Criminal suspects are falling over all the time.'

Bernie's jaw felt as if it were broken, but the pain in his stomach was worse.

Lorenzo flung the moped into top gear and set off for the police station with Bernie running and stumbling behind. He slowed down when the lights of the station came in sight and Cissie Curlewis and Michael Dempster stopped in amazement.

'My God, is that you, Bernie?' Dempster said.

Bernie was so breathless he could only shake his head, and almost dropped to his knees.

'I've got the rapist!' Lorenzo shouted as Chief Flyte screeched up in the squad car.

'We all suspected him,' Cissie said coolly. 'Come on, Michael, we have all those sludge runs to check this evening.'

Bernie was gasping when Delgado pushed him into a chair and adjusted the light so that it shone into his face.

'I am going to get medals for this,' Lorenzo exulted. 'I am going to be interviewed by Dan Rather and Barbara Walters. I—'

Chief Flyte bustled in and pushed Lorenzo aside.

'So, it's been Professor Bernard Lefkowitz all the time.'

'I caught him,' Lorenzo said.

'Yes, yes,' Flyte said, and smoothed the red bristles that passed for a moustache. 'What we need is a full confession from him before Poldowski gets here—'

'And takes all the credit.'

'Eggzactly.'

Bernie tried to focus but it was almost impossible with the glare of light in his eyes.

'I am going to sue you for illegal arrest and anything else my father can think up. I have rights!'

'We must get him to confess now, preferably in writing,' Flyte whispered.

'Let me try a little of this, Chief,' and Lorenzo opened and closed his fist.

'Hang on a minute. I'll interrogate him first,' Flyte replied, and put his face very close to Bernie's.

'Lefkowitz, I want to ask you three questions. Think very carefully before you answer. How old are you, Lefkowitz?'

'Thirty-four.'

'Married?'

'No.'

'Gay?'

'No.'

'He's the rapist all right. Get Poldowski over here. We've got the little bastard cold.'

It took Poldowski less than an hour to check Bernie's story. At first he thought Lorenzo might have caught the right man, but Tobby had regained consciousness in the ambulance, and two of his officers found Deb and Muffin in the cafeteria where they had just finished nailing Bernie's pants to the bulletin board. Deb insisted that Bernie had tried to rape the three of them in the dormitory, but Muffin made a blubbering confession when one of the women detectives offered her a Mars bar with almonds.

Reluctantly, Chief Flyte found an old pair of dungarees and a pair of loafers for Bernie, and Poldowski offered to drive him back to Sufferin in his car. Bernie now felt as though there was a vice in his stomach twisting his guts into a knot of excruciating pain. Waves of nausea almost made him lose consciousness and he began to shiver and sweat. Poldowski looked sideways at him, recognized the symptoms and said hastily, 'Will you be all right if I let you out here?'

'Anywhere,' Bernie said huskily.

He found himself in front of Mollock as Poldowksi swung round and headed back for the police station where he intended to say a great many things to Chief Flyte and Lorenzo Delgado.

Bernie was bent double with pain but he managed to stumble up the stairs and into the elevator. He had a key to Martin's apartment, and in that apartment he knew there was a bathroom. His hands left sweaty prints on the metal walls of the elevator, and he half crawled to Martin's door. He was drowning so agonizingly in a stinking nausea that he no longer cared who saw him – except that one flickering part of his brain prayed that Mariana would be asleep. It was almost one o'clock in the morning and no one was about – then he heard the noise.

.There had been occasional grumblings from the other tenants about Martin's resonant lovemaking but no official complaint had ever been lodged because nobody wanted to mention the name of Lenore Marcus. Now, Bernie heard the clamour. A menagerie of mating baboons would have been restrained by comparison with these whoops and whimpers, whines and gasping howls that expired in a flurry of whinnying whistles. Bernie only hesitated for an instant as the agony in his belly coiled ready to explode. If he opened the front door very quietly, he could slip across to the bathroom and they would not even be aware of his presence. The ululation rose to a piercing shriek and Bernie unlocked the door and crept across the living room to the bathroom. He would have to go through the bedroom and – why, he wondered in anguish, did so many people enjoy making love with the lights on?

Bernie was transfixed by what he saw. At first it was a pink snout and one round eye, and then he saw it all. Naked on a tumbled bed, Martin was wrestling with a large Miss Piggy, gnawing and chewing on her ear, and flailing himself with a long stiff hairbrush flecked with blood.

'I have to use the bathroom. I'm going to be very sick.'

Bernie felt as if he were flushing every organ in his body down the john, and he was grateful that he could lean over the bath and vomit at the same time. He had gone beyond exhaustion to a state of insensate calm where he no longer felt as though he had a body. Slowly, he got up and stepped into the shower. A faint stirring of life came back to him as the icy water struck his flesh, and he found it was difficult to open his mouth. In the bathroom mirror a haggard face stared back at him, and across the side of his jaw a deep stain was already beginning to purple. There was a robe on the back of the door and he wrapped himself in it and tottered into the bedroom.

Martin was sitting bolt upright against the pillows wearing a crisply laundered pyjama suit, buttoned to the top with the collar folded over to cover as much of his neck as possible. His knees were hunched up, his arms locked around them so tightly that his knuckles were like a ridge of white bone. There was no sign of Miss Piggy. Sighing, Bernie sat down beside him and put an arm around Martin's shoulders.

'I'm sorry I woke you up, Martin. You were having a terrible nightmare.'

Martin looked wordlessly at Bernie and began to cry silently. Slowly, as though relating a story about someone else, Bernie told him about the party and the ivy leaves, Lorenzo Delgado, and being arrested as the rapist. It now seemed that the worst part of all was when he had to run like a stray dog, stumbling and falling behind Lorenzo's moped. Every part of his body was beginning to ache and he wondered if some of his teeth were loose, but his mouth was still so painful that he could not bear to touch the gum with his tongue.

He told the story and still Martin was silent. Sighing, Bernie heaved himself up and said he had to get back to his own apartment.

'Do you mind if I borrow some of your clothes, Martin?'

There was still no answer from the bed and Bernie slowly dressed himself in clothes that were not reeking with vomit and dung.

'I must go now, Martin. It's almost two thirty and I have a heavy date this evening.'

Martin looked at him with such pain in his eyes that Bernie felt as if he had just tied his friend to the rack and turned the screws.

'Women are so strange,' Martin said quietly.

'So are we,' Bernie said.

Martin began to cry again and told Bernie that he had never known a woman. All his life he had been terrified of them, so he had learned to invent stories that kept them away from him. In California he said he had a virulent form of herpes and visited the clinic every week. But two women who did have herpes suggested he might like to date them, and that was when Martin accepted the offer of a job at Pequod. Everyone believed he was the lover of Lenore Marcus, and the women had left him alone.

'Martin, you have never—'

Martin shook his head, and Bernie held his friend against him.

'Sometimes – sometimes—' he said lamely, 'it takes longer for some people to reach sexual maturity.'

'It'll never happen for me,' Martin said mournfully.

The fear now stood in the front of Bernie's mind and he turned to Martin.

'Are you the rapist, Martin?'

'No.'

'You're not lying to me?'

'I swear it, Bernie. I – I think about women all the time. And I think about you. I've loved all your women. Felicity is wonderful. I used to have such fantasies about her, but now, all I can see is Mariana. Oh Bernie, I love her so much and it's hopeless, it'll always be hopeless.'

'There'll be someone – there always is,' Bernie said. 'Look, none of this ever happened. Let them all think you're getting it on with Lenore if that's what you want.'

'Please—' Martin breathed.

'I must get back to Sufferin and try to sleep. I'll have to cancel my classes tomorrow – I mean, today.'

'Bernie, I'm glad you're my friend.'

Everything was very still as Bernie walked back to Sufferin. The air was crisp and he could smell the meadow flowers and then he thought of Mariana. A few hours sleep and he would be his old self again. All he needed now was to put his head on the pillow and it would be like taking chloroform. As he put his key in the lock he could feel sleep folding around him and he walked into a wall of wood. He switched on the nightlight in the hall, but he was not mistaken. His doorway was filled in with wood, something had been jammed into the lobby and he was barred from his own home. The wood extended three quarters up the entrance of the door to a narrow dark space. Behind it was his bed and his white sheets waiting to wrap him in sleep. Everything broke in his head at the same time and he banged at the wooden obstruction, cursing and yelling.

Somewhere from inside his apartment he heard an irate voice, 'Cool it, man! People are trying to sleep!'

'This is my apartment! I'm sick and I'm exhausted and I want my bed!' Bernie shouted.

He looked up at the bleary, unshaven face of Chip Frauenfelder peering down at him from the narrow space.

Bernie staggered back across the hall, 'You! What are you doing in my apartment?'

'It's the furniture, Bernie. Sally and I have split up and she grabbed Daniel. Bernie, she has taken my son away from me. Well, I had to get some leverage against her so I had all the furniture moved over here. I knew you didn't have anyone living with you, and I have to get my son back, Bernie. You can understand that, can't you? I'm a father.'

There were rustlings and sounds all over the building and Stefan opened his door behind Bernie.

'It is a quarter of three which is unquestionably the time when the body's vital forces are at their lowest ebb.' He was wearing a long white nightshirt which made him look like a wrathful Jehovah.

'I can't get into my apartment,' Bernie said tearfully.

'You can,' Chip said. 'Just climb up and there's a crawl space. I left some room for you.'

'I want my apartment now!' Bernie shouted.

'I think you'd better sleep on my sofa and then I'll call Melvin Grimes first thing in the morning and have all this removed,' Stefan said ponderously.

'But if Sally knows where the furniture is she'll grab it, and then I'll never see Daniel again,' Chip wailed.

'You can settle your domestic problems in the morning, Professor Frauenfelder. Now, Bernie, I'll give you a blanket.'

Bernie could no longer see clearly and Stefan guided him to a sofa where he collapsed and was alseep within seconds. Muttering, Stefan covered him with a blanket, and went back to his own canopied bed.

'Oh, blessed Michael, open that woman's eyes! Let her see that what she loves is not a man but a depraved and bedraggled little pervert who should have been castrated when still a child.'

When Bernie woke, Stefan was pouring coffee into wide china cups.

'Bernie, you look appalling.'

Bernie looked imploringly at the coffee and Stefan handed him a cup.

'Your apartment is now vacant. I called my friend Melvin Grimes and he came over with two of his men and removed the Frauenfelders' furnishings together with their owner. I might add that the Frauenfelders are now reunited and have discovered a common cause. Last night Daniel caught the train and is now with Chip's parents in Philadelphia. The boy said that he was going to charge his mother and father with child abuse and moral delinquency and Chip's parents are going to assist him. I really think,' Stefan said thoughtfully, 'that Daniel will be much better off with his grandparents, don't you agree, Bernie?'

Bernie could only nod for he had the cup to his mouth and the warmth of the milk coffee was calming his stomach like a soft hand. His jaw still ached but he could feel that none of his teeth were loose or missing.

'Stef, I'm very grateful that you took me in.'

'My boy, what I did for you, I did for Felicity. Yes,' and he looked at his watch, 'she'll be on her way to the airport now.'

The coffee had invigorated Bernie and as he stretched his legs Mariana came spinning into his head. All he needed now was a few hours' sleep and he would be ready for the evening. And when he thought of that he had an immediate erection. He was grateful that he had a pillow on his lap but Stefan shook his head and said, 'Bernie, I do not have a cold disposition, but I have always been discriminating. I would say that as a sex object you would find it difficult to attract a man in prison, or in the navy. What I shall never understand is why a woman of such artistic perception as Felicity should be so unfastidious in her amatory pursuits.'

Bernie could only smile sheepishly, for behind closed eyes he could see Mariana bending backwards towards him, her arms outstretched.

CHAPTER TEN

If the plane had been delayed, Felicity would undoubtedly have gone off to the nearest motel with Chuck for she was feeling decidedly scroomish. She didn't particularly like his ears, which tended to flap, and he smelt like wash day at her old boarding school where gallons of bleach reduced everyone's clothes to an institutional dinge, but she had almost convinced herself that it was natural for a swim coach to be redolent of chlorine. She did, however, respond with some passion when he kissed her goodbye. I must, she told herself, be very careful not to fall for the first handsome stranger who makes a pass at me. And she tried to remember a particularly nasty fairy tale by the brothers Grimm which told of the curse placed on a proud princess that made her fall in love with the first walking object that staggered into view, or another version of the same story that put Titania in bed with a furry character called Bottom.

There was no danger from anyone in the economy class of the plane that morning. Felicity was seated next to a chatty old nun with a clanking chain of rosary beads and a set of false teeth that had obviously decided to take up residence in Felicity's lap, and all around her a geriatric collection of tourists that apparently belonged to an obscurely medical tour group. They spent the first hour checking their pill boxes and exchanging the latest pharmaceutical information on heart medicines, and then scuttled back and forth to the toilets to make sure their diuretics were working.

The Swissair flight was already waiting when Felicity changed planes in Paris, and instead of the geriatrics every seat was now bulging with burly young skiers. Spring was late this year and there was still snow in the Alps. Miserably, Felicity wondered where she belonged among the generations. Certainly not with the old tourists intent on seeing how their bladders could withstand European travel, and definitely not with these yahooing teenagers sprawled in the aisles or energetically rolling bottles under the seats.

It was already dusk when she arrived in Geneva, and nightfall by the time she cleared customs. She found a phone book and discovered that the Villa Francesca was midway between Lausanne and Vevey, and wondered whether to phone or arrive on the doorstep unannounced. Stefan had urged the element of surprise, so Felicity shouldered her duffle bag outside to the cab rank. A few questions and she realized that a taxi would cost more than a small king's ransom, and the next bus was not due to leave before nine. The skiers were herded off into two chartered buses and Felicity settled down on her duffle bag to wait.

'If you're going to the Villa Francesca I can get you there in half an hour.'

It was an American voice, and Felicity saw her stranger. He was not dark, but everything else about him spoke of chauffeured limousines and the kind of luxury she had known only once in her life.

'How did you know I was going to the Villa Francesca?'

He could be a white slaver or the local version of a rapist and murderer, but more importantly, how did he know she was on her way to visit Taraq ben Mollah? She had been asking a number of people about Lausanne, but she hadn't mentioned the Villa Francesca.

'I was waiting to phone and I looked over your shoulder and followed your finger down the book.'

He smiled disarmingly and Felicity began to think of the nine o'clock bus to Lausanne, and then having to hitch a ride to the Villa if she were lucky.

'You said half an hour – do you have a helicopter handy?'

'No, but my car is outside and my boat is at the quay. And in case you're wondering who I am – my card.'

Only the most refined white slaver would carry an engraved card, and Felicity accepted it with a smile. His name was James Baker, and he was a financial consultant with an address in Washington and another at the Villa Francesca.

'I'm Mr ben Mollah's assistant, for want of a better term.'

Felicity handed him her own card and he seemed impressed.

'Must I call you Dr Norman?'

'Yes,' she said engagingly, 'until we get on formal terms and use first names.'

He didn't even smile, and simply raised an eyebrow. It was then she noticed what was so odd about his appearance. Undoubtedly, he was a remarkably good-looking man, but his face was so narrow that when he turned sideways his eye seemed to be looking directly at her. All she could think of was an ancient Egyptian painting with a figure drawn from the side, striding off to the left and a frontal eye resolutely fixed on the viewer. He was very tall with fair hair that could have been silver in the flaring lights of the airport, and his clothes were superb: a black cashmere coat, yellow kid gloves and a soft hat at exactly the right angle. While she was admiring him, he had beckoned to a chauffeur who asked reproachfully if the duffle bag were Madam's only luggage. There was a large Mercedes at the kerb and Felicity settled back to indulge herself. 'I may possibly end up in a Kasbah brothel but I am going to enjoy myself hugely now,' she thought.

'I didn't quite get what you meant about not using your first name,' he said, and Felicity groaned inwardly. Bernie had warned her about southern gentlemen and from his accent she felt she had at last met one.

'James,' she grinned, 'I have a peculiar sense of humour. I tried to lose it when I was in America, but every now and then it pops up again.'

'Ah, I see – an English sense of humour,' and then he laughed.

James Baker was definitely not a ball of fire but he was certainly streets ahead of a chlorine-soaked swim coach and the campus vivisector. His age was a little puzzling, but she decided on something between late thirties and early forties.

The chauffeur loaded their bags into a speedboat at the quay and left them, and Felicity's pleasure became bliss when James Baker said he preferred to take the wheel himself. The boat plunged into the darkness and Felicity cried out with joy as it crashed against the water and then hurtled smoothly into the darkness.

'You're not afraid of speed, Felicity?'

'I think it's wonderful.'

'I see. You believe in living dangerously?'

Felicity cringed slightly as she always did when a conversation seemed about to crawl from one cliché to the next.

'If I thought this were dangerous, James, I would probably be overboard and swimming for shore now, but you don't seem a very reckless man.'

'Really?' He turned, and she thought it was like the face of a thoroughbred horse with a long narrow nose and the disturbingly oblique eye. 'You're quite right,' he said. 'A good financial consultant must be cautious by nature.'

And also remarkably poised, Felicity thought. She did not really believe that he'd been leaning over her shoulder when she went through the phone book, and now he did not seem in the least interested why she would be calling on Mr ben Mollah.

'It won't be too late to speak to your employer, will it?'

She hoped that would trip him into an admission, but he shrugged and said that Mr ben Mollah kept an open house for art dealers and art historians. It seemed he was inordinately proud of his collection of erotic paintings and delighted in showing them off to visitors.

They docked at a private wharf where a uniformed servant stood ready

129

to take their bags. High above them Felicity saw terraces rising up to a baroque pink mansion floodlit against a darkness that could have been sky or trees. Was this how James MacNeill Whistler felt when he first came to Speke Hall, to love and paint? For one instant Felicity sensed that if she turned quickly she would see him at her elbow, dressed like a dandy and sporting a monocle on a black silk cord.

'It's a remarkably fine house,' James said.

'Late eighteenth century Italianate with original mouldings,' Felicity observed.

James seemed a little put out and added quickly, 'It was built by a Russian nobleman for his mistress in 1782. After that it passed through a number of hands until Mr ben Mollah bought it six years ago.'

'And how long has he been collecting?' Felicity asked.

'For as long as I've known him,' and James did not seem prepared to tell her how long that was.

The house had obviously been restored by people with taste and a knowledge of the period. Felicity half expected to see embroidered divans and gilt hookahs, but the furniture was French and the Aubusson carpets and the tapestries were original. James told her casually that dinner would be at eight and Mr ben Mollah expected his guests to wear black tie.

She should have packed more carefully, Felicity thought, as she disgorged the contents of the duffle bag on the bed. A maid was hovering in the background and Felicity handed her a long skirt of cotton voile and a matching shirt.

'I really think these need a touch up with an iron,' Felicity said.

The maid examined them with pursed lips and said she thought they needed washing first, and Felicity agreed.

'Five minutes in the washing machine, ten in the dryer, a quick press, and they'll be good as new.'

The maid was outraged and flounced off carrying the clothes by her fingertips, but Felicity was right, and at ten minutes before eight she had splashed in a gargantuan marble bath, combed her hair so that it plumed about her head and was dressed in the soft blue voile. Downstairs the maid reluctantly admitted that the English madame had style, and Gilles Fresnay, the chef, brightened up considerably. 'Does she look as though she enjoys food?' he said anxiously, and the maid assured him that madame was unquestionably, '*Une femme sensuelle.*'

James Baker was waiting for her at the bottom of the stairs and Felicity wished that he didn't keep reminding her of a variety of different advertisements. Again, she stopped to admire his dinner suit and carved jet cufflinks and James seemed to take her approval for granted. She walked across to the living room and heard him gasp involuntarily behind her. Felicity always said she planned to enjoy her body as long as it lasted, and she saw no reason why other people shouldn't share her pleasure. She never wore slips, and very little underwear. At Pequod she had become accustomed to nervous women sidling up to her in the washroom to whisper that people could see through her skirt. 'I hope they can see my legs,' she always replied. 'I would hate to think I'd lost them.'

'Your employer must be a wealthy man,' Felicity said as a butler offered her champagne from a silver tray.

'You could say that, and then some,' James said.

'He will be joining us for dinner, won't he?' Felicity was beginning to feel ravenous and realized how many meals she had missed since Elizabeth and Alice made their last pot of coffee for her.

'I should perhaps explain to you that Mr ben Mollah is an invalid.'

'I'm so sorry,' Felicity said, and hoped he was not suffering from any heart problems. She had an idea that what she was going to say about stolen art works would be enough to put the most sanguine individual into shock.

'You can see for yourself,' James said quietly.

Taraq ben Mollah must have weighed one hundred and fifty kilos, although the white *djellaba* was possibly concealing a few extra. He was bald and wore thick bifocals, and propelled himself forward with the aid of a surgical steel walker.

Felicity handed him her letters of introduction which he passed to James Baker without even glancing at them. His voice was thick and fruity, and the English was the best grammar school.

'My dear Dr Norman, I am enraptured that you want to see my little collection.' He simpered and ogled her, 'Sweets to the sweet,' he purred.

Felicity almost bit the edge of her glass but managed to smile in return. She could make brilliant small talk when she liked, even though this talk made her think of some rather dim toddlers in high chairs trying to one-up each other. Ben Mollah was clearly enchanted with her and kept putting his head on one side and winking to make her aware that he was appreciative of her figure.

A bell sounded in the distance. Ben Mollah's nostrils flared and he began to salivate slightly in contrast with the sepulchral tone of his voice.

'That is dinner, and I regret to say that since I am an invalid I am forced to exist on a diet so restricted that an ordinary person would die of malnutrition.'

Felicity's heart sank, for the champagne had gone straight to her head making her realize just how much she needed food. The table was decked with spring flowers banked around yellow candles on a heavy damask cloth and the silverware seemed to promise a meal of remarkable elegance. All her fears were realized when the butler arrived with a trolley that he placed alongside ben Mollah at the head of the table. Felicity saw a small mountain of melba toast, a basin of shredded radish, a tureen of what looked like yoghurt, and a tall jug of some hazy liquid that reminded her of the barley water her mother used to make in summer and force everyone to drink. Felicity felt like putting her head on her gold-rimmed plate and weeping with disappointment.

The butler was coughing gently behind her and she moved slightly as an unspeakably delicious aroma drifted across her and on to her plate. It was a *mélange* of cold sea food: delicately pink lobster, golden mussels and pearl-shaped scallops marinaded in herbs and wine.

Ben Mollah was chomping melba toast and craning across the table.

'Eat! Eat!' he shouted. 'And tell me what it is like.'

James murmured to her that ben Mollah had once been a great gourmet but now one of his only pleasures was to see other people eat the food that he could not enjoy himself. He did insist, however, that they describe in the most elaborate detail what he had been forbidden. 'A culinary *voyeur*,' Felicity thought, and proceeded to oblige him, deciding that the customary table manners did not apply and she should speak with her mouth full and empty.

The first course was a miracle and Felicity began to share ben Mollah's enthusiasm. His little eyes were watering as he bathed his head in the yoghurt and told her that he paid a fortune to Gilles Fresnay who was unquestionably the star of the rising young restaurateurs in Paris.

'I pay him as if he were a great film actor, and every night he performs for me,' ben Mollah said, and grazed through the radishes.

Felicity did not want to relinquish her Chastegnel-Montrachet but the butler murmured that there was a 1976 Romanée-Conti to follow. The plates arrived under silver salvers and when they were lifted Felicity felt as though she were in some gustatory paradise. Boned quail were stuffed with a mousse of quail and surrounded by a purée of celeriac and golden potato balls. Ben Mollah asked for a plate to be held under his nose and he closed his eyes and wept.

'Tell me – tell me, what do you taste?' he implored.

It was clear that James Baker was not a very satisfactory dinner guest for all he could find to say was that the food beat the hell out of a McDonald's hamburger, and seemed disappointed when no one laughed. Felicity's fervent appreciation inspired ben Mollah to a frenzy of delight and he rolled in his chair and called for some grated carrot.

'The wine! Tell me about the wine! I have one of the finest cellars in Europe. You don't think the '76 is too young, do you?'

'It already has a bloom,' Felicity said, and the butler promptly filled her glass again. 'The body is enticingly seductive and captures your senses like a lover.' She wasn't quite sure how long she could keep up the metaphorical flow but she was beginning to wish it was the kind of meal where you could ask for seconds. As though someone had read her mind, a tenderly arranged mesclun salad of walnuts, crinkled red lettuce and vinaigrette was placed in front of her.

Goat cheeses and a perfect Roquefort followed in due course and the dessert was a tart of wild strawberries with the perfume of a sunlit meadow. Felicity almost fainted with delight when the butler announced a 1979 Dom Perignon with bubbles so minute that the glass seemed to be fused with crackling light.

'The chef! Where is the chef? Oh, we must applaud him,' Felicity said.

'He gets paid. That is enough,' ben Mollah said, and belched.

'I must find this genius,' Felicity cried. She got up a little tipsily and followed the butler out the door.

She had kicked off her gold sandals and ben Mollah pointed to them and giggled, 'You see, James. She has left her shoes as a token of her love for me. I think she would like me to suck her toes.'

'You must ask her that yourself,' James said tonelessly.

Felicity lost the butler once but managed to find a sliding door that led down to a brilliantly lit kitchen. She burst in clapping her hands, and stopped abruptly.

Sitting on the end of the table was the most desolate figure she had ever seen. The tall white toque dipped forlornly, the starched coat was bleak, and Gilles Fresnay bent over, with his hands on his knees, reminded Felicity of a tragic clown. He looked up at her and she stared into the face of Watteau's Pierrot.

'Are you the genius who created that miracle of art this evening?' Felicity spoke softly to him in French and he replied brokenly with tears in his eyes.

'You ate my dinner?' he said imploringly, 'and you appreciated my work?'

'It was,' Felicity said passionately, 'like listening to Mozart or looking at Degas. Monsieur Fresnay, you are a great artist.'

He stood up and kissed her hands. 'Madame, Oh, Madame—' he began to cry, then suddenly took off his toque and stamped on it.

'But why are you here?' Felicity said. 'You're a genius and yet you cook for that fat old man who can't even eat your food? That's like Beethoven playing to the deaf or da Vinci painting for the blind. An artist must have an audience.'

Felicity sat down next to him and told him about her brief engagement to Neil Monckton who was a very rich and very dull accountant. The only endearing quality Neil had was his enthusiasm for good food and his

133

willingness to pay for it. They used to spend long weekends in Paris eating their way from L'Archestrate to Taillevent, and although Felicity became very plump she was blissfully happy except when she contemplated Neil across the table, or when she found herself sharing the same bed with him where he showed all the finesse of a mating badger.

Gilles told Felicity of the anguish he suffered cooking superb dinners every night and watching those meals brought back to the kitchen untouched, for Taraq ben Mollah seldom had guests. He spoke of his pride that was being crushed, and then he spoke of his wife and her desire for them to have a nest egg.

'A nest egg is one thing,' Felicity said sharply, 'but prostitution is another. You must be firm with her, and tell her that you cannot live without your own restaurant. Oh, Gilles,' she said soulfully, 'I want to be there when you walk from your kitchen temple and take your place in the middle of the tables, and everyone stands and applauds you, and the next day your triumph is in *Le Figaro*, and *Le Canard Enchaîné* has a cartoon showing you wearing the crown of the Bourbons, because only a chef can ever become the real king of France.'

Gilles was staring at her and seemed to be holding his breath.

'You have inspired me,' he said.

'Go forth and conquer France!' Felicity cried.

James came to the door of the kitchen and Felicity suddenly realized she was exhausted.

'I rather think,' she said, 'I'd better go to bed before I drop.'

She vaguely recalled James seeing her to her door but when she kissed him, he said, 'Later.'

'That,' she said passionately, 'is a crueller word than "no".'

The maid was placing a breakfast tray in front of her and Felicity was quite sure there had not been any 'later'. She did not have a hangover which surprised her, but she remembered that good wine and good food had never given her anything but sound sleep and a sweet awakening. 'This is the life,' she thought as the maid poured her coffee and pointed to the flowers.

'The red roses over there are from Mr ben Mollah.'

Felicity saw a large bowl of aristocratic blooms on her bedside table.

'This,' and the maid picked up a single rose by her plate, 'this is from Mr Baker. And these—'

But Felicity had already seen the little bunch of white violets and was smelling them in ecstasy.

'Monsieur Fresnay left word with Alain his assistant that these should be picked and given to you this morning. He said I should tell you that you have changed his life.'

'I hope so,' said Felicity with her mouth full of croissant. 'Art should belong to as many people as possible.'

'While you were asleep, Madame, I took the liberty of arranging your clothes. But are these Madame's?'

Felicity had accidentally thrown a pair of Bernie's shorts and a pair of purple socks into her bag, and now the maid was holding them in front of her.

'They – they belonged to a friend,' Felicity said sadly.

Bernie did not wake until noon, and the horrors of the night seemed more like a nightmare than reality. He was in his own bed in his own apartment and only a few scratches and dents around the walls revealed that the room had been filled with the Frauenfelders' furniture. His jaw ached and his stomach seemed full of ethereal butterflies, but for a man who had been beaten up and poisoned, Bernie thought, he was in remarkably good shape.

Wendy Forsyth was at his door and she promptly invited herself in and poured herself some coffee.

'I'm delighted to see you're in one piece, Bernie.'

Bernie shrugged nonchalantly. 'I'll probably be filing a few charges of assault and false arrest against a number of people in the next few days.'

'Yes, well, get on some clothes and I'll drive you to see Tobby Martin.'

'Tobby Martin?' Bernie's voice almost broke. 'See Tobby Martin? Do you know what she and two of her friends did to me last night? Are you aware that they lured me to their dormitory and then tried to seduce me? And when I refused they—'

'Bernie, Tobby was attacked by the rapist last night. She suffered some appalling knife wounds.'

Bernie was silent and coldly buttered another muffin which he chewed with difficulty.

'We know the whole story now. But she keeps asking for you. Tobby wants to apologize to you.'

'Fine. I accept her apology.'

'But you do want to see her, don't you? After all, she is your student.'

'Now look, Wendy, she didn't behave like my student last night. Are you aware that I was punched by that goon Delgado, that he dragged me across campus on the end of a rope. Oh yes, and I was suffering from food poisoning at the time.'

'Tobby is asking for you, Bernie.'

'I shall see her tomorrow, Wendy. Where is she?'

'Mercy Memorial Hospital.'

'Good, if you see her again today, tell her that I'll call in tomorrow after class.'

135

'Bernie!' Wendy stood up and glared at him. 'You are undoubtedly a cold-hearted selfish little shit!'

This was not entirely accurate, for Bernie had nothing else in his head except Mariana. Even as Wendy was talking to him, he could see her standing on one foot and slowly extending her other leg behind her, then leaning back until her head touched the sole of her foot. And all the time she was smiling at him and the zone of her pelvis shone and throbbed like a lodestone.

Mariana called him in the afternoon and told him she would be there at nine, and he began to tidy the apartment. It was still difficult for him to set last night's events in sequence, but he remembered Martin and tried to call him at his office and then at his apartment, but there was no answer.

Everything was in order. It took him a long time to make the bed, for every few seconds he would see Mariana and had to stop while the vision spun and twisted before him. The bruise on his jaw was a swollen purple stain, but he felt that Mariana was accustomed to injuries, and he recalled what she had told Wendell Grierson about pain. If she noticed it, he would casually mention that he'd had a fight with the local police and then give her a few details about the arrest. He would not mention being tied and dragged along behind Delgado's moped.

Mariana arrived carrying a satchel and slightly out of breath because she had cartwheeled slowly up the stairs.

'It's kind of stupid, but it is amazingly good for your balance, Bernie. You have to take the first step on your hands and then cartwheel to the second. The art is not to miss a single step – and not to slip.'

'Mariana, whatever you do is a miracle!'

He kissed her and she wound herself enticingly around him and stuck her tongue down his throat.

'Bernie, this is going to be a real happening.'

'I know it, darling,' he panted.

'Now, let's set the ground rules,' she said, and began to rummage in the satchel.

'Do you – do you want to protect yourself?' Bernie said delicately.

'Hell no. I never have periods when I'm training. I won't be ovulating until September when I take a month's rest break.'

'You – don't have – to do anything?' Bernie said carefully.

'Bernie, stop worrying. And I hope you don't intend to wrap yourself in plastic, or anything like that. We want flesh to meet flesh, don't we?'

'Oh God, Mariana—'

She produced an exercise book and opened it at what looked like a surrealist sketch of the Milky Way.

'Isn't that just divine,' Mariana breathed.

'I – don't understand what it's supposed to be,' Bernie said, and a flicker of apprehension darted into his mind.

'You know the *Kama Sutra*, don't you?'

'Of course.'

'This is based on the last triadic movement before attaining the nirvanic state.'

'Mariana, we don't need manuals.'

'Please!' she said sharply. 'I'm trying to explain this to you. Louise and I diagrammed the movement. You obviously haven't read exercise charts.'

He tried to put his arms around her but she pushed him away.

'Bernie, because it's the first time for me, we'll do what I want. Now, I am into reciprocity and co-operation in a big way, but you must accept that this is a *rite de passage* for me and I must be allowed to direct it.'

'I can't even see what it is,' Bernie said desperately.

'Get undressed and I'll show you.'

Fumbling, he dragged off his clothes and stood obediently in front of her.

'Now, it is a series of movements in which it is your body that rotates your penis.'

'Mariana! Don't you think that since it's your first time we should try something simpler to begin?'

'Bernie, I did this with Louise last night and we could feel the permutations of auric energy. It was fabulous!'

'Louise!' he shrieked in disbelief.

'I said we went through the movements. I am not a lesbian, if that's what you're thinking. Although, I fail to see why you should suddenly want to introduce a sexist element into this conversation.'

It seemed to Bernie as though the whole building had been struck by a silent earthquake and the room was beginning to slip and tilt around him. Mariana flung off her clothes and jumped on to the bed in one bound. She bounced and rolled on it and told him she liked the springs.

'God, Bernie, we are going to stratoplane right out of the universe on this mattress.'

He walked slowly towards the bed and she looked critically at him.

'You're not in very good shape, are you? And,' her voice rose indignantly, 'I sincerely hope you can do better than that.'

The head of the mighty serpent was bowed and Bernie tried to tweak it upright.

'It's – I'll be fine as soon as I touch you.'

'This is the first movement, Bernie. I want your left foot on my right shoulder.'

It was a torment punctuated only by Mariana's shrill cries. 'Bernie!

137

Shit! Don't you know your left from your right foot. Bend – you have to bend back and push your pelvis against mine.'

'My back is hurting,' Bernie wailed.

'Of course it's hurting. You never work out, do you? Naturally, you're going to feel a few creaks at first.'

He was no longer moving because she was aggressively pushing and shoving him into positions that his body had never thought possible. At one point he felt his chin in the back of his knee, and Mariana said, 'Now, that's better, Bernie. You're getting the idea of it. All right, now we can fuck!'

Bernie tried to throw himself forward, more to untangle himself than to satisfy Mariana, and felt himself falling. He lay on the rug, one leg twisted behind him and a pain so terrible shook him that he almost blacked out.

Mariana sat on the edge of the bed and sighed, 'God, Bernie, you're a real spas. aren't you?'

'Mariana,' he whispered.

'Oh, forget it, Bernie,' she said angrily. 'I just want you to know that you have ruined what should have been a great learning experience for me. I mean – a woman could develop deprivation symptoms as a result of your impotence.'

Bernie groaned and tried to speak, but the pain was choking him.

She threw on her clothes and grabbed the satchel.

'I have never – never in all my life seen anybody in such terrible physical condition. I wonder that anyone with your flab and lack of muscle tone is still able to walk.'

Mariana was gone and Bernie was being dragged across chasms of agony. He tried to call out, but his throat seemed numb and a mountain of fire came down on top of him.

Stefan was bending over him and Bernie tried to speak.

'Bernie, can you move?'

'No,' Bernie moaned.

Gently Stefan placed his hand under Bernie's neck and supported his head.

'Is it your back?'

'Stef – the pain—'

'I gather you fell out of bed.'

Even through his agony Bernie realized that Stefan knew everything and he did not try to answer.

'Now, I'm going to try and ease your leg out from under you.'

Bernie did not flinch and Stefan looked anxiously at him.

'Is that better?'

'Stef, I can't feel my legs,' Bernie said.

CHAPTER ELEVEN

'My doctors like to play games with me,' ben Mollah said plaintively. 'Sometimes they tell me I have six months to live, and sometimes they give me six weeks, and every pleasure is forbidden me. All I have left in life is my food and my art.'

Felicity was almost dancing with impatience to see his collection. She murmured sympathetically and tried to edge past him and into the gallery, but he was blocking the door with his bulk and insisted on giving her in great detail the opinions of his most recent specialists.

James had come to see her while she was still having breakfast and offered to take her sailing. Smiling, he told her that she had propositioned him the night before and Felicity reminded him that he had refused her. 'I hope,' she had said, holding up the single rose by her plate, 'that this is a sign that you'll accept when I next decide to invite you to bed.' James then leaned over the breakfast tray and kissed her and said a number of things which began with love at first sight and ended with madness. If only, Felicity thought, he would stop talking, she could find him very exciting physically. But what she had felt from the moment she woke up in that house was the presence of another James; his eyes were dark and full of a mocking humour, and very different from James Baker's disturbingly oblique gaze.

Eventually, Taraq ben Mollah clumped through the door on his walker, and Felicity was in the gallery. It was, she thought with immediate revulsion, quite the worst collection of junk paintings she had ever seen in one place. One wall was covered with anatomically exact depictions of women being tortured with electrical probes, razor blades and whips in high gloss enamel.

'I am not only a collector, I am also a patron of art, Dr Norman. These are all contemporary works, and this particular artist is a great favourite of mine. His name is Miguel Hauptmann and he was a high ranking and most distinguished officer in the Argentinian army. But there was a change of government and he, poor man, had to retire from military service and take refuge in Guatemala. I buy at least four paintings a year from him. They are so animated, don't you agree?'

'Yes,' Felicity said. 'You wouldn't find better exhibits in a police museum. But what really interests me are the older works, especially any prints and etchings you may have.'

'Ah yes, I have a comprehensive collection. And some of the older works are – quite interesting.'

James Baker had joined them and he stood easily, looking at Felicity with an expression she found difficult to read.

'I'm concerned with a set of plates signed by Seymour Haden. They are not large and are probably made of copper.'

'Yes, I think there are some things like that. I buy whatever my agent tells me.'

Another room was full of simpering Edwardian belles lurching from the canvas in various states of disarray. Wherever she looked there were bulging bosoms with nipples like sugar roses on a wedding cake: leers, winks and ogles on every side with an emphasis on black stockings, lace fans and meticulously detailed corsets.

'They have such charm,' ben Mollah sighed. 'There was a time when I thought of specializing in the works of that great lady painter, Marie Laurencin, but the Japanese have cornered the market. So, I decided to expand my collection. I like to think of Miguel Hauptmann's paintings as my main course at dinner and these – these are the dessert of strawberries in kirsch with *crème chantilly*, or an éclair with mocha cream.'

He was dribbling and Felicity turned her head and almost gagged. James was obviously enjoying the whole scene and Felicity had the uncomfortable sensation that she was acting according to his directions in a play that he had written for the occasion.

At the end of the room by the window was an easel and a painting covered with a white cloth.

'Now, I must show you my masterpiece! I was told about it last year, but it only came on to the market a few weeks ago and my agent immediately bought it for me. She has just this minute come to me. It is a work of incomparable beauty and such – such exquisite taste.'

He thumped to the easel and pulled off the cloth. Felicity was greeted with the simpering pout and peach-down buttocks of *La Petite Joyeuse*.

'I cannot tell you how I have longed to own this painting. I saw the photo of it and I had to have her. The moulding, the colour, the light and shade, yes, the *chiaroscuro* of the flesh is incomparable. Oh, she is delicious!' Ben Mollah leaned over his walker and kissed the canvas twice. 'But so tasteful, don't you agree?'

Felicity thought that James laughed but she was not sure, and she began to think very rapidly indeed. If she were lucky, this painting could be her key to the other treasures, so she made several approving

140

noises and then asked to see the rest of the collection.

Ben Mollah seemed reluctant to leave Bottoms and remained for some time stroking the canvas, but after a few subterranean grumbles he tore himself away from her and clumped into a third room.

'These are, I am told, of great value, but I do not prize them as I do some of my other paintings. There is nothing here to be compared with *La Petite Joyeuse*— Ah, Dr Norman, sometimes in one's life the incomparable jewel is bestowed upon one, and it is a foretaste of that paradise where I shall soon be surrounded with houris like my precious little *Joyeuse*, please Allah.'

There were glass cases around the walls and Felicity ran from one to the next, and suddenly they were before her.

'Please, open this case! These are what I want to see!'

James stepped forward with a key and Felicity picked up the first copper plate. Somebody had once thought they were a set of decorative wall hangings and had framed them, but this plate still had black rubbed into the lines and she could see the picture in reverse. She held it to the light and sighed with relief: it had not been scored. Three naked figures were dancing in front of an Elizabethan timbered house, a man wearing only a wide, soft brimmed hat and on either side a woman. One was Frances Leyland, her long dark hair thrown back, and on the other side, the shorter figure of her sister, Elizabeth Dawson. In the background, under a tree, a swarthy dark satyr sat dejectedly playing on a set of pipes. The plate was signed Seymour Haden but on Elizabeth Dawson's finger there was a butterfly.

Felicity closed her eyes for a moment and held the plate to her breast.

'I call these my curios,' ben Mollah said, 'but as works of art they do not touch my soul.'

'These plates are by Whistler,' Felicity said quietly. 'In this one you can see Whistler himself with his lovers, Frances Leyland and her sister. Behind them is Speke Hall where Whistler came to paint for Frederick Leyland, Frances' husband. The butterfly is Whistler's signature.'

'This Whistler came to this man's house to work for him and seduced his wife and sister in law?' ben Mollah said pointing pudgily at the figures.

'Oh yes, and Frances Leyland loved him for the rest of her life.'

'This man Whistler should have been killed for what he did!'

Ben Mollah recited all the punishments that Islamic law meted out to fornicating criminals like Whistler as Felicity picked up the other three plates. One showed Frances Leyland lying like a Japanese courtesan holding open her kimono on a rumpled bed with Whistler about to climb in alongside her. In the corner was a tall armoire and through a top panel the face of Frederick Leyland peered in anguish at the lovers. A butterfly

141

had come to rest on Mrs Leyland's wrist and as she reached out to her lover with one hand she smiled at the butterfly. The other two were nude studies of Frances. In one she had stepped from the model's chair to stand beside Whistler and admire his portrait of her, while Frederick was a grimacing carved figure at the side of the mantelpiece, and the fourth was a simple study of her lying with legs parted as if she were sleeping after love, a butterfly resting on the tumbled sheets.

'They were expensive so I bought them, but now I know their story I do not care for them at all,' ben Mollah said.

Felicity placed them carefully on top of the case and looked at his other curios. There was a Boucher water colour of a milkmaid and her lover on a bank beside a stream, and one small etching that looked remarkably like a Rembrandt with his young wife under a tree and a cornucopia of fruit and flowers between her legs. Felicity took them both from their cases and placed them alongside the Whistlers. She stopped and asked for a small icon to be removed from a case. James was at her elbow and opened it with his keys.

'I do not see what you find to interest yourself in these, Dr Norman,' ben Mollah said irritably. 'I would like you to discuss La Petite Joyeuse with me. Perhaps you can tell me about the artist, this master, Jules Pascin? Where can I find other paintings by him?'

The gold and jewelled frame of the icon was not as brilliant as the painting of Christ raising the young girl from death. She gazed up at him with adoration and all around her the family wept or raised their hands in wonder to a dazzling blue heaven where the sun and moon and a cluster of stars hung like painted toys on a Christmas tree. Felicity was sure it was a Stroganov but only Stefan would be able to determine that. Carefully, she placed the icon with the two prints and the plates.

'I do not know why I agreed to buy that,' said ben Mollah pointing to the icon with a fat finger. 'It has a pretty frame but there is nothing erotic about the figures. My agent told me it was a prelude to sex, but I like to see more in a picture. Now, let us go back to La Petite Joyeuse.'

Without her asking, James picked up the prints and the icon while Felicity carried the plates. Panting with the exertion ben Mollah pushed himself back to Bottoms.

'You must be able to tell me much that is interesting about this painting, Dr Norman.'

'Indeed I can, Mr ben Mollah. In the first place, it was stolen from the art gallery of Pequod College. If you look behind it you will see our gallery number on it.'

'Stolen!'

Ben Mollah gasped and asked for a chair which James put under him and then handed him a box of pills.

142

'Most, if not all, of the works displayed here were stolen and then sold to you.'

'They are mine! All mine!' Ben Mollah flung out his arms and screamed like a demented child.

'No, they are not yours, and when they are returned to their owners you will undoubtedly be prosecuted for receiving stolen goods.'

'James, who is this woman? Why is she saying these terrible things to me. You are my adviser. What shall I do with her?'

'I would listen to her very carefully and agree to whatever she wants.'

'I cannot part with my little *Joyeuse*. She is my life!'

'Mr ben Mollah,' Felicity said slowly. 'I know a way to give all your works here a provenance—'

'What does she mean?' Ben Mollah turned imploringly to James.

'She means that she knows how these can be legally made yours, Mr ben Mollah.'

'Tell me! Tell me quickly!'

'I can provide proof of sale from two previous owners for all the works here provided you let me have these,' and she pointed to the small pile that James had placed on a desk.

'Have them? Why should I give them to you?'

'Not give them to me. Let me have them on loan for five years.'

'Ah—' Ben Mollah was chewing his thumb and apparently enjoying the taste of it.

'You will be able to keep Bott—, *La Petite Joyeuse* and all the rest of your collection. You said yourself that these were not of great interest to you.'

'And if you – disappeared, Dr Norman, then I would be able to keep them all.' Ben Mollah put his head on one side and showed a set of yellow teeth.

'No, you would not, Mr ben Mollah. If I drowned out there in the lake or died in my sleep, a great many people would descend upon you and seize everything here.'

'It's an excellent suggestion, Mr ben Mollah. I'd take it if I were you,' James said.

'For five years, you say,' ben Mollah said miserably.

'Which will pass like a flash,' Felicity smiled.

'You really do seem pleased with this painting, Mr ben Mollah,' James added and gestured to the canvas.

'Do not touch her!' ben Mollah cried. 'I do not want anyone to touch her except me. She is mine.' Gently he stroked the peachy posterior of *La Joyeuse*.

'And she will remain yours forever if you agree,' Felicity said.

'I'd go along with her if I were you,' James added again, and Felicity could not help but smile gratefully at him.

'I do not like this. I have been cheated and now I am to be cheated again,' ben Mollah grumbled.

'The final joke will be on your agent, Mr ben Mollah. Once these works are given a provenance you can get a tax break on them.'

'Ah, is that so?' And he brightened up.

'I'll guarantee it,' James said.

'You have been a great help to me, James. I hope you are not deceiving me in this.'

'Mr ben Mollah, Dr Norman is an art historian, she is interested in these – curios – for their historical value. She is not suggesting that you lend her any of the master works here. What I would advise is that you let me deal with your agent in future. If you recall, I warned you on more than one occasion that I thought he was over-charging you.'

'Kill Tom Kucich!' ben Mollah cried.

'I'm sure we can find some more paintings by Jules Pascin through reputable dealers,' Felicity added blandly.

'Another *Petite Joyeuse*?' ben Mollah said. 'I would like a brunette next time. Let everything be done immediately!' And he clapped his hands, 'Prepare the necessary documents for this provenancing, James.'

A bell rang and Taraq ben Mollah jumped, 'Lunch! That is the first bell for lunch! Be at table in half an hour,' and he thumped off.

'I think I know where there's a box that will contain these nicely,' James said.

'You have been wonderfully helpful,' Felicity smiled.

'I would do a lot to please a woman like you.'

'Can I see the box? I'd like to pack them myself.'

'I insist on doing this for you, Felicity. And you can consider me an expert.'

'I would still like to—'

'No, this is man's work.'

She was about to snap out an insult but smiled thinly instead. Whatever happened she would not let a little temper spoil her triumph.

Immediately after a lunch of cold pheasant and a rhum baba decorated with crystallized fruits which she ate alone for ben Mollah, since James had pleaded business upstairs, Felicity raced back to the gallery. James was just about to clamp down the lid of a small tea box.

'It's all right,' he laughed. 'Everything's in here. Look for yourself.'

Felicity checked and had to commend James on his packing, for it was almost as if he had designed the box with special padded compartments to hold the plates.

'I wanted to get this done before our fat friend changed his mind. I hope you talked a good lunch for him.'

'James, you've been absolutely smashing about this.'

'Thank you. And I meant what I said this morning.'

Felicity leaned over the box and kissed him with a passion of love for another James, but James Baker did not seem to notice the difference, and trembled slightly as he clamped down the lid.

'Now, this will go to our agent in New York, and he will send it on to Pequod. Is that where you want it delivered?'

Felicity was puzzled, 'Why must it go to your agent?'

'Normal business practice,' James said. 'Felicity, would you like to sail this afternoon? Ben Mollah always sleeps after lunch.'

In the fine cold air, it was like sailing through curtains of crystal on the lake with the French Alps on one side and the Swiss Alps disappearing into cloud beyond the prow of the boat. James Baker was impressive at the tiller and sent the little craft spinning into the wind, jibbing so swiftly that they almost flew across a surging swell of jade green water. Felicity asked him where he had learned to sail and he replied that he had been given his own boat when he was eight, and at twenty-five he had helped crew in a transatlantic yacht race.

When they moored it was sunset and the pink stucco of the Villa Francesca was reflecting the last warmth of the sun like a jewel. Felicity shuddered involuntarily because she remembered as a child carefully picking an apple so red that it glowed in her hand, but when she bit into it her teeth sank into a bulbous and lividily white maggot.

'It is a very splendid house,' Felicity said.

'A pity it's owned by such an old crook,' James said sourly. 'But that will change.'

'If you don't like him, why do you work for him?' Felicity said, and half expected him to say that it was money. Instead, James frowned and said that he stayed with ben Mollah for the good of society.

James Baker was a very odd combination of verbal fatuities and something poised and watchful like a hunting weasel that perplexed and almost frightened her.

Taraq ben Mollah was in a very good mood at dinner and browsed through a tub of grated carrot and raw cabbage as James and Felicity dined on paupiettes of sole in sorrel sauce and a Florentine cake. As soon as the butler handed her coffee in a cup of translucent Limoges china, Felicity bounded off to the kitchen to applaud the chef.

'Hee! Hee! She has done it again,' Taraq ben Mollah indicated the sandals that Felicity had kicked off under the table. 'Tomorrow, she will definitely ask me to suck her toes.'

A different man ran across the kitchen to greet her, kissing her hands.

'My wife agrees! Oh Madame, I thought she would be so angry, but she understood and we are going back to Paris. She thought it was I – I who wanted to stay here. But now she tells me that she cannot bear

Switzerland and she has been pining for our beloved Paris. Ah, I am leaving this purgatory and returning to la belle France.'

'And about time too,' Felicity said gleefully. 'When are you handing the old boy your notice?'

'He will get it tomorrow morning with his – what he likes to speak of as his breakfast. And if I told you what he eats for his first meal of the day you would be sick!'

'I'm sure I should, Gilles.'

'But you, Madame, you gave me the courage and the hope.'

Felicity sat on the kitchen table and ate a great many *petit fours* with him until James came down the steps and complimented Gilles on his dinner.

Gilles merely shrugged and said rapidly to Felicity in French that the American had the palate of a pig.

'Come on, Felicity,' James said. 'You mustn't spend all night in the kitchen. I think we can find better things to do, don't you?'

'We could have an early night,' she whispered.

'And tomorrow morning we'll take your precious box into Geneva and arrange to have it flown back to the States.'

'Oh, yes please,' she breathed. 'Where is it? It's in a safe place now, isn't it?'

'Would you like me to bring it down to your bedroom?'

'Yes – yes, I really think I'd like that very much.' And she swore that she heard another James chuckle just behind her left shoulder.

'It shall be done.'

Felicity knew that he would arrive with the box and when he did, he would expect to stay.

Two of Taraq ben Mollah's doctors came as they were going upstairs and James whispered that the old goat was on his last legs.

'I heard one of them say that his heart was a lump of congealed fat – like the rest of his body.'

'James, can I expect you in half an hour?'

'With the box.'

'Oh yes, I want James to sleep with me tonight.'

He shook his head slightly as he often did so when she spoke to him, but obviously thought this was an English variation of baby talk and said softly, 'James wants to go beddy-byes with you too, honey.'

Outside her window Lake Leman was a silver shield, the moonlight so radiant that the houselights looked sallow by comparison. 'Oh James,' she murmured. 'This is the night of the nocturnes, all black and silver, and I want to dance naked with you through the garden.'

She heard the door open and close and when she looked round James was carefully placing the box in the huge walk-in wardrobe where her few clothes were trying to look at home.

'I don't want either of us tripping over it during the night,' he said, and Felicity saw that he was only wearing a white towelling robe.

'Why don't you warm the bed for us,' Felicity said. 'I'll only be a moment.'

She remembered the diaphragm which had been thrust upon her at the insistence of Wendy Forsyth.

'Sensible girl,' James said from the bed. 'I don't want you to be anxious while you're having fun.'

That, Felicity said, is definitely not what Bernie would have said, and it certainly wouldn't have occurred to James McNeill Whistler.

She took the diaphragm between thumb and third finger as she had been instructed and carefully squeezed a thread of cream around the rim. She bent over and pushed and the diaphragm slipped from her fingers and flew across the room.

'Damn!' she muttered, and retrieved it from the bath to begin all over again. Once, she thought it was about to go in when it shot sideways and stuck to the mirror. No matter how she squeezed, or stood, lifting one leg on to the edge of the bath and then the other, all she succeeded in doing was smearing herself with the cream that smelt like floral detergent. She made one more effort, gripped the diaphragm with both hands and then tried to hold it in place. This time it seemed to be reluctantly entering her vagina. She released one hand, pushed with the other, and the diaphragm spun in circles like a frisbee and slapped itself fast to the ceiling.

James was calling to her from the bedroom, 'Need any help in there, honey?'

'No! No, I'm coming now, James.'

She looked up at the diaphragm winking at her from the ceiling and hoped she wasn't fertile.

'Oh boy, I love a woman who smells clean,' James said, and threw himself on top of her.

Somewhere, James had studied behavioural psychology because, as he made love by numbers, he kept saying, 'You're enjoying this, honey! This is great for you! Don't let yourself go yet, you're going to enjoy yourself more in a minute.'

The sales talk did not compensate for some of the most uninspired missionary style lovemaking that would have made the inmates of a women's prison yawn. Felicity wished she could wriggle out from underneath him and vanish under the bed, anywhere that she wouldn't have to listen to him telling her how great she was feeling, while stirring her inside with something that felt like a blunt pencil. She tried to think of another James and instantly she saw the dark eyes and felt his arms around her.

'Oh James, I've always loved you,' she said.

'Likewise. Likewise, honey.' James panted.

He was finished at last and fell back on the pillows, saying that he would now sleep like a log for eight hours straight.

Felicity decided to have a bath because the combined aroma of James Baker and spermicidal jelly was nauseating. He was almost asleep when he half lifted his head from the pillow and said, 'Wasn't that the greatest, all time screw you've ever had, honey?' And promptly fell back and began to snore lightly.

She had to get some air into her lungs and went out on to the balcony. There was a clink and clatter directly underneath her and she leaned over and saw Gilles weighted down under a load of copper pans.

'Gilles!' she called.

'Ah Madame, I am taking my pans. If he is very angry tomorrow morning he may not let me take my saucepans, and these are mine.'

'Very sensible,' Felicity said, and had a sudden idea. 'Gilles, do you live anywhere near the airport?'

'If it is anything I can do for you, Madame, you have only to ask me.'

'There's a box up here and if it left this evening then I would be so relieved.'

'Wait – I shall come up and help you carry it down.' He looked up at her and grinned. 'Are you, perhaps, taking a few little souvenirs?'

'These were packed for me with Mr ben Mollah's permission. I'll meet you downstairs.'

Gilles had a truck at the side of the house and he lifted the box into the back of it.

'Wait – wait, just a moment,' Felicity said urgently. 'I must change the address on it.'

Felicity was determined that the box would be delivered to Stefan de Mornay and not to some company called Palermo Enterprises in White Plains. How did she know if those people would send on the box unopened, and what if they did open it and damage the plates? No, Stefan would look after them until she got back to Pequod. She ripped off the labels, borrowed a pen from Gilles and on each side of the box she wrote Stefan's name and the address of Pequod College.

'Oh God, this is going to cost a fortune to send air freight. All I have in cash is a hundred dollars.'

'That will be more than enough,' Gilles said. 'I have some good friends at Air France. They will take your box on the eleven o'clock flight to New York, and the hundred dollars will pay for it to be delivered to your friend. But there is one thing I would like you to do for me – in the kitchen.'

'Anything,' Felicity said.

'Write me a good letter in English to Mr ben Mollah explaining why I have left.'

'We'll do it now.'

It was an elegant letter and as she wrote it, Gilles made coffee and insisted she have a little caviar on toast to make her sleep.

'I shall drive to Geneva with your box and talk to my friends and, with luck, it will be in New York tomorrow morning. Naturally, it will have to pass through customs, but I do not think that there will be any difficulty there.'

'Gilles, will you let me know when you're going to open your restaurant?'

'I shall insist that you come to my opening night, Madame.'

'Felicity – please call me Felicity.'

'That is the name I shall always hold in my heart.'

He looked round at the glistening kitchen and smiled. 'This was my gilded cage, my prison, and now I am a free man. Will you give Mr ben Mollah my letter?'

'Oh, I'll leave it on the hall table for him. That's where the butler puts all the mail.'

Felicity ran up to her bedroom and waved to Gilles as he circled the driveway and drove round to the front gates. A few seconds later she saw the lights of his truck on the climbing hill to Geneva.

James was still snoring gently when she came back to bed and she looked at him and thought how beautiful his body was and wondered why he had never learned to use it for love. Sighing, she ran her bath, and sat dreaming of Bernie in the fragrant water. He did know how to scroom, and he knew when to be silent and when to murmur something in her ear that made her choke with laughter.

Carefully, she rolled James to the edge of the bed and covered him with a sheet and slept. In one dream she was riding in the front of the truck with Gilles and when she looked over her shoulder, James McNeill Whistler was relaxing against the box, smoking a long black cheroot. In another she was dancing with Bernie and James, and as they passed her from hand to hand, Bernie and James became one. She woke laughing and saw James leaning over her.

'Felicity, the box has gone!'

'Mmm,' she murmured, and stretched her toes.

'Did one of the servants take it downstairs?'

'No—'

The maid came in with a tray and was about to back through the door when she saw James, but Felicity beckoned her to the bed.

'It must be the effect of Gilles' food. I'm always ravenous in this house.'

She poured her coffee and examined the array of jams on the tray.

James was prowling round the room, looking in cupboards and even under the bed.

'I put it in the wardrobe last night.'

'I know you did,' Felicity said with her mouth full. 'And it's probably three miles up in the air now.'

'What the hell do you mean?'

He seemed about to take hold of her by the shoulders and shake her, and Felicity suddenly felt afraid. She looked down to push his hand away from her and paused – across the side of his palm there were teeth marks.

'You attacked me – you were the man in my room at Pequod!'

'Where is that box?'

'My God! You're the man who murdered Betty Levin and attacked that student. You—'

'I searched your room and you caught me. I was trying to get out but you kept hanging on to me. Now, where is the box?'

'I saw Gilles leaving last night and he took it to the airport in Geneva for me. I was anxious for it to be on its way.'

'I told you I would take it to the airport myself!'

'James, there are a number of things I'm beginning to find out about you. One is that you are a lousy lover, and the other is that you are a liar and possibly the rapist who's been killing women at Pequod.'

James was taut with rage and seemed on the point of striking her. Felicity picked up a knife from her tray.

'I'd prefer to use this on my croissant and not on you,' she said bleakly.

'Damn your interference,' he said.

'The box will arrive a little earlier than expected. Is there anything wrong with that?'

'Everything. You stupid interfering bitch! I've spent months, years, setting up this operation, and you had to interfere.'

'Then you are not Mr ben Mollah's loyal financial adviser.'

'Taraq ben Mollah specializes in laundering dirty money through a variety of banks that he controls throughout the Middle East. He has lately undertaken to accept huge sums from the Mafia in America.'

'Palermo Enterprises?'

'That box must arrive at a certain time. God, I better make some phone calls.'

He flung open the door and Taraq ben Mollah almost knocked him down.

'Where is she? I will kill her now with my bare hands.'

'Cool it, Mr ben Mollah. What's happened?'

'She has taken my cook – I have no food!'

Taraq ben Mollah collapsed into the nearest chair gasping and waving the letter Felicity had written last night.

'Mr ben Mollah,' Felicity said calmly, 'there are many good chefs and I'm sure you'll be able to hire half a dozen if you pay them enough.'

'I paid Gilles Fresnay three hundred thousand dollars a year because he was the best!'

'Three hundred thousand! He should be able to set up a charming little restaurant with all that if his wife has been as frugal as he says.'

James suddenly turned to Felicity. 'You didn't,' he snarled, 'you didn't by any chance change the address on that box, did you?'

'If you gentlemen will leave my bedroom, I shall pack and be on my way.'

'Like hell you will,' James moved towards her, and Felicity picked up the breakfast table and threw it.

She heard ben Mollah shouting that she was a thief and must die, and James shouting, and as she leaped backwards from the bed she fell and seemed to be drowning in a sea of black feathers.

CHAPTER TWELVE

Myra sat on one side of Bernie in the ambulance, holding his hand as though it were something she had picked up on the beach by mistake. She stared across Bernie's body at Stefan and said through clenched teeth, 'Is this what you meant by bringing Felicity and Bernie back together?'

'I said it would take a little time,' Stefan put his chin on his cane and tried to think. 'I am inclined to regard this unfortunate accident as an act of God, Myra.'

'Only Bernie would fall out of bed and suffer a slipped disc. Rosa falls out of bed all the time and she never even scratches herself.'

'I said it would require the healing of time for Bernie and Felicity to realize how much they miss each other. Seen in that light you could say this accident is heaven sent.'

Myra merely snorted.

'No, listen my dear. Bernie is not going to be chasing gymnasts or any other kind of female with a slipped disc. I can assure you from personal experience that the pain is frightful and all his movements will be limited for quite some time.'

'And what about Felicity? Do you think a girl like that is going to remain unattached for long? For pity's sake, Stef, the first rich, intelligent young doctor she sees will be such a relief after Bernie that she'll marry him on the spot.'

'Felicity is looking for the Whistler etchings.'

'I – nothing about this makes sense to me, Stef.'

Myra began to sniffle and Bernie groaned.

He remembered very little except Stef holding his head and waves of blinding pain, until a doctor came who gave him an injection of Demeral and said it looked like a job for an orthopaedic surgeon. It was Stef who insisted on Columbia Medical Center and when he was wheeled in, Bernie realized why. Doctors came from everywhere to greet Stef, nurses recognized him and blew kisses to him, and as Bernie lay ignored and moaning in the lobby, the great Wilbur Krushnek descended from surgery to greet Stefan.

Wilbur walked slowly round his old patient. A number of specialists fell in behind him and, within minutes, Stefan was completely surrounded by a perambulation of white coats and green robes.

'Stefan, my boy, when I look at you – when I see you standing there in one piece, I feel as though I'm God.'

A number of the other doctors joined in to claim their part of the divinity, but Wilbur waved them back.

'Gentlemen, this is my masterpiece!'

Stefan murmured his undying gratitude but—

'No!' Wilbur insisted. 'I am in your debt, Stefan. There never was a case like yours, and never will be again, I hope. Four inches of his spine were like peanut butter, femurs like desiccated coconut. Gentlemen, when Stefan arrived he was carried through that door in a box. I mean that literally; the Finns may have designed it as a bed, but I could see at once that they were economizing. If Stef had died, as they expected, they would have nailed down the lid and called for a shovel.'

'Think of me as your Lazarus, Wilbur,' Stefan said gently. 'But I have brought you a patient.'

'Ah – yes. Slipped disc, eh?'

Wilbur had read the sheet at the end of Bernie's trolley and bent down to him.

Bet you feel like hell, eh?' Whenever possible, Wilbur Krushnek always answered for the patient, which saved a great deal of unnecessary confusion. 'Well, when you come out of X-ray I'll tell you whether it is hell.'

Myra was impressed by the attention Stefan was receiving from so many specialists. At first she was adamant that Bernie should be treated at one of the local hospitals, but Stefan had insisted on Columbia where he had been pinned and stitched together after the Helsinki episode. At least she could tell Fiona and the others at bridge that her son was in Columbia and mention some of the doctors. She could also say that Felicity had sent a frantic cable from Switzerland – and – but she would think of the rest as she drove Stefan back to Pequod.

Wilbur was frowning when he carried in Bernie's X-ray, and said, 'I have known people get slipped discs from stepping backwards out of the shower, or walking downstairs, but an injury like this as a result of falling out of bed is extraordinary. I would almost say unique. What position were you in when you fell?'

'I think I had my left foot behind my right ear,' Bernie said simply.

Wilbur gave a very short laugh. He encouraged patients to laugh at themselves occasionally, but he did not appreciate any kind of joke at his own expense.

'Well, you won't be falling out of this bed, I can promise you that.'

Two nurses arrived with something that looked like a hoop of padded steel with pins protruding from it.

'We're going to put your pelvis in this harness, and that will support your back and prevent any movement.'

'How long? How long do I have to wear that thing?'

'Two weeks, and then we'll see what shape your spine's in.'

Bernie lay back and closed his eyes. At least he could flex his toes, and it no longer seemed that he was going to be confined to a wheelchair for the rest of his life; but the pain took his breath away as the muscles of his back clenched, and every nerve throbbed sympathetically. He could not bear to close his eyes for long because he could still see Mariana standing over him with her hands on her hips and jeering. Either he saw Mariana, or it was Lorenzo Delgado looking over his shoulder as he dragged him along on a length of rope.

He lay unresisting as the nurses tightened the pins, and when he looked down the lower part of his body was in something that resembled an instrument of medieval torture. His mother had hung some balloons in the corner of the room, and left after telling him that she and his father would visit him on alternate days to break the strain of travelling. 'I do have your grandmother to look after too,' Myra said, and went off with Stefan on her arm. The drugs had made Bernie drowsy and he rested comfortably on the edge of sleep. The nightmare of the last two days now seemed as far removed from him as a horror movie on late night television, but one image remained with him: Mariana bouncing naked on his bed.

When she was naked, she was as unappealing as an adolescent boy with sharp bones protruding from her hips, and breasts so flat they were like inverted coffee saucers. He had undoubtedly been the victim of an optical delusion when he first saw her, and to have loved her was a form of temporary insanity. Gymnastics was an occupation for the undersized and overmuscled, and as interesting to watch as a troupe of performing fleas. Her conversation was like standing within range of a manic machine gun so different from – and Bernie wondered with a different kind of pain if Felicity were in bed with Chuck Stimson.

The light was hurting her eyes and someone pulled a shade. Felicity put her hands to her head and tried to think. The last thing she remembered was discovering that James Baker was the homicidal rapist of Pequod, but somehow Taraq ben Mollah had been there too. Slowly, she looked around her and at the same time she felt a pain at the back of her head.

154

This room was different, and even with the shade pulled there was a clarity of light that was quite unlike the Villa Francesca. The furniture, too, was strange and vaguely oriental with mounds of silk cushions on a divan.

'Oh my God,' Felicity said, 'It's a brothel in the Kasbah.'

'Hardly, my dear.'

Felicity frowned and tried to focus. At the end of the divan was a woman with black straight hair, wearing white pants and a short blue sweater. She was astonishingly slender and could have been a model for some elegant fashion house.

'Please,' the woman drawled, 'don't afflict me with the obvious. You are not in a brothel, I can assure you of that. This is the summer palace of my late grandfather, Khalil ben Mollah. Out there,' and she pointed to the window with a lacquered hand, 'is the Mediterranean; behind you, the city of Tunis.'

All Felicity could think of was the box. She felt sure that Gilles Fresnay was trustworthy, but had he been able to get it on a plane to the States in time? And why had James Baker gone berserk when she told him it was already on its way to New York? Of one thing she was quite certain: she had not told James that the box was now addressed to Stefan de Mornay at Pequod College. Yet James had been so helpful; he had persuaded Taraq ben Mollah to part with the plates and the other art works, and he had even insisted on packing them for her. Why had he looked as if he wanted to kill her when he found out that Gilles had already left with the box? But if he were the Pequod rapist then he was completely mad, and she – she had actually scroomed with a murderer.

'You seem disturbed. I can understand why. Let me introduce myself,' the woman held out her hand. 'I am Mima Mollah, Taraq's sister. Or, perhaps I should say, disgraced sister. You arrived here by helicopter last night and James told me something of the story.'

'That maniac was here?'

'I would not describe James Baker as a maniac. I have always found him very charming and with sound principles on fiscal matters.'

'Where is he now?'

'He only stayed long enough to deliver you. I think he said he was flying back to the States.'

'Now, let me try to understand what has happened—' Felicity said slowly.

'Have some iced tea, it will help clear your head.'

'All I can remember is a terrific row with your brother and James.'

'I don't know what your quarrel with James was, but I can tell you now that my brother wants to kill you.'

'Kill me?'

'I gather that it was James who dissuaded him and suggested instead that you be sent here.'

'Why in heaven's name would your brother want to kill me?' Felicity cried. 'He agreed to let me have some of his art works on loan. I did nothing underhand or criminal. If we're talking about crime, then your brother should realize he has a gallery full of stolen paintings.'

'Oh, I don't think that would bother fat Taraq in the least. What has given him a heart attack is the loss of his chef.'

'But he never eats anything but basins of greens!'

'He cannot live without food, and at least with that French chef in residence he was able to see it and smell it.'

'Utter madness.'

'Not for my brother, and you were responsible for this cook leaving, weren't you?'

'Yes.'

'For my brother to be without food is like an ordinary person to be deprived of air. It has always been a passion with him—'

Mima stood up to stretch and almost disappeared from view sideways she was so thin.

'It's the reason he always hated me. When we were children we ate exactly the same amounts, but he got fat and I remained the same. As a young man he lived for food and sex and I believe he was one of the few people who could screw and eat at the same time. Now, he has had another heart attack, and, with the help of Allah, he will die.'

'But why am I here? And what's going to happen to me?' Felicity said, and drank some more tea very quickly.

'Nothing at all. My brother wants you here while he decides what is to be done with you, and I have no intention of annoying fat Taraq now.'

'I can phone from here, can't I?'

'No, you can't, my dear. There is a code number to call out and only I know it. As for escaping by foot, this house is well guarded. On one side of us on the beach we have the R. and R. residence of the PLO, and since my brother helps support them financially they provide guards for this house. On the other side there is a Lebanese warlord who has his own guards, and since he too is a good friend of my brother's, you can see why this house is so well protected. But the weather is always delightful and there is very good swimming. Here – you will find every comfort.'

Felicity sat up and felt the back of her head. There was a large sore lump under her hair.

'You must have fallen or else you were hit by my brother. I'm amazed he had the strength. I don't think you have concussion.'

'You're quite serious about keeping me here?'

156

'My dear, I am prepared to guard you with my life. After all, you're my only hope of life.'

'I don't understand.'

Mima sighed and lit a long cigarette, 'My brother has suffered another heart attack, and James told me the doctors have him in bed in an oxygen tent. Fat Taraq controls a series of banks in several different countries. I – I have nothing. But if he dies, and especially if I do not anger him in any way before he dies, I shall inherit the Mollah estate.'

'He is going to die soon, isn't he?' Felicity said expectantly.

'May it please Allah!' Mima raised her hands above her head. 'Unfortunately, he's had other attacks and survived them.'

'But, you wouldn't kill me, would you, Mima?'

'No – no, I would not. If only because you're the first intelligent woman who's ever come here.'

Felicity tried to think and decided to look at the view. Mima pulled the shade and sunlight drenched the room. Outside was a garden with oleanders in bloom and beds of flowers between paths of white pebbles, and beyond the garden, a beach with some Roman ruins to one side and the Mediterranean beyond.

'It's magnificent!' Felicity said.

'The ruins are of an old amphitheatre. You can sometimes find Roman coins on the beach after a storm, and there are still fragments of pottery in the sand. This was once the greatest city in the world – Carthage.'

'What a perfect place for a holiday,' Felicity said.

'I have been here for nine years,' Mima said bleakly.

'But you travel, don't you?'

'Why don't you have a shower, and then we can go downstairs and you'll understand then what this house really is.'

As she stood under the shower Felicity made one firm resolution. No matter what happened she would not try to leave until she was quite certain that the box had arrived and was safely with Stefan at Pequod. As for the rest, she stepped out of the bathroom and saw that her duffle bag had already been unpacked. There was also a selection of long cotton gowns and a number of swimsuits in the wardrobe. The Mediterranean was outside her window and the warm air smelt of salt. If this was a prison, Felicity decided she was going to make the most of it. And she would join Mima in a few prayers for the speedy demise of Taraq. But she would like to call Stefan and – but Bernie was probably having sex on the parallel bars with his gymnast. She put on one of the long white gowns, combed her hair, and walked out on to a marble landing that looked down to a fountain and a tiled court.

*

Bernie's first visitor was Martin who came into the room so quietly that he was at the side of the bed and coughing nervously before Bernie saw him.

'I brought you some books and magazines.'

Bernie sighed and said nothing.

'Is it very painful?'

'There are degrees of pain, Martin. When I lie like this it is only moderately painful. When they take me out in the evening, for a few minutes, the agony sends me through the ceiling.'

'I – Mariana said I should say "Hi" to you.'

'Oh really?' Bernie said bitterly. 'That's very kind of her.'

'She talked to me,' Martin said in a whisper.

'Watch her, Martin. Watch her very carefully. She – she did this to me.'

'Yes, she told me.'

'She told you? Oh God—' and Bernie closed his eyes and tried to wait until the horror had washed over him.

'Everything's fine at Pequod, Bernie. End of term, and all that sort of thing. I – I may be on the edge of a breakthrough with my factoring.'

'Wonderful, Martin. Tell me all about it.'

Bernie stared at the ceiling as Martin talked and wondered if he were going to be locked into this cage of misery and shame for the rest of his life. Mariana had cheerfully told Martin about him, and she hadn't even sent him flowers. He remembered Felicity was so upset once when he had a cold that she began to knit a Fair Isle sweater for him. She never finished it, but she had cared—'

'I still can't accept the simplicity of it, Bernie.'

'It sounds marvellous to me, Martin.'

'I'm going to write it up this evening. After I watch Mariana and Louise.'

Something occurred to Bernie that had been a niggling question at the back of his mind.

'Who is Lenore on with?'

'Me – naturally,' and Martin tried to laugh.

'In reality.'

'Louise, of course. Mariana says it's a big item, but Louise can't come out of the closet because her father's a Methodist minister in Duluth.'

'Lenore is next door with Louise and Mariana—'

'Oh, there are two bedrooms. It's a corner apartment, and Mariana says they don't make a sound.'

'You seem to be very friendly with Mariana?'

'She speaks to me,' Martin said, and knotted his fingers.

'Well, tell her from me that next time she's flipping round in midair, I hope Louise is thinking of something else when she decides to come down.'

'Bernie! That is pretty damn callous!'

'Try sleeping in a steel harness and see how you feel.'

Martin left, muttering, and his father came in to talk about medical insurance and worker's compensation and claims against the college. Every day brought visitors and most, Bernie decided, were there to gloat over his plight. Everyone except Chip and Sally Frauenfelder who wanted him to sign a character reference for them. 'It's the only way we can get Daniel back,' Chip sobbed.

'Chip's been clean, he hasn't touched anything since Daniel ran away,' Sally moaned. 'You can't imagine what it's like being without Daniel.'

'No one will help us at Pequod. I asked Stefan de Mornay, and he said he was an authority on Russian icons, not character. Bernie, I loved that little boy. I used to play with him. I used to tell him stories—' and Chip started to cry.

'Everyone has refused,' Sally said, 'so we've come to you.'

'I am far too ill to sign anything,' Bernie replied. 'What strength I have left I'm saving to sign my will. And I may only be able to initial that.'

Everyone at Pequod remembered Daniel's electrical genius and no one would help bring the family together again. The Frauenfelders left, accusing Bernie of being heartless and unfeeling.

Grierson arrived with a large bundle of essays and exam papers which he placed on Bernie's bedside table.

'You couldn't have had this unjury at a more inconvenient time, Bernie. But, you'll be able to grade these papers while you're here. I remember that once, when I was laid up with a broken ankle, I read three dissertations and wrote an article on Isaac Bickerstaff.'

'I'll do what I can,' Bernie said numbly.

'There has been a lot of discussion about you, Bernie.'

'I bet there has.'

'Yes, the President called me in.'

Bernie tried to avoid Grierson's eyes and failed.

'There was this problem with the students.'

'I was duped! My God! I expected you to be at that party.'

'I explained to the President that there had been a misunderstanding on your part. But, Bernie, senior members of faculty do not fall into traps like that. If you were an assistant professor—'

Oh, and how you must be wishing I were an assistant professor without tenure so that you could scrub me at the end of term, Bernie thought.

'And then – but I daresay you've already seen this?'

Grierson was holding out a copy of the *New York Review of Books*.

'I haven't seen an issue since I came here, Willard.'

'Ah well, you would not have read the review of your poetry.'

'My poetry – in the *New York Review*?'

Bernie was so excited he leaned forward and his back screamed in protest.

'Yes, well, it's not exactly a review of your poetry. It's a paragraph in a commentary on some contemporary verse.'

'Who wrote it?'

'Haskell Jordan.'

Haskell Jordan of the Pulitzer and Guggenheim prizes, Haskell Jordan who had been poet in residence at Harvard and Cornell.

'Would you like to hear it?'

'Please.'

Bernie lay back and closed his eyes.

' "The inanities and inconsequential absurdity of this kind of poetry . . " You realize, Bernie, this is only part of a long survey, "are most readily manifest in *Absence and Omission*, a slender volume by Bernard Lefkowitz. One hopes that a work of this nature is a prank, a flouting of established forms, or at the least, a parodic interpretation of minimalist technique; but it is more likely that Mr Lefkowitz does indeed believe that these fly-specked pages are poems. I see them belonging more to the commercial category of pet rocks, canned air and diet pills." I really think that last part is rather good, don't you? "Pet rocks, canned air and diet pills".'

Bernie's eyes remained closed.

'Well, I can see you want to rest,' Grierson said, 'and you won't forget those papers, will you? I'll send someone along to pick them up next Monday. You should have them done by then. By the way, would you like me to leave the *Review*? It's a good issue, has some interesting stuff in it.'

Bernie heard Grierson leave and hoped that the angel of death would be his next visitor. If he could only jump from the bed and writhe in torment on the floor, if he could stamp and rave, he might have been able to relieve some of his torment. If there were someone to console him, to tell him that Haskell Jordan was a worn out embittered old fart who hadn't written a decent poem in the last twenty years, he would have felt an easing of his pain. But he was alone, and his next visitors were his mother and Stefan.

Myra asked him briefly how he felt, changed his balloons, and settled Stefan into a comfortable chair so she could go and shop for an hour or two. Everyone on campus, it seemed, knew Haskell Jordan's review by heart, and even Stefan was chuckling.

'Ah well, you're young, Bernie, so you can afford to make a few blunders.'

He pulled out a book and settled down to read to Bernie. It was, he said, less fatiguing than talking, and he knew Bernie would enjoy *The Lord of the Rings*.

'I detest Tolkien,' Bernie said.

'Rubbish,' Stefan said. 'This is pure enchantment and it will take your mind off your problems.'

He did not tell Bernie that he had just received a cable from Felicity that puzzled him. It had been sent from Lausanne and it said simply, 'Off to see Europe. Have a great summer. Love, Felicity.'

At first he grumbled that this was the price you paid when you gave any young scholar a cent more than the cost of a round air ticket. But it was the tone that concerned him most. Felicity would have said something about the Whistlers – unless perhaps a previous cable had gone astray. Moreover, she knew every museum in Europe, and had even spent a summer in St Petersburg where Whistler lived as a child. He decided to phone Mr ben Mollah that evening, but for the time being he would be off and away with Strider and the Hobbits . . .

Myra dropped Stefan at Sufferin just as a hefty young man with technicolour tattoos on his arms was lifting a box from the back of a truck. Always interested in other people's packages, Stefan strolled over and saw with a surge of excitement that it was addressed to him in Felicity's baroque hand.

'Upstairs – carry it carefully. Don't knock it against the wall.'

Stefan shepherded the man into the elevator and opened his door with a shaking hand. The box was now standing in the middle of his coffee table and Stefan walked slowly round it. He could see where it had been cursorily opened by customs, and checked the date. There was no airline stamp from Geneva to New York and he frowned. Stefan did not know that the box had travelled free of charge as the personal property of a senior steward who had once been a waiter at the Tour d'Argent where Gilles Fresnay served part of his apprenticeship. Mysteriously, the box had arrived in New York, and somebody must then have paid the artistically decorated young man to deliver it to him at Pequod.

Boxes fascinated Stefan and he approached this one with the delicacy of a surgeon probing the nooks and crannies of the human brain. It was not an ordinary tea box, he decided, but it was designed to look like one. The sides were reinforced with copper strips and the lid was clamped down. He went into the next room and opened a bureau. When he came back he had a roll of chamois leather which he unfolded to reveal an array of scalpels, fine chisels, and even smaller pliers.

Cautiously, he peeled away the US Customs seal and opened it where it had been examined. Slowly, he removed the lid, checking every few moments to make sure he was not marking the wood. He could see the padded containers, and there were other treasures inside. His heart was now pounding so erratically that he sat down and tried to calm himself. Then, with his fingertips, he extracted the plates and placed them on the sofa.

'Felicity!' he murmured. 'You have won the prize!'

He laughed when he held the plates to a mirror and saw the dancing figures and Leyland glumly blowing his satyr's pipes.

'You poor fool,' Stefan said to him, 'you should have realized that art outlives the power of money.'

He crooned with delight over the Boucher, and guffawed at the Rembrandt.

'I'm ready to swear that it's genuine. Oh, Archie Macbeth, if only you could be with me now!'

There was something else in the box and Stefan reached down and pulled out the icon. Wordlessly, he held it in front of him, and fell to his knees.

'Oh Felicity! Oh, my beloved child, Felicity. You have found it.

Stefan began to rock backwards and forwards holding the icon before his eyes. 'Prokopi Chirin, icon painter to the Tzar and the Stroganovs, she has brought you from the darkness into the light.'

He began to cry and pulled himself on to the sofa. There he placed the icon on his knees and bent over it, tracing the figures with his finger.

'Exactly as it was described in the 1896 catalogue. Everyone thought the Bolsheviks had destroyed the icon and melted down the frame, but God protected your work, Prokopi. And now Felicity has given it into my hands.'

He marvelled at the precise and fervent painting, the figures that stood lightly on their toes like dancers, vibrant souls about to leave the earth, and for a time he leaned back and held the icon to his heart.

'Felicity! Oh, my Felicity,' he murmured over and over again as the tears ran down his face.

Something about the box still disturbed Stefan, and, wiping his eyes, he placed the icon carefully on a desk and walked around the table again. For many years Stefan had prided himself on being a smuggler of incomparable skill, and this box was waking old memories. He extracted a long, folding metal tape from the chamois roll and began to measure every side of the box, inside and out. He sat back on the sofa and smiled wolfishly. It was concealed by the copper stripping and the cardboard containers that had held the Whistler plates, but unquestionably the box had a false bottom.

162

As he made himself some tea, he spread out the tools and selected five of them. Thoughtfully, he sipped his glass of tea and decided where to enter the box. It would take time, he knew, and his hands were no longer capable of fine or very strong work, but he set about removing the copper stripping down two sides of the box. Working by fractions he lifted off the stripping and pulled back the wooden frame. At first he thought that someone had packed silica gel into the bottom of the box to protect the contents from damp, but silica gel was always kept in porous paper containers, and this was in long plastic tubes.

He drank another glass of tea more slowly than the first and looked for a darning needle in his sewing box. He licked the needle and poked it through the plastic, then pulled it out and put it to his tongue. It was not silica gel, and if it was not, then it must be heroin or cocaine.

It was nightfall when he made his way over to the art gallery and, at the corner of Botany Meadow, he met the President and Lester Marcus.

'I am so concerned about the gallery these days, that I make a point of checking the alarm system myself,' Stefan quavered.

'Good idea, Stef. Fred Cadwallader's very upset about that French painting being stolen,' the President said.

'It's Lefkowitz,' Lester snarled. 'Lefkowitz is behind all of this, and don't tell me again that story about a student party. Remember what the black kid was saying when they put her in the ambulance. She was saying 'Bernie', and I say Bernie Lefkowitz is the maniac. Things have been pretty quiet around here since they took him off to hospital.'

'Lieutenant Poldowski cleared him,' the President said.

'What we need are some New York cops on this case.'

The two went off arguing and Stefan let himself into the gallery and rummaged around in the storeroom until he found two bags of silica gel.

When he returned to his apartment, a little breathless after so much exertion, he removed the plastic tubes and filled the space with freezer bags full of the silica. It was almost midnight when he repacked the box and clamped down the lid. Replacing the icon had been an agonizing decision, and for almost an hour he wavered, and considered putting another icon from his own collection in its place. But he knew the contents were described in the customs declaration, and he did not have anything that resembled the image of Christ raising the dead girl to life.

He put away the tools and sat down to admire his handiwork. The box now looked as it did when the tattooed young man placed it on the coffee table. There was not a mark to show where the stripping had been removed. Stefan realized he was hungry and went and made himself a plate of scrambled eggs. Dining out as often as he did, he kept very little food in his kitchen.

At first he thought of flushing the dope down the sink, but decided against it. The drains in Sufferin were often blocked and Melvin Grimes was always threatening to make the tenants use buckets to carry water to their apartments. The incinerator? But there was generally someone popping down to the basement with bags of rubbish, and he could not risk being seen there. Besides, the incinerator was lit at irregular intervals, and he could not wait until it was burning. He was very tired, and went off to his canopied bed. If he prayed to his icons, Stefan knew that when he woke they would have given him an answer to the problem.

The next morning, Stefan strolled over to Botany Meadow with a cloth-wrapped bundle in his arms. A beefy young student was industriously clearing one corner and Stefan walked over to him, dabbing his eyes with a large, embroidered handkerchief.

The student looked up and sideways because he knew Stefan de Mornay by sight and reputation.

'My dear boy,' Stefan quavered, 'I have come to ask you a favour.'

The student was obviously uneasy, and coughed.

'Have you ever owned a cat?' Stefan said plaintively.

'I'm allergic to cats,' the boy replied.

'My cat was my friend and my companion for many years. It is dead now, and I cannot bear to see it carried off with the trash, or burned with other people's rubbish. Would you, as a great favour to me, bury my cat here?' Stefan held out the bundle to the student.

'I'm not sure I can do that, Professor. You see we regulate the fertilizer here. We'll be seeding this tomorrow for a five year growth period and—'

'Surely a cat provides the best kind of organic fertilizer? I can assure you that I never fed Grisha on anything except chopped liver and boned flounder.'

The student said he was not sure – and Stefan began to whimper. This was too much for the student, who began digging furiously.

'I would like to put my old Grisha in his grave myself,' Stefan said, and dropped the bundle in the hole, then leaned back on his cane as the student buried it. He sauntered towards Sufferin, greeting friends on the way, knowing that the student would report the whole incident to the Professor of Botany, Miles Wabash, and Miles would not forget that he owed his tenure and promotion to Stefan. Miles would shrug and say that poor old Stefan was losing his marbles, but a little bit of cat would not affect the planting in the meadow. Ashes to ashes, Stefan mused, and the fruit of the opium poppy has returned to the earth. Getting rid of the dope had been easy; the difficulty now would be waiting for someone to call about that remarkably designed box. In his apartment, he pulled out another drawer of his bureau, and checked a small ivory-handled pistol.

CHAPTER THIRTEEN

Mima, as Felicity found, was not the most engaging companion. She began most remarks with a sneer and ended them with an insult. So, when Felicity saw a dozen women lolling round the fountain, and others watching television and painting their nails, she immediately asked if the palace was a harem.

'That depends on how you choose to interpret the term. Being European, you doubtless imagine a harem to be full of luscious young women and delectable slave girls. A harem was quite simply a house of women, and the inhabitants were mainly old or middle-aged; unwanted aunts, unmarried cousins – all the discarded women that the nearest male relative was obliged to protect were taken into the harem. What you see here, is what you would find in an average upper class harem.'

'I thought they had been abolished,' Felicity said, and looked disapprovingly at a motley collection of young women dabbling their feet in the fountain and giggling.

'This harem was founded by my grandfather who was a most virtuous and merciful man. His brother killed his daughter when she had an affair with a young gardener, and Khalil the Merciful wept many bitter tears for his niece. He left this palace as a refuge for fallen women.'

'You mean – they all got dumped here because they had a quick klorg? Some of them look like children,' Felicity said.

'All of the women here have disgraced their families, and most of them would now be dead if it weren't for this house. But the families send them here and the Mollah estate cares for them.'

'This is a civilized country, isn't it?'

'Remarkably so – but these girls come from backward areas and very poor or very devout families. They are really very fortunate to be here, and they know it. Every Muslim girl is told the story of the Sultan Ibrahim of Turkey who heard that one of his concubines was having a secret love afair with a janissary. When he couldn't discover the culprit he decided to punish the whole harem. The girls were murdered in batches, tied up in sacks weighted with stones and carried to the Water

Gate where small boats carried them out into the harbour. There were two hundred and eighty women in those sacks and only one of them escaped because her sack was loosely tied and she managed to wriggle free. It was she who carried the story of the massacre to a passing boat bound for France. But it did not need her story to spread the news. One of Constantinople's divers was lowered from a boat to inspect a wreck at the bottom of the harbour and there he saw a great number of bowing sacks, each containing the body of a dead woman standing upright on the weighted end and swaying to and fro in the current. My nurse told me that story when I was a little girl – I have never forgotten it.'

'That was hundreds of years ago!'

'The moral code is the same.'

'To keep women as slaves?'

'As slaves or chaste wives and daughters.'

'Horrible—'

'Mind you, this is not a harem in the true sense. This is more a palace of tears.'

'Oh what?'

'When the sultan, or the master of the harem died, all of his women were sent off to another house – and that house was known as a palace of tears. So you see, the girls here are remarkably lucky. They have good food, entertainment, every comfort—'

'But this is a prison.'

'What more can women like this expect? I told you, they are ignorant, stupid and lazy. Don't waste your pity on them.'

'It's barbaric,' Felicity said.

'It is remarkably humane, when you consider the alternative for most of them. What man would pay a dowry for damaged goods. If they had money, that would be a different matter, and husbands could be found for them in the light of the present depressed economy.'

'But what do they do?'

The women were lolling like sleepy kittens in the sunlight that filtered down through a fretted roof. Occasionally, one of them would get up and stroll across to one of a dozen different television sets placed in darkened alcoves.

'That is what they do,' Mima said bitterly. 'They are animals – animals who sleep, eat, and refuse to think. Most of them are illiterate. Some of the older women take to house cleaning to occupy their time, but that is all.'

'And your brother pays for all this?'

'The Mollah estate does. Do you know anything about entail?'

'Not really.'

167

'Then it would be pointless for me to explain, but the maintenance of this house is part of the Mollah inheritance. When my brother dies I shall have to support these—'

Felicity was about to ask Mima what she had meant when she spoke of being a disgraced woman, but decided to wait for Mima to tell her.

'If you want to talk to them, you will find that they all have a little English, since they spend hours every day watching American television. But I would not bother myself with them if I were you, a cage of monkeys would be more interesting.'

Mima clearly enjoyed her company and they swam and walked around the ruins of the old amphitheatre. Occasionally a head and a rifle would appear from behind the rocks but when Mima waved and called out in Arabic the heads vanished. It could, Felicity felt, be an idyllic existence. She basked in the water and dived for shells, and in the evening some of the women would sing in a wavering falsetto as they ate on the wide terrace. It was also, as she soon found, stupefyingly boring. Even her thoughts began to float lazily through her head, drifting from one random image to another fragment of memory that could have been a dream or a recollection of something she had once known or imagined. The sound of the warm sea became the pulse of her own body as she drifted across the water and stood with her feet sinking into the wet sand. A small crab scuttled away from her and it seemed that she had been watching it for an eternity of time. 'A land in which it seemed always afternoon. All round the coast the languid air did swoon, breathing like one that hath a weary dream.' Only when she thought of Whistler did the images fall clear and sharply before her eyes and she decided she must paint or read, or do something to save herself from the Lotus-eaters. After two days she began prowling around looking for a book and found herself outside Mima's door. It was ajar and she stopped short as she saw Mima bent over a desk in a booklined room.

'I came to the right place,' Felicity said. 'I was looking for something to read.'

'Are you interested in economics?'

'Only in a general way.'

'These are mainly books on business and finance. But you'll find a little fiction on the shelves by the window. I am devoted to Ayn Rand and Agatha Christie.'

Mima had obviously been checking some graphs and Felicity saw a computer flashing stock market prices on her desk.

'Are you an economist, Mima?'

Mima sighed, lit a cigarette, and turned slowly to face Felicity.

'Why don't you ask me the question that is always in your mouth?'

'All right – why, in heaven's name, are you here?'

'I am a disgraced woman.'

'Disgraced? Did you rob a bank, commit murder, plagiarize someone else's work? Those are disgraceful acts, but you're educated.'

'Oh yes, I was always more intelligent than fat Taraq – by the way, he is now unconscious,' she said brightly. 'But when he was given books, I was given dolls. I fought for my education and finally my father permitted me to read economics at London. Already I had my idols: Milton Friedman, Frederick Hayek – above all others, Milton Friedman. Every word he spoke, every line he wrote, was engraved on my heart. At the London School of Economics, I fell in love with a young lecturer from Liverpool and I gave him my virginity, but I would never, never give him my mind. He was a Marxist, and we quarrelled all the time about Milton Friedman. Those were terrible days, Felicity. Eventually, he threw me out and failed me on my term paper. It would have been better if he had tied me in a sack and drowned me in the Bosporus. I had no degree, and I was disgraced, so my brother sent me here. Fortunately, my father was dead then so he did not know that I had dishonoured the family.'

'But if Taraq dies?'

'Then I shall inherit and run the Mollah estate,' Mima said brightly.

'And what about the women here?' Felicity said.

'They will live as they have always done.'

'That is absolutely monstrous! You treat them like badly trained house pets. Surely, there are things they can do?'

'I told you – the older ones take to house cleaning.'

'I mean work. Creative, satisfying work. There must be dozens of local crafts they could learn. Why aren't they weaving, or making pots, or – or—' Felicity waved helplessly because she had never really made a study of the local cottage industries in this part of the world.

'Why don't you ask them what they want to do?' Mima said drily, and blew a funnel of smoke into the air.

'You wouldn't mind?'

Mima laughed, 'My dear Felicity, you are so ingenuous.'

'I am not so ingenuous as to call myself disgraced because I scroomed with a scruffy LSE Marxist!'

'He was not scruffy! He was, I accept, a Marxist. But he had a red beard and he looked very poetic.'

'I bet,' and Felicity recalled a number of economists who'd tried to chat her up in the pubs around Kingsway.

Mima called the women together and they assembled round the fountain, yawning and combing each other's hair. Felicity looked at them and felt a slight sinking because when they were gathered together they did look like a collection of sleek brown puppies. Yasmin, the youngest,

169

was rolling on her back, sucking her thumb, while her special friend, Fatima, was sprinkling drops of water on her belly.

'Quiet, all of you!' Mima clapped her hands and the giggles subsided. 'The English lady is going to ask you some questions, and I want you all to answer her with truth in your hearts.'

In case they had not understood her English, Mima repeated it twice, slowly, in Arabic.

Felicity began to wish that Wendy Forsyth were with her. She would know exactly what to say and how to reach these brown, sleepy young women.

'I've been here with you for long enough to realize that life here is – well, it's worse than monotonous, it's dead boring.'

The women sighed and nodded.

'However, it needn't be like this. There must be things you'd like to do,' Felicity began awkwardly, and the women giggled. 'No, please, listen, let me put it this way. What is it you want?'

There was a sudden hush over the group and Yasmin stopped sucking her thumb and stared at Felicity with round dark eyes.

'What do you want?'

Yasmin rolled over twice and landed at Felicity's feet. She smiled up seraphically and said, 'Sex!'

Instantly, the other women began to whisper and then to shout the word until the whole palace was reverberating with their voices.

'You see,' Mima smiled.

'No, I don't,' Felicity said. 'If sex is what they want then they should have it.'

'But they are disgraced.'

'Balls! You're an economist, and if you can't see how to resolve this problem, I can!'

Stefan waited three days, but no one came and nobody called him by phone. He refused two dinner invitations and glumly ate scrambled eggs so he could spend his evenings at home; but the box remained in the middle of the coffee table, while he ached to open it again and remove the Strogonov icon. When he finally managed to get through to the Villa Francesca, a butler answered and said that Dr Norman had already left and Mr ben Mollah was critically ill and could not speak to anyone except his doctors. It was all very unsatisfactory, and Stefan's agitation grew. He expected more from Felicity. She should at least have called to find out if the box had arrived safely, Stefan brooded petulantly, but she was young and thought only of her pleasures, and could not imagine an old man's nerves and natural anxiety.

He was just about to eat his eggs when there was a hammering at his front door, and it was not the deferential knock of someone at Pequod who knew his position and respected his power on campus. This was very different indeed. Carefully, he pushed his plate aside, picked up his cane and tottered to the door, calling faintly, 'Please, please wait. I have to find my cane. I can't move without my cane.'

The door was barely open when James Baker pushed his way in, followed by two men in dark suits.

'There it is!' James shouted, and pointed to the box.

'Gentlemen, really, I must protest this intrusion,' Stefan cried and held his hand to his heart.

The older of the two men came up to him and presented a search warrant.

'Are you Stefan de Mornay?' he asked.

'I am Professor de Mornay, chairman of Art History at this college,' Stefan said, and tried to draw himself upright but failed. 'What is that paper you are prodding me with?'

'Search warrant.'

James Baker was tearing at the box, and Stefan cried out, 'How dare you touch my property! That box has just been delivered to me. It contains art works.'

'You haven't opened it?' the younger of the two men said.

'I am waiting for my assistant from the gallery to open it,' Stefan said, and held out his broken hands, 'I cannot open a match box with these poor wretched hands.'

'Were you expecting the box?' James said.

'It was a wonderful surprise,' Stefan beamed at him. 'Oh please, please be careful,' for the younger man was tearing off the copper stripping.

'My God, I should have known she'd do something like this,' James said, examining the address.

The box was up-ended and the plastic bags fell out. Stefan leaned forward and said, 'The art works must be in another compartment. What a very curious box. And what is that white powder? Of course, silica gel.'

The older man had opened one of the bags, tasted the contents, and was spitting vigorously.

James was on his knees clawing at the box.

'I packed it myself,' he screamed. 'The heroin was in tubes.'

'So you told us,' the older man said. 'But this isn't heroin, is it?'

'Somebody switched the contents!' James shouted.

'That box was opened at the top by customs,' the younger man said. 'No one else has touched it.'

'I would very much like to know what this is about,' Stefan quavered. 'I insist you open the box and let me see if there are indeed any art works inside. Your sordid interest in drugs does not concern me, but I must know if the art works are safe.'

The older man pulled down the rest of the stripping and Stefan collected the plates, the two prints, and the icon and carried them over to his desk. None of the men seemed interested in anything except the plastic bags of silica gel.

'You say you packed the box yourself, Baker?'

James seemed bemused and kept reaching around inside the box.

'The best planned sting in years,' he kept saying.

'I shall demand an explanation,' Stefan said. 'These precious plates and prints could have been damaged.'

'Can you keep your mouth shut for five seconds?' the younger man said to Stefan.

'I beg your pardon,' Stefan replied huffily. 'If you mean am I aware of the meaning of confidentiality, I can assure you that as a responsible officer of this college—'

'A certain Taraq ben Mollah has been laundering money for the Mafia, and this – this,' he pointed to James, 'this investigating officer from the IRS persuaded us to let him have two million dollars worth of heroin that we had just taken off a Panamanian ship in Miami. He was going to use it to trap the owners of Palermo Enterprises.'

'It was a perfect plan,' James shouted. 'You would have picked up the Palermo brothers on drug charges and I would have been able to stop the cash flow to ben Mollah.'

'Except that we stake out Palermo Enterprises for over a week, and nothing happens,' the older man retorted.

'And nobody could trace this box from Geneva to New York,' the younger man added.

'I told you about the woman, Felicity Norman. She switched the contents.'

'Felicity Norman? Are you referring to one of my most esteemed colleagues?' Stefan said.

Both men were now staring at James, and the older said slowly, 'I think it's time you told us what happened to two million dollars worth of heroin, Baker. We work for the FDA, and we have to account for that dope.'

'Are you accusing me of stealing it?' James shouted.

'You said you packed that box and nobody opened it except the customs officer, and you can see by the seal where he examined it.'

'That bitch Felicity Norman has the heroin!'

'Well, you may be able to convince our director of that, but he's never shown an interest in fairy tales,' the older man said, and the three of them left with the remains of the box.

Stefan whistled and took a few jigging dance steps round the table before he winced and sat down suddenly at his desk. He held the icon reverently in his hands and bowed his head before it.

'Oh Felicity, you have the blessings of heaven in your heart. Our Lady of the Sign has guided and protected you.'

Felicity and Mima drew up the plans together, or rather, Felicity insisted on checking Mima from the most rapacious exploitation of human beings she had ever known. They agreed on the general principles and Mima had the forms printed with the registered title of the Cultural and Rehabilitation Centre for Disadvantaged Women, (CRCDW) setting out the terms under which the house should be run. Mima argued that if the women had what they wanted, they should not receive any of the profits of the business. But Felicity said that the enterprise must be run on co-operative principles, and Mima promptly ran to her shelves and produced a dozen different books proving that co-operatives had a lower growth rate than single or corporately owned businesses. Felicity insisted that the women receive a minimum of forty per cent of the gross profits, and Mima said that the percentage should come from net, but by the end of the week Mima had reluctantly agreed to a percentage from the gross.

Every day Felicity fought with Mima and at night she dreamed that she was being throttled by an exceptionally slender boa constrictor. The house was to be discreetly advertized as a rehabilitation centre, open to interested visitors in the afternoon and evening, but with certain provisions: for every hour spent in bed with a man, the women had to spend an equal amount of time in the classroom learning to read and write. And Felicity undertook to give the classes.

At the first lesson, Mima sauntered into the empty classroom in an impeccable trouser suit of powder blue linen, and looked at the blotched and scribbled slates.

'I see you're progressing,' she said mockingly.

'They are learning.' But Felicity would not admit how slowly they learned, and how whenever she turned her head a spitball would land just behind her ear, and a storm of giggles break out in the room.

'I'm teaching them to count first.'

'Count? Surely it is more important to read?'

'We'll work up to that. It's very important that they know how to count money, particularly when they'll be working for you, Mima.'

Mima shrugged, 'You have not the slightest appreciation of supply side economics, have you?'

'I know what's fair.' And she found herself sounding like an embattled shop steward. 'I would also like to know when you are going to allow me to phone my friends and tell them I'm all right.'

'Perhaps quite soon,' Mima smiled. 'Every night I call the Villa Francesca and the doctor tells me my brother is very close to death.' She sighed contentedly. 'When he dies, you are free to do whatever you want.'

'When do you plan to open this house?'

'The end of next week. I have already called some interested clients—'

'They know it's going to be expensive?'

'Naturally – but I have also had another idea. This morning I phoned UNESCO and it may be possible to get the whole operation subsidized. The gentleman I spoke to in Paris was most helpful and said he would be happy to fly out here and examine the whole undertaking.'

'I need an extra teacher. I can't do it all, Mima.'

'I shall hire one immediately. An instructor in religion. These women must learn the principles of the Koran.'

Mima picked up one slate with neat rows of sums on it.

'I am not sure that counting is so necessary for them, Felicity. Surely, it is more important for these women to be religious, to appreciate poetry and learn to read Shakespeare.'

'Oh no, Mima. First they count – then they read. Feminism is based on economics. If a woman doesn't have her own money she can never be free.' And that, Felicity realized, was what Wendy Forsyth used to say.

Every night Felicity was so tired she could barely find the strength to walk down the beach and fall into the water, but the women were learning, and some of them had begun to read. Against Mima's protests, she took the financial pages of *The Times* and used them to teach reading. For some it was only days before they had grasped the meaning of money, others were slower, but by now they had all learned every paragraph of the CRCDW by heart.

As she floated in the water, Felicity could smell the flowers from the garden with a sudden intrusion of musk and patchouli. She raised her head slightly and saw Mima standing ankle deep in the water and crying.

'Mima, is anything wrong?'

'My brother—'

'He's dead?'

'They are feeding him intravenously. Oh, why can't those doctors realize what any kind of food will do to him! He'll recover.'

Felicity walked slowly out of the water. 'And that means I have to be killed.'

Mima shook her head and wept, 'He was dying, the doctors told me so, and now they are feeding him?'

'Is he conscious?'

'No.'

'The doctors could be keeping the corpse kicking as long as possible in order to pad out their fees.'

Mima wiped away her tears with the back of her hand and smiled, 'You really think so, Felicity?'

'After all, they're trying to cheer you up too, aren't they? I mean – they think you're concerned about your brother.'

'Of course, I'm concerned. Ah—' and she gave a long sigh.

'Intravenous feeding doesn't mean they're injecting pâté de foie gras and turtle soup into his veins. It means glucose, a few nutrients and water—'

'If that is what they are giving him, he will die very quickly,' Mima said with considerable satisfaction. 'Come, let us swim together,' and they kept pace together down the path of the moonlight.

When Wilbur Krushnek told Bernie that he would have to be moved from the pelvic harness into traction, he decided he no longer wanted to live. However, suicide seemed extraordinarily difficult with both legs attached to pulleys and weights. He thought of breaking a glass and slashing his wrists, but the glass was plastic. He fought to hold his breath and suffocate himself, but no matter how he strained, oxygen and life fought their way back into his lungs. Whenever Martin arrived he tried to rejoice with him over his unintelligible discovery, but the acclaimed genius of Martin Harris only served to make the miserable failure of Bernie Lefkowitz more unendurable. There had been a lead article in the *Scientific American* about Martin's factoring method, and he was receiving invitations to lecture in exotic places like Beijing and Melbourne. He had been told that he was going to receive an award from the National Science Foundation, but none of this seemed to give him any real pleasure. He sat beside Bernie's bed, cracking his knuckles and tying his legs in knots.

'Oh yes, it's all right, but what do I do next, Bernie? I've spent all my life trying to crack the factoring code.'

'Try a unified field theory next, Martin.'

'You have a brilliant mind, Bernie,' Martin said slowly.

'Oh sure – I think up pet rocks and diet pills in my spare time.'

'I enjoyed your poems – I still do.'

'Please, don't mention them again. I'll never be able to forget this episode but I'd be grateful if you didn't talk about it.'

'I – I have another problem,' Martin anguished, and began to tear his hair. 'Well, it's not exactly a problem, it could be the most wonderful thing that ever happened to me and I still don't understand why it did, but it may disturb you, and you're my best friend.'

The problem burst into Bernie's room in a scarlet jump suit and promptly stood against the wall and elevated one leg against it until the foot was at right angles to her head.

'Sorry, darling. I had an argument with some stupid man who didn't want to let me park the car where I knew I had a perfect right to be parked. So I got so angry I just picked him up and dumped him in the nearest trash can.'

Bernie stared with horror at Mariana and then saw Martin gazing at her, slack-jawed and with bulging eyes.

'Has he told you yet, Bernie?' Mariana turned and stretched the other leg.

'Told me—'

'I'm going to marry Martin. Daddy read all about Martin in *Time* magazine and he approves, so we'll have a big formal wedding at the end of the summer.'

'How's that going to affect the auric force?' Bernie said bitterly.

'Martin and I are both virgins, Bernie. That's why it went wrong with *us*. But Martin—' she leaned over backwards, placed her hands on the floor and smiled up at her betrothed, 'Martin is the yin and I am the yang so the auric force will be in total and complete harmony.'

CHAPTER FOURTEEN

Pequod drowsed through the summer months, the walkways shaded
plane trees, the air above Botany Meadow iridescent with butterflies a
tumbling striped bees. Bernie borrowed a cane from Stefan and the t
walked slowly along Science Road and across the meadow before brea
fast.

'You must overcome this depression, Bernie,' Stefan said. 'God
heavens, when they carried me into Columbia, my spine was lik
cottage cheese, but I survived.'

Bernie shook his head and remained silent.

'I shall make you some coffee and we can sit and draw inspiration from
the icons.'

A troup of gymnasts leaped and vaulted past them on their way to an
early morning workout and Bernie grimaced.

'The college may sleep academically in summer,' Stefan said wearily,
'but the gymnastics go on.'

'God help Martin Harris,' Bernie said bitterly.

'I've made it my business to meet Miss Ashmole,' Stefan said thoughtfully. 'She has an original mind. I doubt if it is a mind of quality, like
Felicity's, but original – yes. What I admire most about her is the
intensity of her will. Quite an astonishing attribute in one so young.'

Bernie moaned and Stefan tapped him on the arm. 'The summer is
almost over and she will be back with us soon.'

'Then it will be her turn to jeer at me, won't it? Bernie Lefkowitz – the
all-time loser.'

Stefan did not answer because he was becoming very concerned about
Felicity's silence. One postcard and nothing since – not a single question
about whether the Whistlers had arrived safely. Perhaps the icons would
help. He was grateful for Bernie's company with so many of his friends
away on summer vacation. If only he had a private income he would
have enjoyed a quiet trip to England, but there were still medical bills
unpaid, and he expected to die owing his doctors money. The two

followed their canes back to Sufferin, and Bernie seemed to lean more heavily on his stick than Stefan.

The Stroganov icon stood on a carved wooden stand and Stefan paused in front of it with hands clasped, and prayed for some minutes before making coffee. Bernie held one of the Whistler plates to a mirror and wondered when Felicity would print from it. The dancing figures seemed caught in a world of laughter and love that he could never hope to enter or enjoy, and he felt like a ghost whose punishment was to move unseen in a house of cheerfully indifferent people. The phone rang as Stefan was setting out the coffee mugs and he asked Bernie to answer. Felicity's deep voice rang through the room and Bernie began to shake.

'Oh my God, Felicity, it's you!'

'Bernie! Bernie, I'm all right. They didn't kill me!'

'Kill you? What are you saying? Who—'

'I'm perfectly safe now – Taraq ben Mollah died this morning and his sister inherits everything.'

Stefan had picked up the phone in the bedroom and shouted, 'They're all here, Felicity. Oh my dearest, dearest girl! Your plates are on my desk, and the icon is the crown of my life.'

'Felicity, where are you?' Bernie cried.

'I'm in Tunis.'

'Tunis!' Stefan and Bernie shouted together.

'It's the Cultural and Rehabilitation Centre for Disadvantaged Women, and it's on the beach, and please come and get me. Mima is so stingy she won't give me my air fare.'

'I'll be there at once,' Bernie said. 'Oh Felicity, I love you.'

'I love you too, Bernie,' Felicity said, and the line began to crackle and fade.

'You must go today, Bernie!' Stefan cried, and pointed to the door.

'I've got a credit card, but I haven't any money.'

'Speak to your parents,' Stefan said. 'Tell them you are going to bring Felicity home.'

It was astonishing, but Bernie did not feel his back until he drove up to his parents' house and heard his mother screaming. Bonnie Wintergreen was in the middle of the living room sobbing, Josh was on the phone, and Myra cut short another scream and glared at Bernie.

'Did you have to come at a time like this? Can you never do anything right, Bernie?'

Bonnie was now having hysterics and Myra walked up to her and slapped her with such force that she span across the room.

'All you had to do was look after Rosa! Hardly a difficult job. And now you've lost her!'

Josh put the phone down and took Myra by the elbow, 'Cool it, Myra,

Fred Cadwallader just walked into his garden.'

Instantly, Myra controlled herself and spoke through clenched teeth while Josh frowned at Bernie.

'Your grandmother has wandered off somewhere.'

'She may be dead in the harbour by now,' Myra said, and suddenly became much calmer.

'I left her at the synagogue the way I always did,' Bonnie wailed, 'but she wasn't there when I came back.'

'You should never have left her for an instant,' Myra said.

'It's odd,' Josh said, 'I've just spoken to the rabbi and Hadassah never has a meeting there on Wednesday.'

'Call the police, Josh.'

'Yes, I think perhaps I should,' Josh said slowly.

'I,' Bernie knew it was not the best time to ask for a loan, but he plunged in, 'I need some money.'

'You need – what?' his father said slowly.

'You have the chutzpah to come here asking for money when you know what that slipped disc cost both of us?' Myra added.

'I need the money for an air fare – one round ticket and a one way ticket back here to the States. Felicity called me from Tunis, she needs me and I'm going to bring her home.'

Myra stumbled and had to reach out to the mantelpiece for support.

'From your mouth to God's ear,' she said quietly, then her voice rose and she stared at her son, 'Bernie, you're not lying to us?'

'Ask Stefan. He was there when Felicity called.'

'Now, I want to know a little more than that before I sign another cheque,' Josh said belligerently.

Myra unclasped the pearls from her neck, pulled off her rings and her watch and threw them at Josh. 'If you need money, take these! Didn't you hear your son? He's going to bring back Felicity!'

Mima received the news about her brother's death late at night and came capering in to Felicity's room. 'Fat Taraq has gone and I am free!'

'Good. Does that mean I can go too?' Felicity said, and looked around for her duffle bag.

'My dear Felicity,' Mima embraced her and kissed her on both cheeks. 'You have been like a sister to me, and I was hoping you would be here when the house opened, but believe me from my heart, I can understand your wish to join your friends.'

'I'd like to phone first.'

'The dialling code is 23768.'

'Thank you, and I'd also like to fly back to the States immediately.'

'Whatever you wish, name it and it is yours,' Mima said expansively.

'Oh, fat Taraq is dead at last and it was you, my beloved Felicity, who laid him gently on the knees of Allah. The doctors told me that he regained consciousness two days ago, but all he said was that he wanted a certain painting to be placed beside his bed.'

'I need some money for an air ticket,' Felicity said.

'Money? I cannot give you money,' Mima said firmly.

'I have slaved here teaching those girls, I have mastered basic finance so they could defend themselves against you!'

'I asked that they be taught religion and Shakespeare. You deliberately defied my wishes and now I have Fatima demanding that she be allowed to see the books every week.'

'What's wrong with that?' Felicity shouted.

'You have turned these silly animals into grasping, avaricious women who have nothing in their heads except money and sex.'

'All right, I have friends who will help me.'

'You can have two overseas calls – no more,' Mima said, and walked off singing.

Felicity walked down to the beach after she had spoken to Bernie and stood for a long time with the waves rustling over her feet. She could tell by Bernie's voice that he loved and wanted her, but there was a difficulty now that he might not appreciate. Felicity had known for the last two weeks that she was pregnant, and so she stood for a long time with her hands on her belly and looked at the sea as one calm resolution flooded her mind: she was not going to lose her child, even though the father was the homicidal rapist of Pequod College.

Mariana accomplished the impossible that night and spun six times in mid air before she swooped into Louise's waiting grasp. Then, as if to challenge the pinnacle of her ability, Mariana flew up again and reversed the spins, and for one dreadful instant it looked as though she was plunging head first into the canvas, but Louise caught her as her chin almost grazed the floor. The crowd exploded, and laughed and cried at the same time, stamping and calling Mariana's name over and over again. The Olympic judges agreed that the women's aerial pairs gymnastics should be accepted as an event, and the crowd of little people stood on the benches and cheered.

Glittering in a silver body-suit, Mariana turned to every side of the gymnasium and smiled so brilliantly that it was as if she were coated with mercury. Then, still waving to the audience, she leaped across the benches to Martin who was sitting next to Lester Marcus and cracking his knuckles.

'I want you all to meet my fiancé, that genius of mathematics, Martin Harris!' Mariana shouted and yanked Martin to his feet. 'I wish we could invite all of you to our wedding, but I know we'll carry your love and best wishes with us always.'

Lester called for three cheers and reached up to slap Martin's back, 'You are the most fortunate man in this country – in the world!' he shouted.

'I know it. I know it,' Martin mumbled, and tried to sit down.

'And I just want all of you out there to realize one thing,' Mariana's smile was a beacon illuminating the whole gymnasium, 'my fiancé and I have saved our virgin bodies for marriage. We have not squandered ourselves on futile fornications. We have made a meaningful commitment to the auric containment of our psychic space, and the purity of our virginal selfhood has not been contaminated or polluted by illicit sexual gratification.'

The crowd began to scream rapturously and Martin turned to the people in front of him and babbled, 'I had to tell her I was a virgin or she wouldn't have married me. I had to say I was, but I'm not. I'm not.'

After a long session of passionate foreplay in his apartment that left Martin gasping, Mariana suddenly jumped out of bed and said she had to go back to the gym.

'But – but you trained – and you did your stretching, Mariana,' Martin said faintly.

'Yes, but Louise and Lenore are still there and I forgot to tell Louise that she mistimed my last drop by at least a tenth of a second. You don't think that was a stunt when I came down after my reverse spins, do you?'

'Is it – is it so important?' Martin said, and tried to bury his face in Mariana's pubic hair.

'Important! And you're supposed to be a mathematician! I must tell her now or by tomorrow it will have become a mindset, and tomorrow night she may miss by a half-second, and I'll be on the receiving end of a broken neck.'

'Are you sure they're in the gym?' Martin said. 'Maybe they're next door—'

'No, Lenore gets a big turn on when Louise rolls her round on the canvas after the routine. They'll be there.'

'You will come back soon, won't you?' Martin said plaintively.

'Yes, I am coming back,' Mariana grinned, 'and if I see Miss Piggy anywhere around I'll cut her ears off.'

Louise denied that her timing was off and Mariana insisted they go over the routine with Lenore watching and holding a stopwatch. Half an hour later, Louise grudgingly admitted that she was wrong and Mariana threw a towel round her neck and skipped out of the gym and down Science Walkway. She began to flick the towel from side to side and

181

hum, taking short dance steps. The darkness took shape behind her, and suddenly hands were round her throat digging into her trachea. Mariana fell to her knees gasping for air as a voice muttered obscenities in her ear.

She pretended to be fainting, and felt the man's grip relax as he began to tear at her clothes. Instantly, Mariana twisted and kicked backwards and heard the man grunt. She jabbed with her elbow and butted with her head and the man bent double. His face was covered with a ski mask and there was a flick knife in his right hand.

'You shitty bastard!' Mariana cried, and threw herself at him feet first. He tried to stab with his knife but she turned in midair and brought her fist down on his wrist. Rolling as she fell, Mariana spun out of his range, but he was almost as agile as she was, and tried to trip her by the ankle and drop on top of her. Mariana feinted – he slipped and lost his balance, and she stamped on his arm with the whole weight of her body. The knife clattered on the stone and Mariana grabbed it. As he lunged for it, Mariana kicked him in the throat. Choking, he collapsed backwards and Mariana kneeled on his chest.

'You crazy shithead! There's only one way to fix your problem!'

The knife flashed as Mariana held it high above her head and then flashed again as it came down. The man screamed and continued to scream.

Turning the corner on his evening walk, humming the sorcerer's theme from *Swan Lake*, Stefan de Mornay was struck by the flying balls of the Chairman of the Board, Lester Marcus. Mariana was still leaning over him and spitting on his screaming face.

'Mariana! Leave at once. Go, quickly!' Stefan bent down and took her by the arm.

Mariana got up slowly and looked at the figure writhing at her feet.

'He had it coming to him,' she said.

'And you will get more than you ever imagined if you don't go at once. Get rid of those clothes, and forget what happened here. Leave everything to me.'

Mariana vanished and Stefan knelt in the blood pulsing from Lester's groin.

'Listen to me carefully, Lester. Do as I say, do whatever I tell you and I can save you.'

Lester moaned and Stefan nodded.

'Very well.'

Scrambling to his feet, Stefan began shouting for help and Lorenzo Delgado came chugging down the walkway on his moped.

'The rapist! I saw him! He went towards the Science buildings!' Stefan waved his cane and Delgado wheeled around, his siren wailing. 'And call an ambulance,' Stefan shouted after him.

Stefan wrapped a large embroidered handkerchief around his fist and thrust it against the gaping bleeding hole.

'Dear heaven,' he prayed, 'don't let him bleed to death before the ambulance arrives.'

Bernie fumbled his way off the plane at the Tunis airport and was almost blinded by the light and the flies, but he managed to find a row of taxis and asked the driver if he knew the Cultural and Rehabilitation Centre for Disadvantaged Women.

'Who does not?' the driver said, and drove off at a speed that sent needles of pain up and down Bernie's back.

He screeched to a stop in a pall of dust, and at first Bernie found it difficult to see where he was as he paid the driver, remembering to bend his knees before picking up his bag. A high, whitewashed wall loomed over his head with an iron studded wooden gate, and at the side, a polished brass plate with CRCDW on it and presumably the same letters in Arabic. He rang a bell and an elderly woman opened the door and told him in faltering English that the house was not open until tomorrow.

'But I'm a special guest of Felicity Norman. She phoned me – and I've flown here from the States to see her.'

The heat and the jetlag were making him dizzy and he did not understand why he should be asked to produce his credit cards, but he obediently opened his wallet, and the woman smiled and ushered him into a shadowed courtyard with a fountain and baskets of flowers.

Fatima had all the makings of a financial genius and Felicity knew she could trust her to keep an eye on Mima and check the books regularly. Her duffle bag was packed, she had tinted her hair, and all she had to do now was explain to Fatima that she had to hire a substitute teacher.

'A business teacher,' Fatima said. 'I shall interview her myself.'

'I did my best,' Felicity said apologetically.

'It was very good as an elementary class, but now we need something more advanced.'

'You will watch Mima, won't you?' Felicity said in a lowered voice.

'She is a vulture, Dr Norman, but the vulture only feeds on the dead. We are alive and if she tries to peck at us, we will stone her.'

The doorkeeper coughed and Fatima waved her away, 'Not now, we are in conference.'

The quiet of the house was shattered by a piercing cry and Felicity heard her name called.

'Bernie! Bernie, where are you? I'm coming!'

She ran down the stairs and heard another cry from one of the guest rooms.

'Bernie! Oh, my God!'

Two of the women had tied him by the wrists to the wall and taken off his pants. Yasmin was kneeling in front of him with bent head.

'What are you doing to him?' Felicity shouted, and pushed Yasmin aside.

'This is not fair!' Yasmin cried. 'He say he wants the rack, and we bring him in here—' she gestured to the whips and manacles furnishing the room.

'My back! I told them I was in pain. Oh Felicity, help me!'

'This is not a client,' Felicity said angrily. 'This is my very special friend.'

'It is not fair,' Yasmin pouted, 'the management should not take the best ones from the staff. I shall speak to Fatima.'

Bernie was loose and fell into Felicity's arms.

'I have missed you so much,' he cried.

'Bernie, I knew you'd come.'

They laughed and kissed as Felicity gently led him up to her room where he collapsed on the bed.

'I want to scroom so badly,' he said, 'but I have to sleep – I haven't slept since you left.'

'We'll scroom in the evening when it's cool,' Felicity murmured, and pulled a sheet over him. 'Before you close your eyes, Bernie, did the box arrive safely?'

'Oh yes—' he said drowsily. 'The dancing figures and Stefan's icon—' and he slept.

He was much older than she remembered him last, but that was probably because there was a furze of bristles round his face: the white scrolls above his ears were wider and reached around his head like wings, and he was gaunt. She unbuttoned his shirt and gently stroked his chest and the black hair looked as though he had accidentally spilled cigarette ash on it. His penis was still wet from Yasmin's lips, be he did not wake as she undressed him and placed a sheet over his body.

He woke once and she gave him some iced water which he gulped, then immediately fell back on to her arm. The light was leaving the room now and she walked out on to the veranda and stared at the crimson sea where every wave had a margin of gold, and the beach shone like Aladdin's cave in a Christmas pantomime. How could she tell Bernie that she was carrying a child? She looked back over her shoulder to the bed but he had turned on his side and was sighing in his sleep. Slowly, she walked down the steps to the garden and was about to put her foot on the gold sand when James Baker reached out and took her by the arm.

'What did you do with the heroin?' he shouted hoarsely.

It was not the James Baker who had spoken to her in Geneva: this man, too, had changed. His pale hair was lank and his clothes looked as

184

though he had slept in them for several days. The light-blue eyes were ringed with dark shadows and he was unshaven.

'The what?' Felicity said, and remembered that this man was a rapist and a homicidal maniac.

'You opened the box, you changed the contents—'

'I didn't open the box, James, I simply altered the address. I wanted Stefan to have it, not some people in White Plains.'

'You know where it is!' he screamed and began to shake her.

Felicity tried to remain very calm as she thought of Betty Levin and all the others he had attacked.

'James, I am ready to swear that I did not touch that box other than to remove the labels.'

'They think I took it. I spent weeks in Washington being interrogated and they wouldn't believe me! They think I stole the heroin and I've hidden it somewhere. Oh God,' he moaned, 'it was the greatest sting operation ever planned. I would have framed ben Mollah and they would have caught the Palermo brothers, but they said I was lying.'

'I don't know anything about this,' Felicity said.

'You are the only one who could have opened the box! You took the heroin!' James shouted.

'Seth, you bum, let go of her or I'll throw this at you!'

Bernie was leaning over the veranda with a chair in his hands.

'You're in it too!' James wheeled, and pointed at Bernie.

Bernie ran down the stairs and slapped Seth across the chest with the back of his hand.

'You're dead! Dead! We sat shiva for you!'

'Just tell me what you did with the heroin. I had to escape from the States. There's an arrest warrant out for me! They think I'm a criminal,' James was almost crying in a frenzy of rage.

'Is it dope dealing this time? Were you trying to frame someone?'

'It was a sting,' James said. 'We would have got ben Mollah and the Palermo brothers.'

'Bernie, your brother is dead,' Felicity said, 'you told me that a hundred times.'

'He is dead,' Bernie said. 'When he left Harvard he went to Washington for a year to work for the government. He didn't tell us that he had joined the IRS. My father used to spend hours with him explaining his tax shelters, talking about his clients. He told Seth everything because he was the eldest son and he trusted him. Then—' and Bernie slapped him again, 'Seth put my father and his clients in to the IRS. My father was wiped out, some of his clients went to prison. The rabbi came to the house, the whole family was together, my uncles, even Rosa, and we sat shiva for him. We all thought mother was going to die of grief because

Seth was her favourite. Felicity, it's something that can happen in a Jewish family or in the congregation when somebody does something so appalling that he is declared to be dead. Nobody mentions his name after the ceremony, it's as though he had never been born. Felicity, we sat round a table and said the prayers of the dead for Seth.'

'I did my duty,' Seth shouted.

'You're a fucking Nazi!' Bernie cried.

Mima joined them, frowning, 'I detest arguments and I do not permit . . . ' She recognized James and smiled. 'My dear James, you come on the wings of Allah. Did you know fat Taraq is dead?'

Bernie pointed at his brother and said slowly, 'You are dead, and you will remain dead as long as there is one member of this family left to curse your name.'

'James, I need your help so badly,' Mima crooned. 'You know all Taraq's business. Stay and help me—'

Mima was lacing her fingers with James and he looked down at her and told her slowly that he was a fugitive.

She shrugged and smiled at him, 'James, I always meant to ask you – what do you think of Milton Friedman?'

'The greatest economist since Adam Smith,' James said bemusedly.

'Marvellous! I shall protect you, James.'

'Mima—'

'Take her offer,' Bernie said, 'it's the best you'll get. Corpses must come cheap in this part of the world.'

'I do not know who you are,' Mima said to Bernie, 'and you are not welcome in my house.'

'We'll be leaving tomorrow morning,' Felicity replied.

Mima and James walked back into the shadow of the house and Felicity suddenly felt sick.

'I think I'd like to stand in the water for a moment,' she whispered.

'Let's see if we can swim to the horizon and back!' Bernie shouted, took her by the hand, and ran down into the sea.

Myra had just finished talking to Felicity and Bernie and was putting down the phone when she heard Josh park with a scream of tyres and run up the steps.

'They've found Rosa!' he said gasping.

'She was a very old lady,' Myra said consolingly, 'and you were always a marvellous son to her.'

'She's not dead,' Josh said, and sat down. 'She's in Israel.'

'Josh, it is our promised land,' Myra said. 'But let me tell you about Felicity and Bernie. They—'

'My mother has eloped with the shammas of the synagogue in Hicksville. We thought she was going to Hadassah meetings but she was screwing with the shammas. They are in Israel.'

'Oh my God,' Myra stifled a scream.

'My eighty-four-year-old mother has run off with a seventy-six-year-old caretaker and is living on a kibbutz.'

'You can get her back,' Myra said.

'The caretaker used to set type for the New York *Daily Worker* and he was a card-carrying Communist. He is a widower with four sons: two of them are rabbis in Israel, one is in the army, and the other is a public servant. They now have a stepmother with a fortune of nine million dollars. Tell me how I should get her back.'

Josh buried his head in his hands and Myra sat on the edge of the chair beside him. The house was very quiet and Myra felt as though she had just taken a miraculous pill that had left her ten pounds lighter, and twenty years younger. Rosa was gone, and she would never have to listen to that cackling voice again or hear her clumping around upstairs looking for capitalists under the bed.

'Josh, I know what a blow this is to you, but we're not ruined financially, are we?'

'Of course not,' Josh said, 'but we have just lost nine million dollars.'

'But think what we're getting, Josh. Bernie and Felicity are flying back to the States now. They phoned from the airport in Paris. Oh Josh, Felicity is coming back to us.'

Josh did not raise his head and Myra stroked his hair.

'Honey, we've been through some tough times, but perhaps this is a blessing.'

'You call losing nine million dollars a blessing?'

Myra put back her shoulders and smiled. They would have the wedding in New York, a white silk huppa decorated with lily of the valley and the reception here at the house. Lights down to the front gate and an orchestra with the food catered by Antoine Guérard.

Bernie had gone to sleep on Felicity's shoulder within minutes of the plane taking off and when he woke he murmured, 'I am crazy about the perfume of saffron.'

He was floating on a warm golden cloud and felt happiness wrapped around him like a second skin. The lights were dimmed on the plane, and when Bernie reached up to touch Felicity's cheek he realized she'd been crying.

'Felicity, if you like I'll go up to the cockpit and ask the captain to come down and marry us now. If sea captains can marry people, the pilot of a jumbo jet should be able to do a slap-up job.'

'Bernie, I'm pregnant.'

'You can't be. We only scroomed last night.'

'I am carrying your brother's child.'

The engines of the plane droned and somewhere behind them a baby began to cry fretfully.

Bernie turned to Felicity and kissed her on the mouth.

'I had to tell you,' she whispered.

'Well, the way I see it,' Bernie said, 'Seth covered for me once when I was fourteen. I reckon I owe him one.'

Stefan stretched out his hands to the small group who had gathered in the auditorium of the art gallery. Mariana was balancing on her toes and holding hands with Martin who seemed to be looking across their heads to some horizon beyond the galaxy. Myra glowed in a linen sheath as Josh chatted quietly to Fred Cadwallader and Goldie Van der Klonk. By the door, Lieutenant Poldowski stared sourly at them all. He was convinced that most of them knew who the murderer was, but it wasn't because nobody was talking. This bunch never stopped talking, like that silver-haired old fox, Stefan de Mornay.

'You are all welcome to the Pequod Art Gallery.'

Felicity had just printed the four Whistler etchings and pinned them to a cork board to dry, and Stefan waved Archie Macbeth back into the small crowd.

'Later, Archie, we will discuss print runs later.'

'Stefan, you promised—'

'This is a moment for rejoicing,' Stefan said, and smiled. He had never looked so well, everyone was agreed on that. His white hair was thick and lustrous and he was wearing a suit of bottle-green velvet with a ruffled shirt.

'You see before you the etchings of James McNeill Whistler which our esteemed colleague Dr Felicity Norman, soon to be Dr Felicity Lefkowitz, has given to the gallery.

'Get it right, Stef,' Felicity murmured to Wendy. 'It will be the Drs Felicity and Bernard Lefkowitz-Norman,' and Wendy smiled approvingly.

'But this afternoon I want to inform you of a great and generous gift which our beloved patron, Lester Marcus has bestowed upon the gallery.'

Stefan swung slightly and indicated a wizened, hunched figure in a wheel chair with a blanket folded across his body. Lester Marcus looked like a dead monkey, staring at his hands with eyes like pebbles.

'Lester Marcus was tragically struck down by an unknown assailant here on this campus.' Mariana smiled at him and raised her left leg at right angles to her body, slowly rotating her ankle until her toe was pointing to the ceiling. Stefan continued, 'But from his bed of pain at the Columbia Medical Center, he did not forget this college and the art gallery. He has given five million dollars to the gallery for a special collections room which will be known as the Betty Levin Russian Room, and a two million dollar discretionary fund to be placed at the disposal of the director of the gallery. I must say,' Stefan coughed slightly and dabbed his lips with an embroidered handkerchief, 'Lester Marcus has displayed his personal confidence in me by appointing me to the board of Conspic Industries.'

Fred Cadwallader turned to Josh and whispered, 'I think Marcus lost his brains – not his balls.'

Stefan may have heard this because he smiled at Fred and said, 'As you know I have dedicated my life to the preservation and the collection of Stroganov icons. Consider the role of Felicity Norman in this amazing enterprise: she has worked in the tradition of the great icon masters who always travelled with their apprentices and were slowly initiated into the mystery of the craft. She has been the apprentice of James McNeill Whistler; now, before our eyes, she has brought his art to life. This is the mystery of art that cannot exist without the interpreter.'

Felicity smiled at him and slipped out the side door to wash the ink from her hands. Myra had been watching her with a slight frown, and followed her.

Stefan placed his hand across his heart and slowly intoned, 'For myself, I like to think that I am following in the tradition of that illustrious family of Russian merchant princes, the Stroganovs, which moved from Novgorod to Solvychedgodsk in 1470, and—' he realized he was losing the attention of his listeners and leaned forward to say, 'To put it bluntly, the Rockefellers, Nuffields, Carnegies and Mellons of this country didn't make their millions for the endowment of banks and factories, they left their money to the arts, and in years ahead Lester Marcus will be recognized as one of the great patrons of the arts in this country.'

Felicity was shaking the water from her hands when Myra handed her a towel.

'Whose child is it?' she said.

Felicity was about to say that it was James McNeill Whistler's child, but she realized this was a truth she must always keep to herself.

'It's Seth's baby,' she said simply. 'It happened in Switzerland.'

Myra was silent for some moments and then she put her arms around Felicity.

'You're not angry?' Felicity asked.

'Bernie will make a wonderful father,' Myra said, 'he was such a lousy son.'